The Bull of Mithros

ANNE ZOUROUDI was born in England and has lived in the Greek Islands. Her attachment to Greece remains strong, and the country is the inspiration for much of her writing. She now lives in the Derbyshire Peak District with her son. She is the author of the Mysteries of the Greek Detective series: *The Messenger of Athens* (shortlisted for the ITV3 Crime Thriller Award for Breakthrough Authors and longlisted for the Desmond Elliot Prize), *The Taint of Midas*, *The Doctor of Thessaly*, *The Lady of Sorrows*, *The Whispers of Nemesis* and, most recently, *The Feast of Artemis*.

BY THE SAME AUTHOR

The Messenger of Athens

The Taint of Midas

The Doctor of Thessaly

The Lady of Sorrows

The Whispers of Nemesis

The Feast of Artemis

The Bull of Mithros

Anne Zouroudi

B L O O M S B U R Y

LONDON · NEW DELHI · NEW YORK · SYDNEY

First published in Great Britain 2012
This paperback edition published 2013

Copyright © 2012 by Anne Zouroudi
Map on p. vi © 2012 by John Gilkes

The moral right of the author has been asserted

Bloomsbury Publishing, London, New Delhi, New York and Sydney

50 Bedford Square, London WC1B 3DP

A CIP catalogue record for this book is available from the British Library

ISBN 978 1 4088 3148 9
10 9 8 7 6 5 4 3 2 1

Typeset by Hewer Text UK Ltd, Edinburgh
Printed and bound in Great Britain by CPI Group (UK) Ltd, Croydon CR0 4YY

www.bloomsbury.com/annezouroudi

For Will

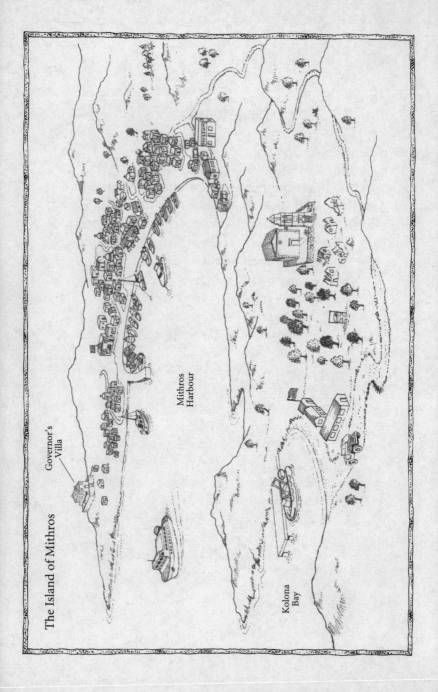

The Island of Mithros

Governor's
Villa

Mithros
Harbour

Kolona
Bay

DRAMATIS PERSONAE

Hermes Diaktoros	–	The fat man, an investigator
Enrico and Ilias	–	Crew aboard *Aphrodite*
Remo and Ricardo	–	Crew aboard a visiting boat
Vassilis Eliadis (Uncle Vasso)	–	A wealthy philanthropist
Lemonia Bousali	–	Uncle Vasso's housekeeper
Manolis Chiotis	–	A stranger
Spiros Tavoularis	–	A coastguard officer
Loskas Vergas	–	A bank clerk
Makis Theonas	–	A butcher
Captain Fanis Andreadis	–	An army captain
Skafidis, Kastellanos, Lillis and Gounaris	–	National Service conscripts
Professor Philipas	–	A museum curator
Lukia	–	Professor Philipas's wife
Olympia	–	A nurse
Tavros	–	Proprietor of a waterfront taverna
Milto Rokos	–	A musician and smallholder
Socrates Rokos	–	Milto's father
Kara Athaniti	–	A friend of Hermes, an archaeologist
Nondas	–	A kiosk owner and fisherman

GLOSSARY OF GREEK WORDS AND EXPRESSIONS

agapi mou – my love
agori mou – my boy
ambelopoulia – a dish of songbirds
amessos – immediately
chairo poli – formal greeting
Despina – Miss
embros – hello (on telephone) (lit. forward)
frappé – iced coffee whipped to a froth
kafenion – café
kai – and
kalé – familiar form of address
kali mera (sas) – good day (plural/polite form)
kali nichta (sas) – good night (plural/polite form)
kali orexi – bon appétit (lit. good digestion)
kali spera (sas) – good evening (plural/polite form)
kalos tou, kalos irthes – welcome
kamari mou – expression of affection, lit. my pride
koproskilo – dirty dog
kori mou – my daughter
koritsi – young lady
kouklos/koukla(ra) – handsome/pretty (lit. doll, m/f)
koulouri – a circlet of bread or pastry

Kyria	–	Mrs, Madam
Kyrios/Kyrie	–	Mr, Sir
malaka	–	common term of abuse
mankas	–	derogatory word for 'gentleman', a spiv
meltemi	–	seasonal summer wind
mori!	–	expression of shock or surprise
mou	–	my
panayeia (mou)	–	by the Virgin
pedi mou	–	my child
pedia	–	lit. children; affectionate address to a group
poustis	–	slang for 'homosexual'
raki	–	home-made spirit distilled from wine-skins
salone	–	living room
tavli	–	backgammon
Theé mou!	–	my God!
Theia	–	lit. Aunt: term of respectful and affectionate address to an older female
to chronou!	–	here's to next year!
vlaka	–	fool
volta	–	promenade (lit.walk)
yammas	–	cheers
yassou/yassas	–	hello or goodbye (singular and plural/polite forms) (lit. your health)
yiayia	–	grandma
zaharoplasteio	–	pastry/cake shop

'Thou seest how sloth wastes the sluggish body, as water is corrupted unless it moves.'

Ovid

PROLOGUE

The struggling bird was dangling from the twig, beating its free wing as it strained for flight, but the glue held both its feet fast, and pinned it by its last few tail-feathers. The quinces in the branches were the yellow of ripe pears; a scattering of lost feathers littered the tree's roots.

'Be careful with it,' said Spiros. 'Don't kill it.'

As Loskas reached out, the bird's fluttering became more frantic, its call more desperate.

'You're frightening it,' said Spiros.

Loskas withdrew his hand.

'You do it,' he said. 'It might bite me.'

'What if it did?' said Spiros. 'You'd never feel it. Look how tiny it is.'

The boys changed places. Loskas put his hands behind his back.

'Why don't you pull the twig out?' he asked. 'If you got the twig out, we could get hold of him.'

'It's a her,' said Spiros, peering amongst the foliage for the twig's end.

'How do you know it's a her?'

Spiros looked at him with faint derision.

'By the markings,' he said, and pointed to the oval of tan plumage on the bird's head. 'It's a female blackcap. The male's head's black.'

He reached in amongst the leaves.

'Don't get glue on you,' said Loskas. 'Don't get it on your clothes.'

The limed twig had been set low amongst the tree's natural branches. Spiros tugged it free, and drew out the long, straight switch, half-coated with linseed glue.

The tac-tac of the bird's distress call was growing fainter.

'Poor thing,' said Loskas. 'Let's let it go.'

'We have to clean it first,' said Spiros. 'It can't fly, covered in glue.' He laid the lime-twig on the ground and crouched beside it. 'If you cover the glue in dirt, it loses its stickiness.'

Taking care around the bird, he trickled sandy soil over the grey gum.

Somewhere in the orchard, an eager voice called out.

'There're more birds!' said Loskas. 'Makis has found more birds!'

'Go and tell him to bring the traps over here,' said Spiros. 'And tell him to stop yelling, or someone'll hear.'

Hampered by hand-me-down shoes, Loskas set off at a run. By the time Spiros finished neutralising the trap, the bird had stopped moving. Afraid that trauma had killed it, he placed the pad of a finger on the bird's chest. He felt only the ridge of a fine bone, but his touch provoked a silent opening and closing of the bird's beak, and a beating of its free wing, which gained it nothing but the loss of one more feather.

Spiros closed his hand around the bird's body. Poking through the loop of his thumb and forefinger, its head moved from side to side, its beak fitfully opening.

Amongst the orchard's trees of citrus and olive, Loskas

and Makis were squabbling. Spiros touched the bird's delicate feet, and realised how easily he might damage them. Holding his breath, one by one he prised the claws from the glued switch, and, relieved to have caused no apparent injury, freed the feathers of the caught wing and the tail. With the bird liberated, he stood up, and rolled the lime-stick in the dirt with the toe of his shoe.

'What're you doing?' The voice close to his back made Spiros jump. Socrates had a way of doing that, of creeping up unseen on the other boys. He tried to look over Spiros's shoulder, but being younger, was too short to see. 'What have you got?'

Spiros showed him the half-dead creature in his fist. Loskas's and Makis's arguing was growing closer.

Socrates looked down at the dirt-caked stick.

'That's one of Vassilis's traps,' he said. 'If he catches you, he'll thrash you! What are you going to do with the bird?'

'Let it go,' said Spiros.

'What for?' asked Socrates. 'Why don't you keep it?'

From between the orchard trees, Loskas and Makis approached, each carrying a switch almost as long as they were tall. Makis's had caught a ruby-masked goldfinch, worn out with its struggle and almost dead. Loskas's held a redstart, newly trapped and still battling.

'*Mori!*' said Socrates. 'You're stealing all Vassilis's birds!'

'We're not stealing them,' objected Spiros. 'We're setting them free. And he's got no right to trap them anyway. He doesn't even live here.'

Loskas and Makis laid down their lime-twigs. Loskas began to cover his in dirt, as if he were an old hand at the job.

'This is where the most birds are,' said Socrates. 'You've got to lay the traps where there're birds. But I don't see why you'd let them go. We could sell them, same as he does.'

Loskas paused, his fist full of soil.

'How could we sell them?' he asked, curiously. 'We don't have cages to put them in.'

Socrates tongued an adult 'tut' at Loskas's stupidity.

'To eat, *vlaka*,' he said. 'We could sell them to eat. Vassilis makes good money from them. He gets a thousand drachma a pair.'

The other three looked at him. Spiros's expression was of distaste, but Socrates had caught Loskas's and Makis's attention.

'They're good to eat, fried,' said Makis. 'Or you can pickle them, in jars. My *yiayia* does that, but I don't like them pickled.'

'And we haven't got a jar,' said Socrates.

'If we sell them to eat, we'll have to kill them first,' said Makis.

'That's easy,' said Socrates. 'I've seen him do it. You smash their heads, like this.' He squeezed his thumb hard against three fingers. 'Or you just pull their heads off.'

'You leave them alone!' warned Spiros. 'We're not killing them, we're setting them free! Loskas, you get them off the twigs. Then we'll go and wash them at the well.'

'You'll never get that glue off with just water,' said Socrates. 'You have to have that special stuff.'

'What special stuff?'

'Listen!'

The boys became still. On the track between the houses and the orchard, a young man whistled, and called a dog to heel.

'He's coming!' said Loskas. 'Run!'

The birds forgotten, he headed off towards the furthest trees. Long before they reached the orchard's cover, Makis had overtaken him.

Socrates snatched up the traps Makis and Loskas had abandoned.

'Go,' he said.

Spiros was anxious to follow the others.

'What are you going to do?' he asked.

'He doesn't scare me,' said Socrates. 'He takes our oranges, so he owes us.'

'But what are you going to do?'

Vassilis was very close; the boys could hear him curse his disobedient dog.

'He steals from my family, I can steal from him,' said Socrates. 'And I can outrun him, any day. Go. I'll keep him off your back.'

'Let's both go,' said Spiros. 'We can set the birds free in the hills.'

'Go, and I'll slow him down. Loskas needs a head start, and Makis'll cry like a girl, if he thinks he's in for the strap. Tell him I'll make sure he doesn't get caught. And I'll be right behind you, don't you worry.'

So Spiros didn't wait. As he made off, Vassilis came into the clearing, and seeing Spiros heading away and Socrates holding the lime-sticks, the young man himself began to run.

'Thief!' he shouted, aiming for Socrates. In spite of his boots, he moved fast. 'Rob me, would you? *Koproskilo!* Give me my property!'

'Come and take it!' taunted Socrates. 'Here!'

He yanked the goldfinch from the switch, but the bird was badly stuck, and left behind a toe, and a spray of feathers. Socrates launched it gleefully into the air, looking up to see it fly away and thwart Vassilis; but the exhausted bird fell back to earth with a thud, and lay half-stunned and floundering at Socrates's feet.

'*Malaka!*' shouted Vassilis. 'I'll teach you to steal from me!'

He lunged for the boy. Socrates dodged him, and dropping the lime-sticks, set off after his friends; but the young man had longer legs, and quickly caught him. He held Socrates by his arm, so tight it hurt; and when the boy struggled to get away, Vassilis pinched his ear-lobe, and that hurt more. Socrates stopped his struggling. Vassilis released his arm, but used the pressure on his ear to make the boy turn and look up at him. Vassilis wasn't tall, but he had the island's broad and powerful build.

'I should have known,' he said. 'Wherever there's trouble, there's you. Do you know who I am?'

The boy tried again to pull away. Vassilis squeezed his ear-lobe, and Socrates yelped.

'I asked if you know who I am.'

'You're Vassilis,' said Socrates.

'But you can call me Vasso,' said Vassilis, almost kindly. 'And those birds are my property.' He tugged Socrates's ear to stress his point, and Socrates winced. 'Those little birds are my ticket out of here. People pay good money for them. And we all want to make money, don't we?'

The boy said nothing, so Vassilis increased the pressure on his ear, until Socrates answered, 'Yes!'

'You could make some money too,' said Vassilis. 'If I have a good season this year, I'll be off this island by spring. You could help me have a good season, by keeping your thieving friends away from my traps. Do you think you could do that?'

Keen to avoid more pain, the boy nodded.

'Then you and I have a deal.'

Vassilis let go of Socrates's ear, and tousled his hair. He reached into his pocket, took out two one-hundred drachma coins and held them out to the boy.

Socrates took them.

'Let's you and I be friends,' said Vassilis. 'You look after my traps, and I'll look after you.'

Socrates clenched his fist around the money, and rubbed his ear.

'I didn't hurt you, did I?' asked Vassilis. 'If my father had caught you thieving, he'd have tanned all your backsides. I've let you off lightly, because I trust you. But if I catch those boys at my traps again, I'll hold you responsible. Got it? Now go.'

He gave the boy a playful clip to the side of his head.

Overhead, the rainless clouds were breaking up. Socrates sprinted after his friends. As he disappeared amongst the trees, Vassilis whistled his dog and walked back to the lime-sticks, where the goldfinch and the redstart cried their despair.

One

In Mithros's harbour, no boat ever came or went unnoticed. By early summer, when the heat was beginning to bite and all risk of storms was past, the number of visiting craft increased fivefold, and by August, doubled again. Some left with the dawn, and some arrived in the small hours (the great ferries of the Zoutis line – whose routes were lengthy, and so were prone to delays – never docked before midnight, even when running to time). But the majority arrived as the blue afternoons became evenings, seeking out overnight berths: yachts captained by professional wanderers, or mishandled by nervous novices ignorant of seamanship and etiquette; luxurious cruisers crewed by lithe men in white uniforms; and local fishing boats bringing home sun-sated tourists from the beaches, legs dangling over the sides and nursing weary children. There were dinghies and cargo-boats, caiques and gulets, and all were watched by some-body, somewhere: by the coastguard's duty officer, self-important on the quay, or feet up in his office with its view of the harbour's full stretch; by the town councillor's boy who collected the mooring fees, cycling unhurriedly from berth to berth on a brakeless bicycle; by the post-siesta crowd in the *kafenions* and bars, who – whether sailors or not – passed judgement on the competence of the arrivals' manoeuvrings.

But not every boat that came to Mithros entered the harbour. Some wanted peace, or privacy, and found their way instead to the remoter coves and bays around the coast – bays like Kolona, a wide-mouthed stretch of water narrowing to a stony beach, beyond which, set some way back, was a hamlet of run-down cottages and their church.

On a day in midsummer, where Kolona's aquamarine shallows ended, a German yacht lay at anchor. As noon approached, a second vessel sailed towards the beach, cutting its engines to anchor on the same line as the yacht. On the roof of its wheelhouse, a Greek flag fluttered; at the stern was a tattered flag of red and black. The boat showed the dilapidation of long travel: the fenders were battered, the exhaust smoked black with burning oil, the port-holes were blind with salt spray. As the anchors dropped, the captain switched on the bilge-pumps, fouling the waters with diesel.

When the engine and the pumps were switched off, the boat was quiet. The crew of four men – one blond, one black-skinned, two Greeks – were subdued. They didn't dive into the cooling sea, or turn on music; there was little talk between them, and no laughter. One clattered crockery and cutlery, and laid the table on the canopied stern; another brought out feta, salted cucumber and bread, which they ate in near silence. The blond fetched beers from a cooler, but got no thanks as he passed the bottles round. They finished their food, and cleared the plates, and sat back down at the table to light cigarettes.

From the trees behind the shore, cicadas shrilled. The men drank more beer, but stayed sober; when they spoke, they kept their voices quiet. The sun went down, and the temperature fell a few degrees towards tolerable. As the stars came out and the gibbous moon rose, one by one the men all went below, and lay down in their narrow bunks to sleep.

Mid-morning of the following day, an islander at the shoreline was mending nets. Over a mound of yellow mesh, flies buzzed after decaying debris: fish-scales and seaweed, dead crabs and discarded bottom-feeders. The islander spread the next few feet of net, and finding a tear, hauled it up over his knees.

The shuttle moved fast as he made the repair, but as he cut the thread with his knife, the day's brilliance dimmed, as if a cloud had passed over the sun. The islander looked up. A figure stood over him. The islander put his hand above his eyes to block the sun, and squinted up at a face he didn't know.

'I'm looking for a relative of mine,' said the stranger. 'Maybe you could help me.'

The islander stitched the next knots in the mesh.

'Who's your relative?' he asked.

'They call him Vassilis Eliadis.'

The islander's fingers became still.

'You're a relation of Uncle Vasso?' he asked. 'I don't see any family resemblance.'

'We're related by marriage,' said the stranger. 'But you do know him?'

'Oh yes, I know him. I know him very well.'

He found another hole, and put the shuttle to work.

'There'd be something in it for you, if you'd show us where to find him,' said the stranger. 'But we'd like you to be discreet. Our visit's a surprise.'

The islander was silent. He stitched, and cut.

'We'll make it worth your while,' said the stranger.

The islander seemed uninterested; but as the stranger turned to go, he spoke.

'I can be discreet,' he said. 'Especially if you make it worth my while.'

'Of course,' said the stranger. 'And I expect you know your way around here pretty well?'

'I should do,' said the islander. 'I was born here, and I've lived here boy and man.'

'There are things we need,' said the stranger. 'Our stores are low, and we need a chandler. Is there one in the port?'

'There are two or three,' said the islander. 'I can show you the cheapest, if you'd like. For a consideration. You'd be taking me from my work.'

The stranger smiled.

'Of course,' he said. 'I think you could be our man.' He held out his hand, and the islander shook it. 'They call me Ricardo.'

'Socrates.'

'Good to meet you, Socrates. When you've finished here, why don't you and I have a drink, and we can talk?'

Some nights later, Ricardo, the blond and the black-skinned man climbed into the dinghy they towed behind their boat. The blond fired up the outboard, and steered towards the shore. At the jetty, Socrates was waiting; as the dinghy drew alongside, he flicked his cigarette into the sea. He stepped aboard, and offered a greeting, to which only Ricardo replied. The engine was never cut; the three made room for the fourth, and they sped away, passing their own unnamed vessel without acknowledgement to the crewman left behind.

In the weak light of battery lamps, he watched them go.

In the dinghy, the blond spoke to Ricardo in a foreign language, and as Ricardo replied, Socrates caught his own name.

'He wanted to know what they call you,' translated Ricardo.

'What do they call him?' asked Socrates.

'Nothing, as far as you're concerned. He doesn't need a name.' He jerked his thumb at the black-skinned man beside him. 'But you can call him Remo.'

As they made the turn into Mithros's harbour, the dinghy slowed.

'Vasso lives up there,' said Socrates. He pointed to the highest house on the promontory, where lights blazed at all the windows. 'The Governor's Villa.'

Ricardo spoke to the blond, translating what Socrates had said. The blond's response was short.

'He wants to know where to go,' said Ricardo.

'Over here,' said Socrates. 'Tell him to find somewhere on this side.'

There were no vacant moorings, but the dinghy needed little space. Between an elegant Turkish gulet of varnished pine and a local caique painted up for the tourists, the dinghy touched the harbour-wall, at a point where stone steps rose from the water. The blond tied up to an iron ring in the wall. The gulet's crew looked down on them mistrustfully.

On shore, they fell in with the casual pace of the evening's *volta*. Amongst the many tourists, Ricardo, Remo and the blond moved unremarked. Socrates walked ahead, assuming without looking that they were following. A shout came for him to join a *kafenion* table, where local men sipped coffee and eyed the girls. Socrates called out, 'Later,' and went on.

Towards the harbour's end, the town was quiet. The three followed him along an alleyway, where drab businesses were doing no trade. In the doorways, the proprietors sat in shorts and cutaway vests which showed their thick shoulder hair; on the balconies above, their women spread their fat white legs under cotton dresses, sighing for a breeze to cool their thighs.

Socrates led on and up through a maze of backstreets, until they reached the lane where the Governor's Villa hid behind its wall. Lit by a streetlamp, the lane at its far end dropped away down the hillside, giving a view of the night-black sea and the silhouettes of islands under the moon. Far out on the water, a boat's navigation lamps glinted green and red.

The villa wall was draped with honeysuckle and jasmine, whose sensual perfume mixed with the stink of cats. From a house below the villa, Kalomiris's piano concerto crackled from a dusty-needled record-player.

Socrates didn't speak, but gestured to the villa door, which had no handle, only a keyhole, and a knocker in the shape of a lion's head. Over its arch, a light burned; given the brightness of the streetlamp, it seemed unnecessary.

Ricardo spoke to Socrates, keeping his voice low.

'Get him to open the door,' he said. 'Don't let him know we're here.'

He led Remo and the blond a little way along the lane, where they stood with their backs against the villa wall, out of Socrates's sight.

Socrates raised the lion's-head knocker, and banged on the door three times. He waited, until at length from behind the door, someone asked, 'Who is it?'

'It's me,' said Socrates. 'I want to talk to you.'

A key was turned, a bolt drawn, and the door opened.

'So you're back, are you?' said Uncle Vasso, his voice full of dry humour. 'What is it you want to say?'

Socrates had no answer to the question, and in several seconds of silence, Uncle Vasso studied him, and realised all was not well. He moved to shut Socrates out; but before he could do so, Ricardo, Remo and the blond reached the door, the blond slamming his weight against it so it could not be closed.

Uncle Vasso's expression was grim.

'*Yassou*, nephew,' he said to Ricardo.

There was no embracing, no back-slapping reunion.

'Shall we go inside?' said Ricardo. He turned to Socrates. 'You, wait over there.'

Socrates shrugged his indifference, and walking away, took a seat on the stump of a pine tree. He lit a cigarette. The three men followed Uncle Vasso inside. There were footsteps on the stone-flagged courtyard; an inner door closed, and there was silence.

On his tree-stump, Socrates listened. In the house below, the record of the piano concerto was stuck; the same uplifting phrase played over and over, until the needle was lifted from the groove, and dropped back on to the record beyond its sticking point.

The silence from the villa continued. Socrates ground out his cigarette, and approached the door; he put his hand to the wood, and found it fastened shut. He pressed his ear against it. There was nothing to hear.

Minutes went by. Growing bored, he wandered to the lane's end, and looked out over the sea. The music from below was coming to its climax, piano and strings playing loudly, and with passion.

Someone screamed.

The sound was startling, short and sharp, there and gone. Unmistakably, it came from inside the villa. Yet as the silence resettled, Socrates doubted what he had heard; as the quiet persisted, he was ready to dismiss the scream as a tom-cat's yowl, or a child in some rough game.

But then there was shouting – a stream of protests, curses and the vilest, foulest language thrown between men – until the curses broke off, and the screaming came again, drawn-out and chilling to the soul.

Socrates ran back to the door and hammered on it. There was no answer. The screaming stopped. As Socrates listened, a new silence grew, spreading to the houses down the hillside where others were now listening, too.

Fast footsteps ran across the courtyard, and the door was thrown open.

The three men emerged, the blond carrying a satchel made from coarse-grained boar-hide. Socrates was in their way, and the blond jarred his shoulder as he went by. Socrates grabbed Remo's arm, but Remo was moving quickly, and easily pulled free. Socrates put out a hand to stop Ricardo, but Ricardo dodged him, giving no acknowledgement Socrates was even there.

'What the hell's going on?' Socrates called after them, but the men were intent on their getaway, and didn't respond. At the lane's end they disappeared, heading back the way Socrates had brought them.

Socrates's instinct was to follow; but somewhere in the house, Uncle Vasso moaned.

Through the courtyard, the villa door stood open. Inside, the kitchen smelled of burning.

He went through the kitchen, into the *salone*. The room was ostentatious in its comforts, flamboyant in its style – a low-backed leather sofa, a lighted drinks cabinet with crystal glasses, a polished oval dining table – yet what drew the eye was Uncle Vasso's collection, his hoard of African souvenirs. On the floor before the fireplace was a zebra-skin, on the hearth a funerary urn decorated with stick-figures. Along one wall hung spears and painted shields, and complex, beaded necklaces in frames; and on all sides were disquieting black masks, the weird, elongated faces of warriors.

Behind a burning icon-lamp, Uncle Vasso sat at the table, roped by his waist and lower legs to his chair. The dead match which had lit the lamp had been dropped on the polished table, but the burning smell – far more intense in here – was not of scorched varnish, but of singed hair.

Uncle Vasso looked up at Socrates. His eyes were swollen with crying, his face was creased in pain, and he held up his shaking hands to show Socrates his roasted skin.

'My hands!' he said. His voice was weak with shock. 'They burned my hands!'

Socrates ran outside, made for the sea's end of the lane, and called down to the house where there had been music.

'Lemonia! Come up here, quickly!'

A woman's voice responded.

'What's going on? Who is that?'

'Come up here, quickly!' shouted Socrates. 'Bring bandages, and honey! Vasso needs help, and I can't stay.'

As fast as he was able through the dark lanes he followed his quarry, kicking off his sandals and carrying them to move faster on the smooth-worn stones. Knowing the shortest route, he had the advantage of them. They, inevitably, would lose their way; they'd keep heading downhill, but they'd hit dead-ends and take unwanted detours. He knew he'd reach the harbour-front before them; even given their lead, he'd be there first.

But then he felt a sting of pain in his foot. He hopped to a stop, and swearing, picked it up. The light was bad, but by touch he found the object which had punctured his sole still embedded in the skin. Leaning against a wall and balancing with difficulty, he pulled out what was buried there, wincing and taking care not to break whatever it was. He held it up to the moonlight: a piece of glass, and the wetness glistening on his fingers could only be blood. Cautiously, aware there'd probably be more glass, he slipped back into his sandals and continued on.

His foot was painful; he limped along on his toes, so his progress was slowed. As he reached the waterfront, he saw his delay had been too long. The three men he was pursuing had already cast off, and the dinghy was mid-harbour. He shouted after them – *kleftes, kleftes – thieves, thieves* – so loudly the diners in the tavernas stopped eating, and the drinkers in the bars turned to stare; but in the whole of Mithros harbour, only the three men he wanted to hear him apparently did not.

Socrates needed to borrow a boat.

At his house a short way back from the waterfront, the postman was sitting on his doorstep in only a pair of shorts, his legs apart to let the air circulate around his genitals.

'Hey, *malaka*!'

The postman squinted over at Socrates.

'Hey, Socrates! Is that you? How're you doing? Long time no see! Come and have a beer!'

He picked up a bottle and waved it in the air, then held it up to the light, disappointed to find it empty.

Socrates stood in front of him.

'I need a favour,' he said. 'I need to borrow your boat.'

The postman's face showed his reluctance.

'When?' he said. 'I'm taking my boys out tomorrow. We're going fishing.'

'Now,' said Socrates. 'I need it now. To stop them.' He pointed after the dinghy, which was by then moving out of sight around the harbour end.

The postman craned forward from his step for a better view.

'Who are they?'

'They're foreigners,' said Socrates. 'Please, fetch me the keys. You'll have it back within the hour, I promise.'

The postman cast around for another excuse.

'I'd be happy to, normally,' he said. 'But I don't think there's any fuel in it. Ask Fotinos. He might have fuel.'

'I need something quicker than Fotinos's old tub,' said Socrates. 'I'll pay you. Five thousand. Five thousand for an hour's rental – that's fair.'

The postman was still doubtful.

'OK, seven and half,' said Socrates. 'Ten, then. I'll give you ten thousand.'

The postman laughed.

'Where would you get ten thousand?' he asked. 'You don't have ten thousand to give me!'

'They owe me,' said Socrates. 'The foreigners owe me money. That's why I need your boat. They're moored over in Kolona, on a cruiser. If they get to it before I get to them, they'll be gone.'

'Ten thousand?'

'Ten thousand. I promise.'

'And you'll be back inside the hour?'

'Inside the hour. Kolona and back, that's it.'

The postman sighed, as much at the inconvenience of standing as at the risk of loaning his boat. He ambled into the house. Minutes went by. Socrates sat down to inspect his foot. The wound was still oozing blood; his sandal was stained with it. More time went by. He stood up, and called through the window.

'Be quick, *malaka*! For Christ's sake!'

'I can't find the keys,' called the postman. 'My damned wife's been cleaning again.'

Eventually he appeared at the window. He had opened himself a fresh beer.

'Here,' he said, dropping a set of keys into Socrates's cupped hands. 'Remember, no more than an hour. And take care of her!'

Everything seemed to take too much time – the starting of the uncompliant engine, the hauling in of the small anchor, the loosing of the ropes to cast off – and even once all that was accomplished, the boat moved slower than Socrates had anticipated; what had always struck him as being a fast boat seemed to chug through the water as if dragging three others behind.

He reached the outer waters of Kolona Bay. The moon was high in the sky, and as he drew close, its dim light showed him the inevitable: Ricardo, Remo and the blond already aboard their vessel, the engine fired and the boat moving forward on to its upcoming anchor.

Socrates began to shout, though over his own engine at full power he could barely hear himself.

Their boat's anchor was up, and she was leaving her mooring.

Socrates stood up in the stern, and steered at the oncoming vessel; but the postman's boat was beginning to labour, missing and losing power.

Socrates was still shouting.

'*Malakes*! Eh, *malakes*! Where are you going, you sons of whores!'

And then his engine died. Furious, cursing, he went to the control panel, and played for a minute with the switches, until a glance at the gauges told the whole story: he had no fuel.

But the postman's boat glided on, slower and slower, in the direction he had been heading, towards the vessel which was driving towards him at full throttle. Socrates ran back to the rudder. At the other boat's wheel, Ricardo waved him out of the way; but Socrates was helpless to move, and his drifting boat began a turn to port, taken round by the light breeze and the swell until she was broadside to the oncoming prow.

There was a terrible bang. Ricardo never even cut the power.

A flare went up, turning the moon blood-red. A young boy – held back from the water by his distraught mother – screamed, *Papa, papa!* Men came running from the hamlet, and launched their fastest craft. When they reached the place where the two vessels had hit, pieces of the postman's boat were still afloat; but of Socrates, who had captained it, there was no sign.

Seventeen Years Later

Two

The heat of early afternoon made everything still. Close to the islands' shores, the sea rippled with unbroken waves; far out, a crescent of calm water – silky as the skins of swimming bream – was split by the fanned wake of a white ferry, which moved unhurriedly along the arc of its heading, towards a misty smudge of land on the horizon.

Tracking the ferry, a mile or so behind, was an ocean-going yacht. Along her hull, narrow bands of gold and navy blue picked out her subtle curves, and on her prow, her name – *Aphrodite* – was painted in gold.

Leaning on the deck-rail, a man taller than many looked down on *Aphrodite*'s wake, studying the flow and forms of the tumbling sea. From time to time, he brushed salt-water splashes from his clothes: a pale-lavender shirt, and cream linen trousers of Italian design, expertly tailored to disguise a generous stomach. His greying curls required a barber's attention; his sunglasses were of tortoiseshell, round-lensed and giving an air of academia; and on his feet, he wore white canvas shoes, in the old-fashioned style once worn for tennis.

The fat man brought his attention back from the water, and read a pencil-marked paragraph from an old copy of Herodotus. A breath of aromatic wind – fresh with oregano, pine and sage

– riffled the book's loose pages. He glanced forward. The ferry's stern was markedly further ahead than it had been, when he had last looked. *Aphrodite* was losing ground.

The fat man frowned.

A crewman in white uniform appeared from the galley. Dark and balding, he had the lascivious mouth of a satyr, and a mischief-lover's eyes. He gave a short bow.

'*Kyrie*, excuse me,' he said. 'Lunch is ready.'

The crewman led the way to a table on the awning-covered rear deck.

As the fat man followed, he asked, 'Is everything in order with *Aphrodite*, Enrico? Because it seems to me we're losing power.' His Greek was beautifully enunciated, the perfect Greek of TV newscasters, each word a separate entity and given equal importance within his speech.

'We have a little problem with the starboard engine,' said Enrico, pulling out a chair. 'Ilias has shut it down.'

'What problem?'

The fat man sat; with a waiter's flourish, Enrico spread a napkin over his lap.

'The same problem as last week,' said Enrico, pouring the fat man a glass of chilled wine. 'The boy's idle; he didn't fix it properly, and now it's failed again. He should have stripped it right down to the filters, but he botched it instead. So now we're back to running on one engine. Regretfully, that's likely to make us somewhat late.'

The fat man looked around them, at the hazy blue islands which lay to the north, and to the west.

'So,' he said, 'the Fates whisper the suggestion of a change of plan. And who are we to disagree? We'll make a detour, and put in somewhere where Ilias can make a proper repair.'

He looked at each island in turn, considering, and up at the sun, establishing bearings.

'There,' he said, at last, indicating the most distant of the westerly landmasses. 'Tell Ilias to change course. And tell him to make a decent job this time, and to do it quickly, because if we lose that engine a third time, I shall not forgive him so easily.'

By late afternoon, the tamarisk trees were casting shade on the guardhouse terrace. At the top of its pole, the national flag's blue and white lines stirred in the lightest of breezes. Under the tamarisks' feathered branches, the National Service conscripts were relaxing, stripped down to their undershirts or tanned torsos, with camouflage trousers the only gesture to uniform discipline. Gounaris and Lillis had not troubled to shave that morning; Skafidis's beard was some days into its growth.

They had made themselves comfortable, as best they might. Skafidis had created a hammock from a bedsheet, its corners tied with rope between two tree-trunks, and lay in it with his cap over his face, his booted feet crossed at the ankles. When Gounaris dragged his mattress from the bunkhouse, the captain had not bothered to object, so Gounaris lay parallel to Skafidis, on the ground. Kastellanos and Lillis were playing *tavli*, the click of counters and the rattling of dice percussion to the rhythm of cicadas.

The captain sat alone at the unsteady table, and read his newspaper. A transistor radio played music from a Turkish station, the only one they could reliably receive; the announcer's talk was gibberish to the captain's ears.

The solitary boat moored on the bay – a run-down commercial vessel with the scrapings of careless dockings along the hull – had kept its distance. Now the ragged crew (whose raucousness had disturbed the peace all afternoon) were cramped thigh to thigh around a table too small for all six. A bottle was brought to the table; a round of drinks was poured. A pack of cards was found, and the first hand dealt.

For an hour, the crew drank, and played. The more they drank, the louder they became, with shouts of victory and dismay, with taunts and challenges. The soldiers were indifferent; the game of *tavli* was won, and another begun. Gounaris and Skafidis dozed. The captain read the sports news.

'*Malaka! Poustis! Poustis!*'

The captain removed his mirrored sunglasses, and squinted into the blue glare, towards the boat. It was not the insulting words that caught his attention – they were commonplace to him – but the rage behind them. A fist slammed down on the table; a glass clattered to the deck, spilling liquid into the laps of two men, who jumped up and themselves began to shout.

'Gounaris,' said the captain, 'go and get me the binoculars.'

On his mattress, the conscript didn't move.

'Gounaris, do you hear me?' said the captain, louder.

Lillis turned round from the *tavli* board, and prodded Gounaris with his toe.

'The captain wants you, *malaka*,' he said. 'Get up.'

Without trying to hide his unwillingness, Gounaris rose and went slowly to the guardhouse. When he brought out the binoculars, he didn't hand them directly to the captain, but put them to his own eyes to survey the boat.

'There's trouble,' said the young man, smiling. 'Looks like a fight to me.'

'Give me those.'

The soldier handed the captain the binoculars.

But even with the view magnified through the lenses, what was happening on the boat was hard to say. Not all the words being shouted were in Greek, and, whilst all the men were on their feet, some were smiling. There was pushing, and pointing, but all might still be good-humoured, and the shouting might have been no more than banter.

Yet the focus seemed to be all on one man, who was holding up both hands, head down and submissive as a kicked dog. The odds were stacked against him, five on to one. As he lowered his arms, one of the five shoved him in the chest, and knocked him back against the rail; when he objected, the man who had assaulted him stepped up close so they were nose to nose.

No possibility of a peaceable outcome seemed to remain. The conscripts left their dozing and their *tavli* and wandered over to the captain, Lillis in his fraying espadrilles, Skafidis's black boots dusty and unlaced. The captain focused on the boat's stern and studied the unfamiliar flag, then handed the binoculars to the conscripts, who passed them amongst themselves, anticipating entertainment; but the two men on the boat finally gave each other space, and it seemed their quarrel would come to nothing.

The captain put on his sunglasses, and picked up his newspaper.

The man up against the deck-rail laughed, mocking and loud.

The man who had shoved him, punched him in the face.

The man who had been hit swore, and touched his nose and mouth. He looked at the blood on his fingers, and yelled at his assailant.

The assailant grabbed the bloodied hand. The punched man tried to break away, but the assailant pulled him forward, and two others laid hands on him too; another kicked his feet away, and the sixth caught him under the armpits as he went down. Five were on to one, and the job was easy. They heaved him up, and pitched him into the sea.

There was a splash, and the victim sank. Within a moment,

he was back at the surface, blowing water from his nose and his mouth, shaking seawater from his hair.

His crew-mates stood at the deck-rail, laughing; he seemed to take the humiliation in good part, and trod water whilst they joked at his expense, until, bored, they turned away, the man who had hit him sliding his palms across each other: *finito*.

The five crew still aboard went to work, one at the prow untying ropes, another in the wheelhouse preparing to start the engine. The man in the water called up to them, pointing to a ladder lying against the deck-rails, and when the crew ignored him, swam to the stern. He reached for a trailing rope-end to haul himself aboard, but the rope was out of his reach. In frustration, he slapped the boat's hull. He shouted up half-laughing to the crew, but they, treating him as invisible, only smirked and winked amongst themselves. The engine fired, and the anchor-winch started up, covering his pleading with its noise.

The boat began to move, and he swam away a fast few metres to be clear of the propeller. As the distance between man and boat increased, there was no more laughing. The wheel-man opened the throttle, and the boat picked up speed, leaving an arrow of white wake in which the man in the water bobbed up and down. From the rear deck, three crew-men waved their arms over their heads in unkind farewell.

The swim to the beach was not lengthy, but the man took his time, swimming on his back in nonchalant style, glancing round from time to time in hope of the joke being over, of the boat having made a turn to pick him up; but by the time he reached the beach, the boat from which he'd been thrown was out of sight.

He sat for a while at the water's edge, drying slowly in the last afternoon sun, skimming flat stones across the water, looking out at the horizon for the boat's return, until the sky's blue faded, and shifted to the pink of sunset.

Eventually, he stood, and shoeless and wincing on the stones' sharp edges, made his way towards the soldiers at the guardhouse.

The soldiers were dispersing to various duties. The captain was still sitting at the table, and watched the man pick his way across the beach.

When he judged him to be within earshot, the captain spoke.

'*Kali spera sas*,' he said. 'You're trespassing on military property.'

'*Yassas*, Captain.' The man wore nothing but a pair of shorts, and though no longer young, looked as if he had once been very fit, with good tone still in his muscles. 'I apologise, but it's not my fault I'm here. You saw my friends' stupid joke. And it's getting dark, so I'm assuming the joke won't be over tonight. So I must ask you for assistance. Can you offer me a lift to . . .' he cast his eyes along the empty beach. 'Well, somewhere civilised? And could I borrow some shoes, and a shirt? I'm so sorry to have to ask. My friends are idiots. They take things too far, as you've seen.'

The captain studied him.

'That's a nasty cut you have there,' he said, looking at the man's split and swollen lip. 'Do your friends often treat you that way?'

'They drink too much.' He touched the bump on his lip and the scab of dried blood on the cut. 'Sometimes they get carried away.'

'We should introduce ourselves,' said the captain. He held out his hand without moving in his chair, so the man had to step forward to take it. 'They call me Andreadis, Captain

33

Fanis Andreadis. I'm in charge of this unit. What shall we call you?'

Before the man gave his answer there was the slightest hesitation.

'Chiotis,' he said. 'Manolis Chiotis.'

'Ah, Chiotis! One of my favourite singers! You're not related to him, I suppose?'

Manolis waved his hand to dismiss the suggestion.

'Well, *Kyrie* Chiotis,' said the captain. 'I can't take you anywhere tonight. We're on short army rations, and we don't have fuel to make unscheduled trips to the port. But I can lend you a shirt and some shoes, and you're welcome to eat with us, of course. Though you've come at a bad time, where food's concerned. I'm afraid it's Skafidis's turn to cook.'

Lillis claimed that, in civilian life, he knew about engines, and his claim had earned him the job of engineer. As it grew dark, he went to the shed where the generator was housed, and persuaded the motor into life, so its throb became the dominant background noise, drowning out the sea's soft splash along the beach. When the generator was running smoothly, Gounaris threw the power switch, lighting the guardhouse terrace with a string of dim bulbs which drew moths and other insects. Kastellanos found matches, and set anti-mosquito coils smoking under the windows.

The soldiers had dressed down for dinner, all stripped to shorts and bare-chested, in heat which had hardly reduced since the late afternoon. Skafidis spread the trestle table with a plastic cloth holed with cigarette burns, and fastened it to the table-edge with aluminium clips.

Captain Fanis sat at the head of the table, and offered the visitor the seat to his right. Gounaris carried out a Greek salad and a basket of bread. Skafidis brought out plates of spaghetti with meat sauce and a bowl of grated hard cheese.

'When I leave the army,' said Lillis, 'I'm never eating spaghetti again.'

'There's nothing wrong with spaghetti,' said Kastellanos. 'It's only Skafidis's spaghetti you'll never want to eat again. You should try my mother's spaghetti. She makes a meat sauce so good, you'd eat nothing but spaghetti for the rest of your life.'

The young men ate, and talked, and laughed.

The captain and Manolis ate too, but for a while said nothing. The sea before them disappeared into blackness; the sky was lit by a million stars, the magical incandescence of the Milky Way.

'So, friend.' The captain turned at last to Manolis. 'Tell me how you come to be here.'

The soldiers laughed at some joke, and one of them demanded the passing of bread. Lillis called out for a game of poker when dinner was finished.

'Your men are going to play cards,' said Manolis. 'You should tell them to be careful. It was a game of cards which landed me here with you. Look, I really need to get out of here. I'm a businessman, and there are calls I need to make. Surely you have VHF? I could get in touch with someone that way, save you the trouble of taking me to the port.'

'This is the Greek army, my friend, the very dregs of it,' said the captain. 'VHF kaput. You should relax, look on this as a holiday at government expense. Tomorrow at the earliest, you'll be leaving here.'

Manolis wound spaghetti around his fork.

'Maybe you're right,' he said. 'Maybe here's as safe as anywhere.'

'Safe?' The captain looked at him sharply. 'Are you in some kind of trouble, friend?'

'Trouble? No, no trouble. Why should I be?'

'Because your arrival here was unorthodox. And you haven't yet said who your friends are. Hardly an act of friendship, was it, to abandon you that way?'

'Maybe I misled you, calling them friends. Our arrangement was purely business. The boat was a private charter, but the guy who chartered it – my associate – was being cheap. He's always cheap. He sends me a rust-bucket which barely floats and a crew of Albanian cut-throats, and expects me to deliver what he wants. But in fairness I made my own problems. I played cards with them, and I got lucky. In the end I had too much luck for them to stomach. When I cleaned out the mate, he got mad, and when he couldn't frighten me into giving his money back, he rallied the troops and they dumped me overboard.'

'You were lucky,' said Captain Fanis. 'There aren't many places on this God-forsaken island where you'd have got out of the sea and found yourself anywhere but trapped by cliffs and mountainsides. It's not a place for a man without shoes.'

'So what's the name of this place where I've washed up?' asked Manolis, putting the forkful of spaghetti in his mouth.

'A forgotten outpost, and one of the last of Greece's territories before you hit Asia. This unit protects the outermost regions of our country from invasion from marauding Turks. You have landed, my friend, on the island of Mithros.'

Manolis coughed, as if choking on his food.

'Careful there,' said the captain. 'Skafidis likes to lay traps for us in his cooking. Overdoses of chilli, or chicken with all the guts left in. Whole peppercorns are a favourite with him. Maybe you found one of those.'

Manolis took a drink of water.

'I'd no idea we were so far south,' he said. 'Those idiots told me we were somewhere off Astypalea. They read nauti-

36

cal charts worse than they play cards.'

'Do you know our island? Have you been to Mithros before?'

Manolis scratched his ear.

'No,' he said. 'No, I don't know the place at all.'

'Well, now you know our small corner of it, Camp Kolona,' said the captain. 'Established fifteen years ago, by order of the military powers that be. I've been posted here since the day that flag was first hoisted to the top of that pole. But it wouldn't have been surprising if you'd been here before. The tourists come in droves, all hoping to find our famous missing bull. You've heard of the bull of Mithros, no doubt?'

'I've heard of it, yes.'

'If you don't know the story, it's worth hearing.' Captain Fanis poured himself more water, and offered the jug to Manolis, who held out his glass to be filled. 'They say it was only luck it was ever found at all. Whoever hid it – who knows how long ago? – hid it well, so it only came to light when builders went to work in one of the old harbour houses. I could take you there now and point out the place they say it was found, in a box, in a cavity under the floor. So big, no more.' He held his forefingers about six inches apart. 'Just a small thing, not much bigger than your fist, all ebony and gold. An object so beautiful, they say it lit a fire in all who touched it. From all over the island they came to see it, and many went away wanting it to be theirs. Those who'd had it in their hands all said how hard it was to give it back. It created a lust in them, to keep it for themselves. Then it was stolen. Within days of being found, it was gone. Pouf! Vanished. Before the experts got here from Athens with their photographing and cataloguing, it disappeared. And from that day to this, its whereabouts is a mystery. Is that the story as you know it?'

37

'That's about it,' said Manolis. 'The lost bull of Mithros, a tale lacking a happy ending.'

'You should buy a memento of it, whilst you're here. There are some excellent souvenir shops in the harbour. I'll point you to one where they know me. If you mention my name, they'll give you a good discount.'

'I don't have time to play the tourist,' said Manolis. 'Listen, is there really no way of getting me out of here tonight? What about that?' Manolis pointed to a Jeep parked behind the guardhouse, at the place where a footpath to the beach became a rough road. 'I'll make it right with them, if one of your boys would drive me. I'm anxious to get out of here. There's a woman I really need to call, and she'll have my balls on a plate if I don't phone.'

'So you're married, are you?' asked the captain. 'Only you don't wear a ring.'

'I'm not married any more,' said Manolis. 'Ten years of that misery was enough for me. No, the lady in question is someone else's wife. I spent a long time warming her up, and if I'm not careful, she'll go cold on me and all that effort'll be wasted. I see you wear no ring yourself.'

'I never married.'

'Really?' Manolis raised his eyebrows. 'An unmarried man, alone on a beach with all these young men? Don't you worry about your reputation?'

The captain's face hardened.

'What do you mean?'

'It's not about what I mean. It's what others might say that would worry me. Plainly it doesn't bother you. But being stuck here wouldn't suit me, regardless. I like to be where the women are. I like to have something to look at, and there's not much to look at here. But you're wise never to have married.'

'I wanted to be married, once,' said the captain. 'And I often wish that I'd had kids. But then, these boys are my family. I've been father to hundreds of them, over the years.'

'Can you understand, though, the importance of my getting to a phone?' asked Manolis. 'If she cools off, there won't be another chance. So what about it? Would one of your lads drive me? Hey, lads!'

He called out to the young men, but over their joking and baiting, they didn't hear.

'Before you ask,' said the captain, with a smile, 'I should warn you that Jeep has been Lillis's project since the day he arrived. He's tinkered and taken it to bits, and put it back together again, and let me tell you, it's never driven a single kilometre these past three months. You'll come with us tomorrow, in the launch. We head out of here usually by ten. In the meantime, relax, and enjoy your dinner. If you're a businessman, what business are you in?'

Manolis was watching the soldiers, still hoping for an opportunity to enlist their help.

'I turn my hand to many things. You might call me a travelling salesman.'

'We get a lot of salesmen in the islands. Everything from garden pots to snake-oil. What do you sell?'

'I'm in the export business. You name it, if there's money to be made, I'll sell it. I don't suppose you have a beer, do you? I'd kill for a cold beer.'

'I allow no alcohol on this post,' said Captain Fanis. 'Army regs. And if I did, we've no facilities to keep it cold. But this water's from the well here. It's pure, and it tastes good. This boat you were on – what was its name, its registration? When we go to the port tomorrow, we'll radio from the coastguard office and get your crew brought in.'

Manolis shook his head.

'No need, no need at all,' he said. 'It was a joke, a stupid prank. Besides, I don't remember the boat's name. And I didn't ever notice the registration.'

'Where was it bound for, then? We'll get the coastguard to track it down after it docks.'

Manolis put his hand to his head and rubbed his temple.

'Do you know,' he said, 'I've got a lousy headache. I suppose that's what you get for taking a punch in the mouth.' He laid down his fork. 'If there's really no hope of getting out of here tonight, I'd like to get some sleep.'

'I'm sure you would,' said the captain, after a moment's silence. 'There'll be some formalities tomorrow, of course. Since you have no ID with you, I'll escort you to the coastguard station. I expect there'll be some paperwork before you're free to go.'

'I'm no illegal immigrant, Captain,' said Manolis. 'I'm a citizen of this country, born and bred. If you could just take me to the port, that'll suffice.'

'Unfortunately, that won't be possible. The circumstances of your arrival are unusual. The vessel you were on wasn't Greek registered, and you seem unclear as to its port of origin. Besides, you've no resources on which to travel. You'll need either the coastguard or the police to vouch for you, if you want to get funds from the bank. And forgive me for pointing this out, but you don't even have a coin to call your woman. Though I'll be happy to give you change for the phone myself, when the time comes.'

'I'd appreciate that. And thanks for the sandals.'

'That's nothing,' said the captain. 'One of the soles is loose, as you've no doubt noticed. Be careful not to trip over it. If you'd come tomorrow, they might have been thrown out, so you're welcome to them. You'll sleep all right, I'm sure, over in the stores. That campbed isn't the most comfortable in the world, but you'll be better by yourself than lying awake all night listening to my garrison snoring.'

'I'm sure I'll be fine.' He got up from his chair, and looked again to the bottom end of the table. ''Night, lads,' he said, to the soldiers; but they were laughing at one of Skafidis's jokes, and didn't hear.

Captain Fanis watched Manolis go, then turned his attention back to his plate; but as he wound strands of over-boiled spaghetti around his fork, Kastellanos stood up and reached across the table for a basket which still held a slice or two of bread, showing as he did so the leanness of his torso. Captain Andreadis glanced down at his own soft belly, and pinched a little spare flesh through his undershirt. He looked again at Kastellanos, and pushed the spaghetti away, and served himself instead a spoonful of salad. As the captain finished eating, Gounaris cleared away the plates and glasses, and Skafidis brought out a bowl of watermelon, glistening in the light, its black seeds shining. The young men grabbed for the rough-cut slabs of fruit, and bit into it without caring about the juice which dribbled from it; they wiped it from their mouths with the backs of their hands, and from their chests and bellies with their palms, and wiped the wipings on their shorts or their bare thighs, and went on ribbing each other with cruel affection, arrogant and cocky, naive and clear-eyed, optimistic about life as it beckoned them forward: into the next few minutes, where there might be the glory of a victory at poker; into the brightness of the coming years, and the brilliance of the futures which would be theirs.

When the fruit was gone, Lillis fetched a pack of cards in a ragged box, the cards themselves dog-eared and sticky with use, and so many of them nicked and bent that from ace to king of every suit might be said to be marked. All the conscripts had a handful of small change with which to gamble; all approached the game with such excitement, the stakes might have matched the highest in Monte Carlo.

They began to play. The captain watched, and the hot night moved slowly on. The soldiers won or lost, laughed, complained and jeered. Kastellanos threw his cards down, and stormed off in a rage; minutes later he was back, smiling and ready to take his chances, confident of winning back what he'd lost.

'Shall I deal you in, then?' asked Lillis. 'But don't go crying when I clean you out.'

'Deal, *malaka*,' said Kastellanos. 'I'm feeling lucky.'

Lillis dealt the cards, and they studied the hands they'd been dealt.

The lights went out.

They groaned. In the darkness, Skafidis slapped Lillis's head. In the new silence created by the generator's failure, the blow was loud.

Kastellanos fumbled for his lighter, and struck it; by its flame, he found the torch kept on the windowsill for these eventualities. The dark was deep but not complete; a little moonlight, and a faint glow from the stars allowed them, as their eyes adjusted, to see.

'Why didn't you fill it, for Christ's sake?' asked Captain Fanis. 'I told you to make sure there was enough fuel.'

'I did,' objected Lillis. 'It should run for hours, yet.'

'Go fix it, then,' said Skafidis. 'I've got a great hand here, and I want to play it.'

'Forget it,' said the captain. 'It's getting late. Kastellanos, you're on night duty. You'll have to use a storm-lantern as watch-light. The rest of you, turn in.'

The captain made his way to his tiny quarters, and undressed by the light of the lamp which burned before the icon of the Archangel Michael. He placed his boots side by side, folded his undershirt and laid it over a chair-back, folded his trousers and placed them under his mattress to be pressed. The room was impossibly hot; with the door ajar and the window open, still there was no air. In only underwear, he lay down on the old mattress. In the flicker of lamplight, the saint's expression seemed to move from smile to frown.

The captain closed his eyes, and tried to sleep.

At the waterfront taverna, all the tables were taken. In the kitchen, Tavros sweated as he turned skewers of chicken and lamb over the charcoal, and kept an eye on the grilling swordfish steaks. His belief was that personal hygiene was the obsession of homosexuals, so the smell of him, sour and musky, wafted over the food. From time to time, he dipped a paintbrush into a bucket of his special marinade (the secrets of its composition were never revealed, but the smoke rising from the hot coals suggested lemon and a flourish of allspice, maybe juniper and certainly garlic) and basted the seared meat.

Out on the terrace, Uncle Vasso sat in his reserved seat at a table with a clear view of the harbour. A squat man, very overweight and very dark, with oiled grey hair and a dominant Syrian nose, he had (as always) taken some trouble with his clothes, yet still seemed more *mankas* than gentleman. His new jeans were in a very large size, making them too long for his height, and so the extra length was rolled into fifties-style turn-ups. The dark leather slip-ons on his silk-socked feet were vigorously buffed; the open neck of his navy shirt showed a great deal of grey chest hair, and over the shirt, he wore a jacket in pale-blue seersucker, which – being large enough to fit him around the torso – was also too long for him, and reached to his mid-thigh. Disproving Tavros's theory of personal hygiene, he had the Turkish habit of regularly splashing on cologne, and favoured an iris-scented brand ordered from Izmir.

The men with him were talking politics, their solutions for the problems of the state becoming more dogmatic with each glass of ouzo. The dishes before them were empty, except for the oily sauces of stewed beans and okra; the ashtray was filled with crushed-out butts which Tavros had not yet found time to remove.

'Don't tell me that *koproskilo* knows what he's talking about!' said a hotelier. 'He knows less about foreign policy than my grandmother!'

Across the harbour, a late-arriving vessel turned stern-on to a narrow berth, beckoned by the town councillor's boy with a whistle.

Uncle Vasso touched the hotelier's arm. On his hands were gloves of kidskin.

'That boat that's just arrived,' he said, pointing, peering across the water, whose surface shimmered with reflected lights. 'What flag's that she's carrying?'

The hotelier paused in his argument.

'I can't see very well,' he said, 'but I should say that's Luxembourg. Luxembourg, or Holland.'

'I agree, it's Luxembourg,' said Uncle Vasso. He patted the hotelier's arm, and returned his hand to its resting place on the top of his cane.

Tavros carried out an order to the corner table, balancing his tray on a chair-back and announcing each item as he placed it before three men: a half-litre jug of red wine from the barrel; octopus salad dressed with oregano, and a plate of spinach rice; an order of fried *kasseri* cheese and one of courgette fritters; chicken braised with bay-leaves, served with baked figs on the side; beetroot boiled with its own leaves, sprinkled with chopped garlic. He had dipped his own fork into the spinach rice before he brought it out, and tasted it to check the seasoning; now flecks of spinach were stuck between his teeth.

'Can I get you gentlemen anything else?' he asked.

Untroubled by the heat in cool French linen, the fat man smiled up at him. His tennis shoes were freshly whitened; his hold-all – a bag of the type favoured by athletes, in antique but well-cared-for tan leather – was tucked under his chair. Beside him in white uniforms, Enrico and Ilias – a stately blond youth, who cultivated an air of innocence which seemed to draw the girls – sipped Dutch beer.

'Thank you, no,' said the fat man. 'This will do very well, to begin with.'

A young man approached Uncle Vasso's table. His face was lined from the outdoor life; his shirt – faded with washing and the sun – was ripped under one arm, with the sleeves rolled up to the elbows to show strong forearms. There was dust in his hair and in the deep creases at his eye-corners, and he brought with him the grassy smell of the fields. Under his arm he had a violin case, and as he took the chair he was offered, he kept his head low so his hair fell over his eyes. His greeting to the company was brief, and the company, expecting no more from him, went back to its discussion of foreign policy; but on his way back to the kitchen, Tavros called out to him.

'Hey, Milto! Play us something! Give us a tune!'

Milto shook his head.

'Later,' he said.

'What do you mean, later?' shouted Tavros from the grill, coaxing more heat from the coals by wafting them with a piece of cardboard. 'Tomorrow? Next week? It is later! The people want some music with their dinner! Play us something! And make it something light. Something Yiannis can dance to.'

Yiannis – a man of close to eighty, with similarly elderly companions – nodded his delight.

'I'll dance!' he said. 'Give me a tune, and I'll show these women what I can do!'

Milto snapped open the catches on his violin case, and took out an old instrument with mellowed varnish. In the case-lid was the foxed address label of a music shop in Athens, which, given the label's age, seemed unlikely to be there now. He ran a block of resin up and down the bow's fraying horsehair, then put the violin to his chin, and held it there whilst he plucked the strings and turned the pegs to tune it.

'OK, Tavros,' he called through the kitchen doorway. 'I'll play.'

'Of course you'll play, *malaka*,' said Tavros cheerfully, and slammed down a chair above the kitchen steps, and told the girl washing the dishes to fetch Milto something to drink.

Milto sat down on the chair, accepted a bottle from the girl and placed it by his feet. Then he began to play: lilting island dances, and popular tunes all the Greeks knew. For a while they clapped, and tapped their feet. Old Yiannis did his best at a fisherman's dance, and bowed to the company and sat down when he couldn't do any more.

When the customers began to drift away, Milto let his music follow different tracks, and slipped into slower, soulful songs.

Uncle Vasso rose from his seat, and leaning on his cane, made his way to the kitchen, where Tavros was sitting by the till, counting the takings. Uncle Vasso pushed several notes across the counter.

'This should cover my table,' he said. 'What about him?' He jerked his thumb towards Milto, who seemed lost in a doleful melody. 'Has he eaten?'

'Not yet,' said Tavros.

'Take for something for him, then,' said Uncle Vasso. 'Give him some of the stewed lamb, on me.'

'He won't eat it,' said Tavros. 'You know he won't. The peppers are good. Or there's pilaf.'

'Serve him the lamb,' said Uncle Vasso. 'A man needs meat. Tell him I said he's to eat it.'

The fat man drained the last wine from his glass, and rose from his corner table. He sent Ilias into the kitchen to pay the bill, and followed him as far as the doorway, where Milto was finishing his tune.

'You have talent, my friend,' he said. 'Your playing is very good.'

Milto lowered his violin, and bowed his head to acknowledge the compliment. The fat man pressed a banknote into Milto's hand, and Milto thanked him.

A distant church clock struck midnight. The fat man called out *kali nichta* to all those who remained, and followed Ilias and Enrico out into the sultry night.

Kastellanos, on watch, left the storm-lantern burning by the tree-trunk and struggled into the temperamental hammock. He disliked being on watch alone; but as Captain Fanis always said, the probability of invasion was so absurdly low, there was no point in keeping two of them awake. But Kastellanos was a town boy, not used to the sea's strange noises as it ran up the beach stones, and the others, knowing his vulnerability, frightened him with country tales of ghosts and wraiths, which took root in his mind. Gounaris, a local boy, told of a haunting in this very place, where a man had

47

died a tragic and violent death; of how his spirit walked at night playing his fiddle, tempting the living with unearthly music to join him in his world of troubled souls.

The others, when on watch, always claimed to go straight to sleep, and the captain turned a blind eye to their dereliction. Kastellanos, however, could rarely sleep, and in this deeper than usual dark, knew his prospects tonight were poor. He lay wakeful, and saw the captain's lamp go out; he heard the voices in the bunkhouse quieten and fall silent.

He dozed a while, but something woke him. He listened. At first there was only the sea tumbling the stones, and the slightest rustling of the tamarisks. Then he thought he could hear music, down on the shore, and – though he dared not move to look in case the hammock tipped him out – a shadow seemed to be moving behind the storeroom.

He was almost sure enough to sound the alarm; then he wasn't so certain, and dismissed it as his overtired brain. But as he dozed, the sound he'd heard came again: there was a footfall on the beach path, but whether coming, or going away, was hard to say.

Three

First light broke in a line of blazing red, marking the boundary of sea and sky. On the hillside, a rooster crowed, and away below was answered by another, and another.

Uncle Vasso wasn't sleeping. Despite the open window on the seaward side, the first part of the night had been too hot for sleep; then he had slept, but bad dreams had woken him in the early hours. The tablets on the bedside table hadn't helped; a double dose had done no more than make him drowsy.

The lamp had been left burning through the night to chase away the memories of his dreams, but daybreak was now turning the lamplight pale. Through Uncle Vasso's restlessness, the woman beside him had slept deeply. He turned away from her, on to his side; still not comfortable, he settled on his back. Despite his drowsiness, his mind gave him no peace, running in its usual channels of anxiety. When the hammering came at the door, he was immediately alert.

He sat up in the bed, and shook the woman.

'Lemonia! Lemonia! Wake up!'

He put his feet to the floor, and slid out a drawer in the bedside table, shifting the items in there – a paperback book, aspirin, peppermint tablets for dyspepsia – to uncover a black velvet pouch tied with a tasselled cord. He closed the drawer, and laid the velvet bag beside him on the bed.

'Lemonia!' He shook her again, and the woman, still with her back to him, turned her head.

'What is it?' she asked. Her voice was sleep-filled and slow. 'What time is it?'

The pounding at the door came again.

'Someone's here,' he whispered. 'Stay here. Don't come out of the bedroom.'

He wore nothing but underpants; taking a silk robe from behind the door, he slipped it on as he made his way as silently as he was able to the *salone*. He carried the velvet pouch with him. The window on to the courtyard was open, a little; he stood at the gap, and listened. There was nothing to hear but the sounds of early morning: the cockerels crowing in the house yards below, the rustling leaves of a fig tree in the lightest of sea breezes.

He called out, 'Who's there?'

'It's me, Dmitris.' The voice was a young man's. 'Nikitas Floros's Dmitris.'

Uncle Vasso closed his eyes, and let out a breath.

He went barefoot to the house door, and hampered by the stiffness of his scarred hands, unfastened its complicated locks and slid back the bolts. In the courtyard the air was blessed with a little coolness, though the stones were still warm from yesterday's heat. He called through the closed courtyard door.

'What do you want, this time of the morning?'

'It's Pedro. Can you come?'

'What, now? What time is it?'

'Just after five. Please, Uncle, come. I need your help.'

Uncle Vasso hesitated.

'All right,' he said, 'I'll come. Go down and wait for me.'

He heard the boy go.

In the bedroom, Lemonia sat anxiously on the bed, clutching her knees.

'Who is it?' she asked.

He shook his head.

'No one. Only the Floros lad. I'm going down there. You'd better go home anyway, or you'll be seen. It's after five.'

He pulled on baggy trousers and a T-shirt, and slipped his feet into leather pantofles. With the velvet pouch in his pocket, he went outside. He followed the path he knew the boy had taken, down the side of the villa to a short run of steps, before the path turned to pass the houses lower down the hillside. Behind one of the smallest houses was a shed where the door stood open.

Inside the shed, the boy crouched by the head of a donkey, which lay on its side on a straw-scattered floor, its eyes wide, its breathing fast and shallow; there was foam around its grey muzzle, and flecks of blood in the foam. The place stank of urine, and even at that hour, a torment of flies crawled over the animal's eyes. The boy was stroking the donkey's sweat-darkened neck, and as Uncle Vasso approached, the animal twisted its head to look at him, and thrashed its legs in an effort to stand; but it had no strength, and dropped back limp to the floor.

Uncle Vasso stood over donkey and boy.

'We should have done this yesterday,' he said.

The boy looked up at him. His eyes were full of tears.

'He might have pulled through,' he said. 'He might still, if we could get him up.'

Uncle Vasso shook his head.

'That's your sentimentality. You're thinking like a woman. The beast's finished, done. And he's in pain. You let him suffer unnecessarily.'

51

'I wanted to give him a chance!' said the boy. He brushed away tears. 'He's been mine since a foal. My grandpa gave him to me.' He stroked the animal's neck again, and bent down to kiss its ear.

'So he's had his chance, and he's made nothing of it,' said Uncle Vasso. 'And if you're honest, you gave him a chance, as you call it, to spare yourself pain. I can't help him, and neither can you. His time is done.'

He turned his back on the boy. Pulling the velvet bag from his pocket, he loosened the cord at the neck and took out an old Stechkin 9mm. The donkey struggled and thrashed and then lay still. The quickness of his breathing filled the stall.

'Everyone's the same on this damned island,' said Uncle Vasso. 'No one wants to do what must be done. You'd better take yourself outside, son.'

In desperation, the boy looked up at him.

'I want to say goodbye.'

Uncle Vasso was looking through the dirty window. High over the house roofs, swallows swooped and dived.

He sighed.

'He's just a dumb animal, son,' he said. 'Go on. Go outside.'

Head low in misery, the boy obeyed.

Uncle Vasso slipped off the thumb-safety, and put the gun-barrel to the donkey's forehead.

The fat man heard a shot.

He moved quickly to the open port-hole of his cabin. The air was fresh with the cold scent of the sea; as feeding fish rose, soft circles of ripples broke the water's oil-smooth surface, splitting the reflections of moored boats.

On the hillside where the shot had been fired, the walls of the Governor's Villa were red in the early sunlight. For a few minutes, the fat man stayed by the port-hole to see if anything developed; but apart from the swooping of swallows, there was nothing to see.

Nikitas Floros's Dmitris crouched in the dirt by the shed wall, crying. Uncle Vasso stood beside him, and ruffled his black hair.

'It's done, son,' he said. 'He's not in any more pain. Go home, wash your face, and when it gets to a decent hour, fetch someone to take him away.'

The boy rubbed at his eyes with the heels of his hands.

Uncle Vasso searched the rear pocket of his trousers and found money, a few notes. He glanced at it, assessing how much there was, whether it was enough. He held the money out to the boy.

'Here,' he said. 'Buy yourself a new donkey.'

But the boy didn't move; he crouched, still crying, with his hands covering his eyes.

Uncle Vasso placed the money by the boy's feet, and left him.

Four

Captain Fanis woke suddenly, to a room already light and warming with the heat of the day. A bee knocked against the screens which covered his open windows; somewhere close by, a goat's bell jangled.

His watch showed 6.45. As he hauled himself from the bed, he cursed Kastellanos and the unsounded reveille. He found a clean undershirt in the wardrobe, and put on the pressed trousers from under his mattress, then went barefoot to the end of the terrace. He lobbed an empty water bottle, and hit Kastellanos on the nose. Kastellanos woke in shock, and fell out of the hammock.

As he walked back towards the bunkhouse, the captain hid his smile, and shouted, 'Get my coffee on the table in ten minutes, Kastellanos, or I'm putting you on report and cancelling your leave.'

Lillis had left the soap-grey water he'd used to wash his underpants in a bucket. The captain grabbed the bucket as he passed, and took it with him to the bunkhouse, where he slammed open the door, and positioned himself ready to throw the water. The soldiers all knew the drill: the last one out of bed would get a soaking and a wet mattress which would have to be dragged outside to dry. In seconds, they were on their feet.

The captain lowered the bucket.

'You're getting faster,' he said. 'Now get dressed and get moving. Gounaris, you're on breakfast. Get in the kitchen and make sure Kastellanos has got my coffee on the boil. Lillis, go and tell our visitor that breakfast's in twenty minutes. If he wants to eat, he'd better be there.'

But as Captain Fanis sat down to wait for his coffee, Lillis came to find him.

'He's gone,' he said.

The captain looked at him.

'Where?'

'I don't know, sir. But he's not in the stores. I checked the latrines, but he isn't there either. I didn't know where else to look. Maybe he went for a swim.'

The captain looked at Lillis, and then up and down the deserted beach, and out across the empty bay. No one was there.

'Kastellanos!' he called through the kitchen window. 'Have you seen our visitor?'

'No, Captain.'

The captain marched to the latrines, and kicked both doors. One resisted, and brought complaints from Gounaris. The second opened wide, revealing nothing but the wooden bench which covered the stinking bucket. He moved on to the stores, where the campbed had been slept in. No one was sleeping in it now.

'All of you, form a patrol!' he shouted, going to his room to fetch his boots. 'We'll be leaving here in exactly five minutes!'

The captain led the soldiers away from the camp. Where the Jeep was parked, they didn't take the port-bound track, but instead stayed on the footpath which led to the beach's hinterland. The captain carried a stick, and knocked the ground ahead to alert snakes, prompting them to slither away before the soldiers grew too close.

Heading for a neglected orchard of olives, citrus and quince, they crossed a tranche of barren earth which coated their boots in dust. At the mid-point of the empty land, they passed the camp well, walled round in stone and with its metal bucket standing on the wall. The bucket's rope was long, extended with a length of yellow rope tied to the original blue as the water level had dropped.

'You'll be fetching water in a while, Kastellanos,' said the captain.

'I fetched it yesterday, Captain,' said Kastellanos. 'It's Gounaris and Skafidis today.'

'Not since you overslept, it's not,' said the captain. 'You'll take Gounaris's place.'

Gounaris grinned. Skafidis and Kastellanos scowled.

As they walked through the coolness of the orchard, crickets fell silent and sprang from their feet; songbirds stopped their singing, and flew away. Here and there on the olive trunks – fat and twisted, centuries old – one-time owners had carved their initials, in letters now grown swollen and distorted; black rolls of harvest nets wound between the raised roots, and on the branches, the bitter, young olives were mossy green.

'Why are we coming this way, Captain?' asked Skafidis. 'What would he be doing over here?'

'He isn't in his bed at the camp,' said the captain, 'and he left without saying goodbye. That's not polite, is it, Skafidis? He's a man in a hurry to leave us, and I'd like to know why. I don't expect to find him over here, but then I didn't expect him to vanish in the night, either. Most likely he's headed in the direction of town. But if he hasn't, that's a long walk for

56

us in the heat. So we're ruling this option out first because it's easiest for us.' He tapped his forehead. 'You have to use this sometimes, Skafidis. Logic and efficiency. Rules to live by.'

They passed beyond the orchard boundary, and stopped by a campanile which formed the gateway to a church: tall and slender, with a pair of bells suspended in the arch beneath the ornate pinnacle, but of no depth, so it seemed from a sideways angle to be only its own façade. Its last coat of ox-blood render had been some years ago, and now the dark red of the pigment blended naturally with the buff of the building stone where it showed through. The campanile gate opened on to a stony field contained by walls shaded with myrtle and evergreen oak; the dried field-grass had been grazed down to the dirt by goats.

'Gounaris, Lillis,' said the captain, 'go and check the church. Skafidis, Kastellanos, come with me.'

Gounaris pushed at the church gate, which stuck, at first, on the irregular ground. He pushed harder, and, juddering, it opened, squealing on its unoiled iron hinges. Hands in pockets, Lillis ambled through, and followed Gounaris into the church field.

The captain led the others away, down the path, which continued towards houses – a hamlet of twenty or so overgrown ruins. He swished his stick over a stand of barley-grass, provoking rustling as something hiding there slithered away.

'Have a good look round,' he said to the soldiers. 'If he's here, I want him found.'

They went, between them, to every house. At one, the kitchen was no more than two paces across, with tiny window casements still painted a bold green, and thrown open to admit some long-blown-out breeze; the marks of sooty smoke flared over a great oven, with a stone bench adjacent where three members of a family might have huddled for winter warmth. The dropping wall-plaster carried the blooms of seeping damp, and algae grew on the cement between the stones, picking out the pattern they were laid in. The room behind was showered in the debris of the collapsed ceiling, which had exposed long supporting struts of pine, cross-laid with nailed-on planks. The neighbours' house was grander, but its fate had been the same. The roof was part collapsed, creating holes where streaming sunbeams spotlighted symbols of status: wooden shelves against a wall, a staircase leading to an upper floor, and through holes in worm-eaten floorboards, the darkness of a cellar. The windows, here, cast the shadows they had always done, as if through polished glass, into what had been once a beautiful room, and was now rubble-strewn. Another house, of grander status still, had a stone staircase round its side, and an elegant stone arch leading to a veranda; but the staircase could not be climbed for the brush of summer-dead thistles, and the archway was obscured by invading trees.

In the cobbled lanes between the houses, weeds had flourished and died back in the heat to crisp, pale stalks. At the longer-abandoned properties, nothing remained but walls to waist-height, with gardens reverted to meadows. Some had been used as goat-pens, and their floors were ankle-high in sharp-smelling excrement; many were daubed in paint with initials of ownership.

Kastellanos stopped at a house where the outer walls still stood, where the wooden window-frames were square in place and the door was still *in situ*. He looked up at the floor above, at a window which had never had a frame, but had iron bars set solidly into the stonework.

'Look at that,' he said to the captain and Skafidis. 'Why did they put bars on that window?'

'Inbreeding,' said Skafidis. 'In places like this, half of them were mutants and the other half were mad. That's what happens if you screw your sister. I bet that's where they kept the family nutcases.'

'They must have been violent nutcases, to be kept locked up behind bars,' said Kastellanos. 'I don't like this place. Everywhere you go, you can feel them watching.'

Skafidis laughed.

'Who, *malaka*?' he asked. 'There's nobody here. Listen!' He put both hands to his mouth and called out, long and loud. His shout carried through the empty buildings, and when it died, left them in silence, to which all three found themselves listening, as if a response might come from amongst the derelict walls.

'See?' asked Skafidis after a few moments. 'No spooks, *malaka*. No ghosts.'

'I think you're right,' said the captain. 'Wherever our friend's got to, it isn't here.'

'Why are we looking for this guy anyway?' asked Kastellanos, as he and Lillis headed along the track which led to the town. Foraging goats trotted away from them, scattering through the rocks and scrub.

'Because we're following orders,' said Lillis.

'He's long gone by now,' said Kastellanos. He kicked a stone, which skittered and bounced ahead of him, throwing up dust. 'Reached the port and found a boat out.'

'Who knows how far ahead he is?' said Lillis. 'You were on watch. You must have heard him go.'

Kastellanos seemed uncertain.

'No,' he said. 'Well, maybe.'

'God help us,' said Lillis. 'The Turks might have had knives to our throats, and you'd still not have raised the alarm.'

'Should I have stopped him going, then, if I'd seen him?'

'Of course you should've! He's a man with no papers off a foreign boat. We treat him as an illegal immigrant. He must have something to hide to have left us the way he did.'

'Maybe he couldn't face any more of Skafidis's catering,' said Kastellanos. 'And who can blame him for that?'

They walked a couple of kilometres, and stopped to drink. Brown bees buzzed around the dried heads of oregano flowers. The sun beating on Lillis's backpack had heated their water cans, and the water was too warm to give any refreshment. Lillis poured his remainder over his head, savouring the relative coolness of its wetness.

'You'll regret that,' said Kastellanos, screwing the cap back on his can. 'We might have to walk miles yet.'

Lillis squinted along the track ahead of them.

'I don't think so,' he said.

He pointed to where a solitary olive tree spread shade over the road. A figure was slumped against its trunk. When the soldiers were within shouting distance, the figure raised a hand.

'It's him,' said Lillis. 'We found him.'

He set off at a jog. Kastellanos followed behind, at a more measured pace.

As Lillis stood over him, Manolis gave a mocking salute.

'*Kali mera sas*,' he said. 'And thank God you're here. It's hot, and I didn't bring any water. I planned to walk my way into town, but . . .' He held up the captain's old sandal. '*Kaput*. A man with soft feet and one shoe can't get far on this road.' He showed them his bare foot. The sole was cut and bleeding. 'If one of you has something I can wrap my foot in, I'd appreciate it. And it looks like I'll be coming back with you to camp.'

Kastellanos gave Manolis his boots, though they were two

sizes too large. Kastellanos walked easily barefoot, the soles of his feet cured hard by weeks unshod in salt-water, and on rough rocks and cement.

'Ask Lillis to show you his party trick,' he said, when Manolis remarked on his grit. 'He likes to impress girls by stubbing cigarettes out on his heels.'

'And does that impress the ladies?' Manolis asked Lillis. Manolis's shadow fell over an aqua-tailed lizard, which scuttled into hiding in a boulder's cleft.

'Sometimes,' said Lillis. 'Sometimes they've seen the trick before.'

'Your captain says you're the troop's mechanic,' said Manolis. 'What're the chances of you giving me a ride over to the port?'

'None,' said Lillis. 'Even if I could get the damned Jeep to run, there's no fuel. Besides, you'll be going in the launch with the captain, when we get back.'

'I suppose so,' said Manolis. 'Listen, lads, might either of you lend me a boat fare? I'll make it worth your while, if you'll front me five thousand. Ten would be even better.'

Kastellanos looked at him, and, incredulous, shook his head.

'Ten thousand?' he asked. 'On a soldier's pay? You must be mad! Friend, you've been sitting in that sun for far too long.'

The fat man swam away from *Aphrodite*'s mooring. His stroke was confident and fast; his limbs were supple, his skin was tanned almost to copper. Breathing through his snorkel-pipe, he moved across the depths, seeing nothing but the ocean's immense blueness, split by phosphorescent spikes of diffused sunlight.

A few strands of his hair were caught between mask and

forehead, and the compromised seal let in a trickle of water. He stopped, and trod water as he pulled off the mask, and shook it dry. Before replacing it, he glanced back at the view of Mithros's coastline, and high on the promontory, the Governor's Villa caught his eye. For a few moments he studied its graceful architecture, ideal for its enviable position, overlooking the channel between Mithros and its neighbours and the boats passing on the waves far below.

He replaced his mask, and continued to swim away from *Aphrodite*, his target a deserted stretch of coast not visible from the harbour. As he grew close, the water grew shallower, becoming intense turquoise of great clarity. Through his mask the seabed spread below as if he were flying over it, giving a dreamlike view of fine sand and wafting weeds, the silvery flickerings of darting fish, and colonies of black urchins on the encrusted rocks.

A hundred metres offshore, he stopped swimming and lay face-down on the swell, rising and falling as he was carried slowly closer to land. The place was inhospitable, and it would be difficult to leave the water without shoes; the strong waves breaking at the water's edge would knock a man off his feet. By swimming a few strokes here and there, the fat man kept his distance from the danger, and let the water cradle him as he surveyed the seabed and the fish below.

The rocks beneath him were the lava of volcanoes, set into jagged pinnacles and troughs. The sand lying in the narrow passages between them drew amber centipedes and soft, pink slugs. The fat man floated and drifted, seeming content to go with the tide and observe this world from above. But then his eye was caught by a rock different from the rest: a softer stone, paler than the basalt grey of the igneous rocks.

He fanned the water, steadying himself directly over the stone and estimating its depth. Then, filling his lungs deeply, he dived, and pulled down as fast as he was able to the seabed. A school of startled whitebait scattered around him. He touched the stone, and dragged fronds of burgundy weeds from its surface to see what was beneath; and when he was sure of what he'd seen, he swam back to the surface, emerging with a sharp out-breath to clear his snorkel, before turning back in the direction of *Aphrodite*.

Manolis sat on a chair with no back, digging in the dirt with a stick, glancing from time to time up at the sun to estimate how much time had passed since he had arrived back at the camp. Behind him, Lillis was working on the Jeep; metal rang on metal as he knocked a spanner on a stubborn bolt. On the Jeep's wing was an assortment of nuts and bolts he had already removed, and a length of rubber tubing cracked with perishing. On the driver's seat, the radio played the Turkish station. Lillis's hands were black with oil; the sun beat on his deep-brown back, but Lillis didn't seem to care.

'So you think you'll ever get that thing going again?' asked Manolis.

Lillis didn't answer. The bolt he was working on was loose; he fitted the spanner to it, and began to twist.

'Because you're not much of a unit without transport, are you?' persisted Manolis. 'You're not exactly mobile, without wheels.'

Lillis raised his head from under the bonnet. He didn't speak, but pointed with his spanner at the launch tied at the jetty.

'And what happens when that goes wrong?' asked Manolis. 'Are they going to get you to fix that, too?'

Lillis bent back under the bonnet. From the jetty, Captain Fanis shouted, and beckoned to Manolis to come down.

'Thank Christ,' said Manolis. He tossed away his stick. 'See you around,' he said to Lillis, but Lillis didn't reply.

Manolis made his way down the beach, his feet hot inside

the stiff boots the captain had lent him, and sore from the cuts on his sole. By the launch, the captain pointed to a seat in the prow, and Manolis climbed aboard. The captain, Gounaris and Skafidis had put on uniform jackets and caps. The captain took a seat beside Manolis. Gounaris and Skafidis settled on the stern bench.

Skafidis fired the engine, and steered out into Kolona bay.

The engine was loud; the captain made no effort to talk over it, but watched a graceful seagull skim the waves. Manolis scanned the sea around them for other boats. Gounaris was in high spirits – he had plans to pay a visit to some new girl – and he and Skafidis were laughing as they speculated on how far Gounaris might get.

The swell and the head-wind were light, and the launch made good time. As they entered the harbour, Manolis glanced up at the Governor's Villa.

'That's a beautiful place,' he said to the captain, pointing up at the house. 'A house like that would cost a fortune.'

'And the man who owns it has a fortune,' said the captain.

Skafidis cut the power and motored slowly over to the quayside to tie up.

'Who would that be, then?' Manolis asked the captain.

The captain was distracted, uncoiling a rope from under his feet. 'Who?' he asked.

'The man who owns that house,' said Manolis. 'What do they call him?'

'His family name's Eliadis,' said the captain, passing the rope's end to Gounaris. 'They call him Vasso. Why? Were you thinking of asking him for a loan?'

'The thought had crossed my mind,' said Manolis.

When all the men were ashore, the captain addressed Gounaris and Skafidis.

'You two, go and buy everything on that list. You have brought the list, haven't you, Gounaris?' Gounaris held up a piece of paper. 'Tell them you have my permission to sign for what you buy. If you have problems, come and find me at the coastguard's office. Skafidis, get fuel for the boat. And make sure Gounaris doesn't spend all his time where he shouldn't be. We'll rendezvous at – what time is it now?' He looked in the direction of the town-hall clock; but the clock had long been broken, and for weeks had shown the time as five to three. 'Let's say an hour and a half, then,' said the captain. 'Two hours at most. If I'm not here by the boat, find me at the *kafenion*.'

Captain Fanis led Manolis away from the hectic harbourside. They passed a chandler's, where Greek flags in many sizes hung like bunting, and sticky spiders' webs at the window corners were glutted with flies. Outside a tiny grocer's, a woman worked a delicate piece of lace; curious, she watched the men go by, whilst her deft fingers manipulated the bobbins and cotton. Next door, the pharmacy was closed; a well-used card pinned to the door read, 'Back in five minutes'. Between the pharmacy and a butcher's shop – where the smell of meat no longer fresh hung in the air – was a warehouse. A bicycle was leaned against its front; a wooden staircase bolted to the side of the building led up to what had once been a merchant's offices and home. On the wall above the staircase – missing a screw, so it pointed at the ground – was a sign: two crossed blue anchors, between the words 'Hellenic Coastguard' and 'Port Authority of Mithros'.

In the doorway of his shop, the butcher was smoking a cigarette. By his feet, a cat chewed with vigour on a scrap of purple offal, a section of windpipe or bowel.

'Makis, *kali mera*,' said the captain, as he and Manolis passed. 'How's things?'

65

'Oh, you know how it goes,' said the butcher. 'Could be better, could be worse.' He looked at Manolis, who seemed to take his interest.

'The lads'll be in shortly for our order,' said the captain. 'I suppose it's ready for them, is it?'

The butcher nodded, slowly.

'I'll make a start on it now,' he said. 'Just as soon as I've finished this cigarette, I'll get to it.'

The cat picked up the offal, and with it dangling between its fangs, tried to sneak past the butcher into the shop; but with surprising agility, the butcher put out his foot, and gave the cat a light kick which sent it in the opposite direction.

'Damned thing,' he said. 'Yes, it'll be ready. Give me half an hour, and I'll have it done.'

'It'll be sooner than half an hour,' said the captain. 'They'll be here at any moment.'

'I'll get to it, then,' said the butcher, and smacked the back of his neck where a fly had landed.

The captain led Manolis up the warehouse staircase, which rattled and vibrated as they climbed, as if there were only a bolt or two holding it to the wall. Manolis kept a tight grip on the handrail as if it might save him in a fall; but the handrail itself was not secure, with one bracket missing, and loose screws in the remaining three.

At the stairhead, the door to the coastguard's office was propped open with an old flat-iron standing on its end. Inside, the office was fiercely hot. With the rattling of the staircase, the officer in charge had ample warning to prepare himself for visitors, and by the time the captain and Manolis entered the room, his feet were off the desk, his newspaper was folded away in a drawer, an official document was open before him and a pen was in his hand, as if he had been interrupted in writing. A fan on a stand whirred in front of him, its draught lifting the edges of a stack of papers weighted down against the fan and the sea breezes by a handgun in its holster.

'*Kali mera sas*,' said the coastguard officer, formally, to both men; and then, informally, to the captain, '*Yassou*, Captain Fanis.'

'*Yassou*, Spiros,' replied the captain. 'How's things?'

'Oh, busy, busy,' said Spiros. He leaned back in his chair and scratched his belly, which was impressively flat, given his age; he was well groomed, and his uniform, despite the heat, had kept its ironed-in creases. Around the light fitting and in the window casement, flies danced. A clock on the wall ticked the seconds away. 'What can I do for you?'

'We've had a visitor, at the camp,' said the captain. 'This gentleman here.'

Spiros offered a smile, but Manolis didn't catch it; he had crossed the room behind the captain, and was looking out of the window.

'He'll not have found much hospitality with you, I'm sure,' said Spiros. 'Army rations are best left behind in youth.'

'He didn't have any choice,' said the captain. 'His companions ditched him.'

'Ditched him?'

'They threw him overboard and abandoned him.'

Spiros's eyebrows lifted.

'Really?' he said. 'Now why would they have done that?'

'I'll let him tell you,' said the captain, and stepped back, leaving Manolis open to Spiros's scrutiny.

Spiros's eyes narrowed.

'Do I know you?' he asked.

Manolis shook his head.

'I don't believe so,' he said.

'So, let's have it,' said Spiros. 'What's the story?'

'That's it,' said Manolis. 'We argued over a card game. They dumped me, and motored off. As a joke, of course, but those guys don't know when the joke should be over. I swam to the base. The captain offered me bed and board, and here I am.'

Spiros picked up the fly-swatter which lay across the desk, and brought it down swiftly on a bluebottle crawling on the stack of paperwork. He flicked the flattened corpse to the floor; a bloody smear remained on the papers.

'Damned flies,' he said. 'They come up from the butcher's. If Makis would keep the shop clean, there wouldn't be so many.' He exchanged the swatter for a pen, and turned to a blank page on a pad of paper. 'Who threw you overboard, and from what vessel?'

'I don't know their names. They were crew, Albanian. We were playing cards, and they didn't like it when I won.'

'Albanians always are very poor losers,' said Spiros. 'What vessel?'

'I don't know that either. I didn't notice.'

'What port did you sail from, then?'

'Look,' said Manolis, 'I don't see why we need to go through this. I've suffered no harm, and I can see you're busy. If you'll just direct me to the bank, I'll get out of your way.'

'Where are your papers?' asked Spiros. 'Passport, ID?'

'I don't have them. They didn't exactly give me time to pack.'

'If you've no ID,' said Spiros, 'and no passport, and I assume you have no bank-book either, how will you get money from the bank?'

'I'll have to talk to them about that. There is a bank, is there?'

'Yes, there's a branch of the National Bank. Do you have an account there?'

'Happily, yes.'

'But the bank will need ID. You don't have ID. You left it with your Albanian friends and it could easily be misused. I'm going to have to report it as having been stolen.' He put the paper to one side, opened a drawer and pulled out a pad of forms in pastel colours: blue, pink, green and yellow. He scribbled his pen on the edge of the topmost form. The pen didn't work. He pushed it back into his pen-pot, and took another.

'Name?' he asked.

'Chiotis,' he said. 'Manolis Chiotis.'

'Ah, Chiotis,' said Spiros. 'Any relation to the singer?'

Manolis sighed, and shook his head.

Spiros wrote the name in the correct box on the form.

'Address?'

Manolis gave a street address in Thessaloniki.

'OK,' said Spiros. 'Now tell me, so we can track this vessel: what type of craft was she?'

'Just some old cargo boat. It smelled bad. I think maybe they'd been transporting chickens. They were sailing from Volos to Alexandria, and that suited me. I was looking for a cheap ticket, and I got one.'

'You were headed for Alexandria? In Egypt?'

'No. I was headed for Crete. They were going to put in there.'

'Forgive me, *kyrie*,' asked Spiros, very politely, 'but why thumb a ride with a group of foreigners you don't know, when you might easily have made the journey by regular ferry, and not run the risk of being thrown overboard?'

'In retrospect, you're quite right,' said Manolis. 'It was a foolish thing to do. Look, I'm a businessman, and I need to get back to my work. If you would just direct me to the bank . . .'

'I'm not sure how that would help you, immediately,' said Spiros. 'As I say, without ID, you can't access your account.'

'You could vouch for me. Issue me with a temporary card.'

Spiros shook his head.

'With respect,' he said, 'I cannot possibly do that. You might be anyone. I'll tell you what you should do. Call your family – there's a phone booth on the harbour-front – and tell them what has happened, how you're in a bit of difficulty. Ask your wife to send your birth certificate, marriage certificate, photographs, bank-books, anything she's got which will confirm who you are. She can send them to the post office, and you can pick them up there.'

'I don't have a wife,' said Manolis. 'I'll get someone to transfer money to the post office.'

'Ah, but the postmaster won't release funds without ID either, will he? You must have a friend, I assume, who could bring those papers for you? I realise this will all take time, so you'd better make up your mind to spending a few more days with us.'

'I could borrow money,' said Manolis. 'Maybe you'd lend me something? You have my word I'll make it good, when I get home.'

'I would, of course,' said the officer, 'if only my salary would stretch to making loans.'

'But how will I live? I have to eat, and I have nowhere to sleep.'

Spiros looked at the captain.

'I think under the circumstances, the best thing I can do with you is to prevail upon the captain to take care of you. Captain, what do you say?'

The captain frowned.

'How can I do that, Spiros? I run a military establishment, not a hotel for passing travellers.'

Spiros rose from his chair. He smiled at Manolis.

'I wonder if you would excuse us, just for a moment?' he said.

He took the captain by the arm, and led him to a back room, where he spoke quietly in the captain's ear.

'Do me this favour, Fanis. I don't like the look of this guy. I've seen him before, somewhere. I recognise his face. Just take care of him for me for a day or so, whilst I make some enquiries. I can't lock him up – he's committed no offence – but I want to look into his background before he disappears. Look at him; he's anxious to be gone. Left here in the port, he'll blag his way on to some vessel and be gone in no time. Over there with you, it's like house arrest. He can't go anywhere without your say-so.'

'Don't be so sure. He's tried to walk out once already.'

'See? That's my point. From here, the job's too easy. He'll cadge a ride on a yacht, and he'll be gone. Come on, Fanis. It's in all our interests.'

The captain hesitated.

'OK. But a day or two, no more.'

Back in the office, Spiros sat down at his desk.

'You're in luck,' he said. 'I've managed to persuade Captain Andreadis to accommodate you until your paperwork comes through and you can be on your way. You'll find it pretty quiet over there, but you'll be comfortable enough, I'm sure. Why don't you treat it as a holiday at government expense?'

Outside, the captain handed Manolis several coins.

'You'll find the payphone easily enough,' he said. 'I have to run an errand or two. We'll meet as we arranged, in about an hour.'

'There's no point in my meeting you at the *kafenion*,' said Manolis. 'What am I supposed to do there, without money?'

The captain regarded him.

'If you talk fast on the phone, you'll have half the price of a coffee with what I've given you,' he said. 'Otherwise, I suggest you sing a song, and pass round a hat.'

The captain left him, and Manolis made his way back to the harbour-front; but when he came to the payphone, he passed it by, walking on as far as the National Bank branch. He glanced around to see if anyone was watching, and went inside.

Loskas Vergas, the bank clerk, was brewing coffee. He had a special spoon for measuring the powder, and was levelling it with the flat side of a knife. When Manolis opened the door, he turned off the butane burner, and turned with polite professionalism towards his customer. Posters around the walls offered favourable savings accounts rates. Under a glass dome at the back of the office, a small stuffed owl perched on a twig. A fan turned slowly, stirring the hot air.

'*Kali mera sas*,' said the bank clerk. 'May I help you?'

He shuffled on to his high chair at the counter, and looked expectantly at Manolis.

'I hope so,' said Manolis. 'My situation is somewhat unusual. I've lost all my papers in an accident at sea, and have ended up here on Mithros with no means of identification, and no money. So I was hoping, under these exceptional circumstances, you could arrange access to my account.'

'An accident?' asked the clerk. 'Not serious, I hope?'

'Only in that I lost my belongings. But it's vital I get home as quickly as possible. You understand, I'm sure. So if you could see your way . . .'

The bank clerk pulled a face.

'Doubtful,' he said, 'very doubtful. We wouldn't be doing our job if we let anyone walk in here, and take money from your account.'

He looked Manolis in the face, and frowned.

'Do I know you?' he asked. 'You look familiar.'

'I don't believe so,' said Manolis. 'If you could help me, I'd really appreciate it. Please.'

'I could make a phone call, I suppose,' said the bank clerk. 'If you give me some details, we might see. Of course we aim to help our customers in distress, if we can. Otherwise I'm afraid you'll have to get your wife to send some proof of identity.'

He picked up a pen and paper.

'Name?'

'Never mind,' said Manolis. 'Forget it. I'll come back some other time.'

Five

Enrico held the dinghy steady. The fat man picked up his hold-all and climbed from the boat on to the harbour steps.

'Don't expect me for at least a couple of hours,' he said to Enrico. 'And don't get into trouble whilst I'm gone.'

'Ilias asked me to get some parts for his engine,' said Enrico. 'They'll take some tracking down, I've no doubt. And they say they do a decent wine from the barrel here, so I'll see what I can find. After that, I thought I might do a spot of fishing.'

He looked up on to the quayside, where a woman at the attractive beginning of middle age was choosing a copy of *Die Zeit* from a stand of outdated newspapers.

'Be here when I want you,' said the fat man. 'And make sure Ilias's parts take priority over yours.'

Enrico smiled his satyr's smile.

'Of course, *kyrie*,' he said.

The fat man wandered along the quayside, adopting the summer visitors' unhurried pace. From a barrow, a fisherman with a catch of pipefish shouted for buyers; a lorry piled up with bricks rattled by, the driver cursing the dilatory pedestrians. Drying nets were spread along the moorings; outside his shop, a baker yawned.

On the square, under awnings which gave shade like desert tents, a market had drawn in the local traders. Their day's offerings and prices were scrawled on blackboards, and the traders sat behind tables of their produce: cantaloupes and honeydews, apricots, peaches and nectarines; courgettes capped with their wilting orange flowers; scarlet tomatoes, from fist-sized globes to small, sweet cherries; glossy peppers, aubergines and green chillies. The fat man ambled amongst the stalls, stopping to talk where his interest was caught. He bought a jar of thyme honey, and a tranche of waxy honeycomb; he tried slices of several sausages and air-dried ham, and bought two pies of home-made feta and spinach, eating the first as he went along and finding it so good, he followed it immediately with the second.

From the market, he moved on amongst the other dawdling tourists to the shops. Business was good, the range of merchandise eclectic – Caribbean shells and Florida sponges, olive-wood carvings and T-shirts with crude slogans; and everywhere, on every shelf, in every display there were bulls – brass bulls, ceramic bulls, vases painted with bulls, bull ashtrays, bull labels on liqueurs, bull-leapers on plates.

The fat man stopped at a display of postcards and began to spin it slowly, looking at the views of Mithros and the pictures of bulls.

In bad English, a woman called out to him.

'Very nice, very nice,' she said. 'Five cards three hundred. I have stamps. Five cards three hundred, I give you good price.'

'Thank you most kindly,' said the fat man, in his perfect newscaster's Greek. 'When I have made my choice, I shall let you know.'

The woman looked him up and down, taking in his Italian linen suit and the powder-blue polo shirt beneath, and staring for a moment at his shoes.

'Forgive me,' she said, in Greek. 'I took you for a foreigner. My apologies. For a countryman, the cards are five for a hundred and fifty.'

He chose his postcards and paid for them. Further along the harbour-side, a hand-painted sign nailed to the side of a building read, 'Museum', and he went in that direction, through the backstreets. At the church of the Archangel Michael, a white-haired woman, on hands and knees, was scrubbing the steps; when she saw the fat man approach, she sat back on her heels and smiled at him with warmth.

'*Kalos tou*,' she said. '*Kalos tou*.'

'*Kali mera sas*,' said the fat man. 'That's hot work for a day like today.'

'I do it for the saint,' she said, and crossed herself. 'He's been very good to me, and so I'm happy to do what I can for him.'

'Admirable,' said the fat man, 'admirable. Am I on the right track for the museum?'

'Go straight, and then right,' she said. She looked at him with curiosity. 'Where are you from, *kalé*?'

'Athens,' he said. 'Though I spend little time there.'

'You look familiar to me,' she said. 'Have you been in Mithros before?'

'Once or twice,' he said. 'But not for many years.'

'Well, you're very welcome here.' She gave him another smile. 'A handsome man like you is always welcome.'

He followed her directions, to a path that rose in broad stone steps. Ahead, he heard the clip of hooves and the whack of a stick on hide, and in a moment met a young man driving an overladen donkey. The young man's head was recently shaved against the heat (a clumsy shaving, which had left his scalp, in places, cut and scabbed). In almost incomprehensible vernacular, he offered a gruff greeting.

The fat man called after him, 'Am I on the right path for the museum?'

The donkey-driver neither slowed nor turned his head, but raised his hand and made a cutting motion to signify straight on, and called out, *Pano* – up.

The fat man came, at last, to a doorway in a whitewashed wall. One side of the door stood open, and on the other side a sheet of paper mounted with drawing pins gave the museum's opening times. Breathing in to shrink his belly, he passed through the narrow half-doorway into a courtyard shaded by the branches of a pair of fig trees. The courtyard floor was a mosaic of black and white pebbles, its design's perimeter a trail of vine leaves, and at its centre was the circle of a compass with north, south, east and west picked out in diamond points. Around the walls, amphorae high as a man's waist were filled with white geraniums, and appearing to grow out of the wall itself, were long stems of pink valerian. A coiled hosepipe dripped under a brass tap; recent watering had softened the petals of the flowers.

The fat man lifted a bloom of valerian to his nostrils, and as he sniffed its oddly odorous sweetness, a telephone rang inside the museum. There were footsteps on floorboards, and the receiver was picked up from its cradle; he heard a man's voice – *Embros?* – and then only the hum of a conversation conducted at a low volume, so anyone nearby – someone such as himself – would not hear. The fat man released the valerian, and moving silently in his white shoes, crossed to the museum entrance; but his big stature blocked the light, and the man on the telephone looked up from the desk where he had sat to take the call.

77

'I'll ring you back,' he said, and replaced the receiver in its cradle.

The fat man stepped into the room; the man at the desk smiled over at him, politely rather than warmly, and pushed his hair back over his head, briefly leaving his hand on the back of his head as though frustrated or upset. Dressed in a short-sleeved shirt and camel trousers, he seemed a professional man, and though not handsome, was pleasant-looking, a man beginning to soften but only recently past his prime.

'*Yassas*,' he said. 'Welcome to Mithros's museum.'

'*Yassas*,' said the fat man. He looked around. The room was the downstairs of a large house, with most of the dividing walls knocked out and the old pine floorboards bare of paint or varnish. A steep, carved staircase rose to a sleeping-platform crammed with cardboard boxes and parts of the collection which lacked display space: a spinning wheel, a harpsichord, a stringless bouzouki inlaid with mother-of-pearl, a model of a sailing ship with broken rigging. The high ceiling was embossed with plaster flowers over-painted in mushroom gloss; the walls were covered in artwork and posters, and photographs in dark-stained frames: the crews of turn-of-the-century boats, arms folded, proud and mustachioed as they prepared to sail; women in traditional costumes with grinning children at their feet, all enjoying their moment in front of the camera, and all now certainly dead.

Throughout the room were display cabinets of irregular sizes and styles, with treasures of all kinds under their glass covers: shards of crude pottery and nineteenth-century ceramics, official letters, certificates and newspaper clippings, hats and caps, shoes and boots, lamps and small arms from the last war. An anchor was propped against a wall, beneath a splintered plank and a painting of a shipwreck. The collection had the air of final resting places, and yet everything was cared for; the woodwork smelled of beeswax polish, the glass on the cases was free of fingermarks, the labels on the exhibits were all in place.

The fat man held out his hand.

'Hermes Diaktoros, of Athens,' he said. The man shook it, glancing as he did so at the fat man's shoes. 'I see you are admiring my footwear, my winged sandals as I call them. Diaktoros is an ancient word for messenger, and since I carry both the god's name and his epithet, it seems fitting I should also wear his shoes.'

'They call me the Professor,' said the man. 'Professor Philipas. The title's grandiose, for what I do here. I'm really no more than a curator, a caretaker of objects whose value, I must be honest, lies more in social history than anything else.'

'Are you not a university man, then?'

'I've never visited any educational establishment since I left what passes for a high school down the hill. But I'm self-educated. I've taught myself plenty, enough to bore you on the history of many of these objects. I'm a bookworm, and a magpie. The results of that combination are what you see here. Please, feel free to look around.'

On the professor's desk were a few cheaply printed pamphlets, with the print not quite straight on the page and the paper yellowing with age. There was a cardboard box with a slit made in the lid for donations, and a piece of paper stuck to it which read '50 drachma'.

The fat man found several coins in his pocket. He dropped them in the cash box on the table and took a pamphlet. The cover bore a picture of a bull.

'It's a shame my father can't see this place,' he said. 'He's a classical scholar, and would be intrigued by your collection, as I am myself. Would you steer me in any particular direction? My preference would be to work chronologically. My main interest has always been in the ancient.'

'You're unusual then,' said Professor Philipas. 'Most of our visitors want to know about the bull, and nothing else.'

'In Mithros, the bull is hard to miss,' said the fat man. 'Though I confess, the last time I was here – it was some years ago, admittedly – I remember no reference at all to any bull.'

'He was a recent discovery,' said the professor, standing up from his chair. 'Found by chance less than twenty years ago, and tragically stolen shortly afterwards. Where he's been since then, no one knows. Every summer, visitors come in the hopes of being the ones to find his hiding place. But all we have here is a replica – a good replica, but a replica nonetheless. Here, let me show you. It's still our most treasured item, a craftsman's piece in itself.'

The professor led the fat man to a padlocked display case of ancient relics. Both men looked through the glass on to the exhibits below. The fat man scanned the objects – coins with the heads of long-dead rulers, belt-buckles tarnished and weathered almost beyond recognition, a comb carved from bone with the turquoise of its decoration still largely intact. Four glass beads were swirled with what seemed contemporary colours; there were arrow heads from ancient battles or hunts, and a bronze armlet of remarkable size, worn once on the bicep of some warrior.

And at the centre of the case was an ebony bull, small enough to sit on a man's palm, modelled head down ready for the charge, pawing at imaginary ground, so lifelike it felt as if it might charge out of the cabinet, if it were opened. Its horns formed an elongated hoop, with a disc representing the sun held between them, and both horns and sun were of pure gold, as were the animal's hooves, and an object resembling a tongue which hung from its mouth.

For some moments the fat man gazed at the bull.

'This really is a beautiful piece,' he said. 'As you say, a work of art in itself.'

'It was made by a local jeweller,' said Professor Philipas. 'He worked from the memories of those who had seen the creature in the flesh, as it were. I believe the bull to be a representation of Zeus, from the myth of his union with Europa. Do you know the story? Zeus saw Europa gathering flowers in a meadow with some nymphs, and was immediately smitten. So he changed himself into a bull, and carried her off to Crete, where she had three sons by him – one of them the great Minos – before he abandoned her.'

'It is not a story which shows Zeus in his best light,' said the fat man. 'But he was never one to be thwarted in his desires. Do you think, then, this handsome creature originated from Crete?'

'No. I think he was made somewhere in our group of islands, probably around 1400 BC. The Minoan culture spread throughout the ancient world. They built settlements as far afield as Egypt and Israel. In some ways, their culture was way ahead of our own. They recognised the sexes as fully equal. Their famous rites of bull-leaping involved both men and women.'

'You are untypical of the modern Greek male, to be suggesting sexual equality as enlightenment.'

'My wife has strong views on the subject. She has strong views on many subjects.'

'And the protrusion from the mouth – what is that?'

'I believe it's a crocus. The saffron trade was very important to the Minoans.'

'Fascinating.' The fat man leaned down closer to the case. 'What a treasure the original must be – and what a tragedy to have been found, and then lost so quickly. Please, tell me, what happened?'

'The discovery caused a great stir of excitement through-out the island, as you would expect. The bull was found in the basement of a harbour house, during building works. My father was the museum's curator at that time – I have my passion for this work from him – and was already preparing this case in the hope of welcoming him here, though he was still in the care of the man who found him. Then, one morn-ing, the bull vanished, as if he had never been.'

'Stolen?'

'Stolen.'

'And who was suspected?'

Professor Philipas shrugged.

'It was always felt it must be an inside job, by which I mean someone from Mithros. Who else would have known of his existence? He was found in the winter months, when no strangers were around. Secondly, he disappeared on a night of storm and tricky seas. There were no boats in or out, so no one took him away. The next day thorough searches were carried out, and as is the way in these islands, the police had their ears to the ground. But no one knew anything, and no one knows anything to this day. It's as if those who made him came back to claim him. Most believe he's never left this island. Hence the treasure-hunters.'

'Your father was an optimist, if he was preparing a home for the bull here,' said the fat man. 'I don't doubt he would have made an excellent custodian, but surely an object of such quality and value would normally have a place in one of the national museums.'

'I don't doubt you're right. The archaeologists were already on their way when he went missing. You'll find the whole sad story in detail in your pamphlet there.'

'Did you write it?'

'I'm its author, yes.'

'Is it possible the bull came from Mithros itself?'

'Almost certainly not. There's no Minoan outpost on Mithros that I'm aware of. Any such settlement would've been built on the coast, for obvious reasons – trade, transport – and the few spots where the coast is habitable here are all still inhabited. Our longest inhabited site is over at Kolona, and there's no basis for saying the Minoans were ever there, only our own mongrel ancestors.'

'So he was an import, then? Why so?'

'Who knows?'

'How much would you say your little bull is worth, if it were found?'

'Really, I've no idea. To me, he would be priceless.'

'To you, maybe. But I have known far inferior antiquities change hands on the black market for many, many millions of drachma. One item like this would secure a man's retirement quite happily, and let him live in style for the rest of his life. You didn't say who the unlucky man was, who found and lost him.'

'He wasn't so unlucky,' said the professor. 'He was a local man. The house had been in his wife's family for generations, and was her dowry house. Of course he was devastated to have lost his treasure, but his wife came into a legacy some months later, and the family used that money to emigrate. To America, I think.'

Professor Philipas returned to his desk, whilst the fat man spent a while browsing the cases of curios, from time to time asking the professor for more information about objects that piqued his interest. He stopped before a table of stuffed animals: a mountain hare frozen as it ran; a five-legged cat spitting and arch-backed; a number of pretty songbirds posed in leafless branches, overhanging a collection of their eggs.

'I always find it poignant to see creatures this way,' said the fat man. 'This poor bee-eater, for example. How can its skin and feathers capture the essence of the living bird? And to take the eggs of any wild bird is a crime.'

'Really?' The professor looked surprised. 'I find them very lifelike, and people are interested to see the birds up close. They're done by a local man, Loskas Vergas, who works in the bank. He prides himself on his work, and I have to say, I think he's very good.'

'Then you and I must agree to differ,' said the fat man. 'May I ask about the portrait on the wall there?' He pointed out a painting, amateur in its execution, which showed a man of resolute expression in modern dress. 'The face is familiar to me.'

'That's our benefactor,' said the professor. '*Kyrios* Vassilis Eliadis. Uncle Vasso, as he is known. He's a very generous man; without his interest and his donations, the museum would have closed down long ago. He's a Mithros man who spent many years abroad, and made a fortune in Egyptian cotton. Now he's come home, and lets the community benefit from his fortune.'

'He's a popular man, no doubt.'

Professor Philipas smiled.

'He is,' he said, 'and the most sought-after godfather Mithros ever saw. He's known for his generosity to his godchildren. He's a knack of choosing perfect gifts on their name-days. He lives in the Governor's Villa on the harbour promontory – no doubt you've seen it.'

'I believe I know the house you mean,' said the fat man. 'It's a beautiful property. Perhaps I should walk over there, and take a closer look.'

'Not too close,' said the professor. 'He doesn't much like visitors.'

'Is that so? I shall bear that in mind. Professor, I thank you for your time.'

'Are you here in Mithros long?' asked the professor. 'I wonder if you'd come for dinner? I've an archive at home of photographs and archaeology, everything there's no room to display here. My wife doesn't share my interest – I caught her once ready to make a bonfire of it all – so I'd enjoy showing it to someone who'd appreciate it. You'd be most welcome. Though I'd have to give my wife a little notice – she's not a woman who likes surprise guests. Maybe the day after tomorrow?'

'Thank you,' said the fat man. 'It would be my pleasure.'

Professor Philipas picked up an envelope from his desk, removed a letter from inside, and on the unaddressed side drew a plan of how to reach his house from the museum.

'Shall we say eight o'clock?' suggested the professor.

'Perfect,' said the fat man, and took his leave.

Outside the museum, the fat man was undecided which way to go. He might return the way he had come, or turn left, in the opposite direction; but in the end he chose a narrow path which led uphill behind the museum, winding away between the houses.

On this path the day's heat was reduced by the shade of the stone walls which surrounded the houses' courtyards, all irregular heights, and with the work of individual builders a signature in their styles; one builder had favoured flatter, smaller stones, another smoother-cut, squarer slabs, whilst a third had picked at random and produced less competent work, as his walls bowed at their centres, and were in danger of collapse.

Around a corner, the fat man found a painter in spattered overalls, working with easy confidence from a plank balanced between two stepladders. One set of ladders was markedly lower in the lane than the other, and neither was stable on the cobbles; but the painter seemed not to notice the wobble in the plank as he applied green paint to a pair of window shutters. In the heat, the smell of the linseed oil which thinned the paint was pungent.

'Will I find anything of interest up this lane?' asked the fat man.

Comfortable on his narrow plank, the painter looked down, his brush in one hand, his paint pot in the other.

'Depends what you find interesting,' he said. 'Houses. Not much else. Old women with rheumatics and young women with babies. All the action here's in the town, friend, where you must have come from.'

A wasp landed on the wet paint, and was stuck. Carefully, the painter picked it off the shutter by its wings, dropped it on to the plank and stepped on it, crushing it with a twist of his boot.

'Well,' said the fat man, 'I find the architecture interesting. I shall go on.'

'Don't get lost, then,' warned the painter. 'The place is a maze for those who don't know it. Strangers go up that way, and are never seen again.'

The fat man smiled.

'If I lose my way, I'll shout,' he said. 'If you'll be good enough to shout back, your voice will guide me.'

'Gladly,' said the painter. 'But don't be too long. I'll be knocking off for lunch soon, and there'll be no one to rescue you before morning. And who knows what ghosts and ghoulies might have grabbed you by then?'

'Should I be afraid, then?'

86

The painter laughed.

'Only of the widows,' he said. 'There's one or two up here haven't had a man in years. A fit, strong man like you – they'd eat you for breakfast!'

But as the fat man went on, he found himself not amongst houses as the painter had suggested. Instead, he came into an open square with a threshing floor, made – like a dance floor – from segments of stone laid to form a circle. The floor's circumference was surrounded by a low wall of upright stones easy for man or animal to step over, but enough to keep the sheaves of grain in place when tossed in for threshing. At its centre was a pole, and mounted on the pole was a spoked wheel, like a ship's wheel, to which donkeys or mules were tethered as they toiled round.

And around the floor a grey mule plodded. The sound of its hooves was muffled by the crop it was threshing; its long ears twitched to repel the flies drawn to its smell of soiled straw and sweat. Over its mouth, it wore a muzzle of twisted wire, a cage tied to the leather of its headcollar; a rope from the headcollar (whose brow-band was painted in bright checks, with a crucifix dangling on to the mule's forehead) secured it to the central pole. Its head was low, from boredom or fatigue; but when it noticed the fat man, its ears pricked up, its head lifted and it slowed its already steady pace, as if it scented a reason to relax.

But as it slowed, the mule-driver on the far side of the threshing-floor flicked its rump with a switch of bamboo. The mule trotted a few lively paces, then settled back to its previous rhythm, watching the fat man's approach.

The mule-driver's eyes flickered over the fat man, but dropped immediately to the ground, and he bowed his head to one side, showing his wish to let the fat man pass by without acknowledgement.

The fat man walked across the square to the edge of the threshing floor, where he stopped and put his hold-all down at his feet.

'*Kali mera*!' he called out to the mule-driver. 'This is marvellous! It's a sight that's all too rare, these days.'

The mule-driver offered the obligatory greeting, then turned to a cart behind him stacked with brittle stalks of lentils. As he gathered up as many as he could hold, lentils dropped tinkling from their pods back into the cart, along with a scattering of leaves, a few stones and a puff of dust from the field.

He dropped the stalks into the mule's path, where they crackled as they broke under its hooves. The mule attempted to shorten its circle and cut its circuit tight, but the driver picked up his switch, and poked the animal's shoulder to push it out to the wall.

Apparently intrigued, the fat man picked up his hold-all and moved closer to the mule-driver. He held out his hand.

'I must introduce myself,' he said. 'I am Hermes Diaktoros, of Athens.'

The mule-driver held out a dirty, dusty hand; but the hand, as the fat man clasped it, was not hard-skinned, but soft, and his fingers were long and limber.

'They call me Milto,' he said.

The fat man looked more closely at the mule-driver's face.

'I know you,' he said. 'I've seen you before.' He snapped his fingers, as if the thought had just come to him. 'In the taverna. You're the violinist. You play very well, as I said to you last night.'

Milto inclined his head as a thank-you.

'I put a great deal into my music,' he said. 'I hope folks see that in my playing. I go nowhere without my violin.' He pointed to the cart, and there, on the back, the end of a black

88

violin case stuck out from under the unthreshed lentils. 'If I've ever an idle moment, I use it to practise.'

'I'm something of a musician myself,' said the fat man. 'I have a special interest in ancient music, so I suppose you might call me a revivalist. I play the lyre, which is a rare skill these days. Certainly, I meet very few others who play. Is there a history of music in your family?'

'None,' said Milto. 'Most of what I know, I taught myself, the rest I learned from anyone I could persuade to teach me. Mithros has its share of players. My violin was a gift from my godfather, when I was a boy. I began to learn the skill in my father's memory, to make him proud; thanks be to God, music spoke to me, and the more I played, the better I got. I think my father'd be pleased to hear me play now. He never did hear me play. He was taken before I played a single note.'

'I'm sure he would have been proud,' said the fat man. 'And I hope in his absence, your godfather did his best to be a father to you in his own right.'

'He did his part,' said Milto, tapping the slowing mule on the rump once more. 'He's been very good to me. But with the best will in the world, he was no substitute for my own father. The loss of my father is something I'll never forget.'

'Nor should you,' said the fat man. 'May his memory be eternal.'

A silence fell between them, with the fat man seeming pleased to watch mule and man work together, and Milto occupied with his threshing. The fat man reached into his pocket, and took out a pack of cigarettes – an old-fashioned box whose lift-up lid bore the head and naked shoulders of a 1940s starlet, her softly permed platinum hair curling around a coy smile. Beneath the maker's name ran a slogan in an antique hand: 'The cigarette for the man who knows a real smoke'.

'Do you smoke?' he asked, and held out the pack to Milto, who took one.

The fat man lit their cigarettes with a slim, gold lighter.

'I've just been to your museum,' he said. 'They have quite a collection of agricultural memorabilia, though it did strike me that some of the implements which have found their way to the museum are tools I still see in daily use, in certain parts. As you, here, keep the old traditions alive. I applaud that.'

'No disrespect, but I'm no museum piece,' said Milto. He held his cigarette in his mouth, and squinting through its smoke, followed the mule a few paces with the switch, tapping on its rump in an attempt to hurry it on. 'I've a job to do, and to my mind, there's no better way to do it. The lentils need threshing, and here's a threshing floor, and my mule. What's the alternative? A smallholder like me can't afford expensive machinery.'

'You have a smallholding, then?'

Milto gave up on hurrying the mule, which now seemed determined to hold to its own pace, regardless of the switch. He removed the cigarette from his mouth, and waved a hand towards the hills.

'I've a bit of land, not much to speak of,' he said. 'We used to have more. We had land over at Kolona, where I was born. But the well there ran dry, so we moved over here, to a piece of my mother's dowry. There's a tangerine orchard, and that's good; it makes a few drachma, in winter. Then the army took over Kolona. They offered us no money. One day, someone comes to me and says, the army's moved on to your land. They've got equipment, the army; they can drill down, where a spade and a bucket can't go, and they got water back in the well. So I thought I might move back there, but Captain Fanis told me no. He says they aren't in permanent occupation, but the army is the army, so who knows? They don't stop me taking my olive harvest, such as it is. The few trees over there, and the few trees over here, together we get a pressing to last us the year. We'd be better off if the tangerines were olives. But God grants us the part he wants us to have, and that's all.'

He pitched more lentils on to the floor; the mule exhaled, in what might have been a sigh. Milto wiped sweat from his brow.

'It's hot work, today, just standing still. I learned to grow lentils from my father. He always gave a portion of the land to lentils. I remember him saying to me: green crops can rot, or get damaged by storm. Have your dry goods as stand-by, boy, and there'll always be food on the table.'

'A wise man,' said the fat man.

A shadow crossed Milto's face.

'He died a dog's death,' he said. 'Where was the wisdom in that?'

In the harbour, the fat man found the public phone. He took a small notebook from his hold-all, and searched the hand-written entries at the back. Finding change in his pocket, he put coins for a long-distance call into the slot, and dialled an Athens number.

The phone rang out for a long time, until at last a woman answered in bored tones.

'Museum of Archaeology.'

'*Despina* Kara Athaniti, please,' said the fat man. He waited again as an extension rang out. A man in half an army uniform came to stand nearby, obviously wanting to use the phone.

'*Embros?*'

A woman's voice answered the extension. At its sound, the fat man smiled.

He put his mouth close to the receiver, so she would hear him even if he spoke quietly.

'Kara,' he said.

'Hermes!' she said. 'Is that you?'

'The same,' he said. 'How is the most beautiful woman in archaeology?'

'Ready to spend some time with you,' she said. 'Are you in town?'

'Alas, no,' said the fat man, with regret. 'I'm a long, long way from home. Where doesn't matter. I might perhaps be coming there, in a few weeks, but the story's always the same, *koukla mou*. The demands of the work grow no less.'

'Ach, Hermes,' she said. 'I heard your voice, and had already picked out the dress I was going to wear.'

'What colour?'

'I shan't say. If I must wait, so must you.'

'In my mind, I see it,' he said. 'Put it to one side, and don't wear it until I come to take you out. Promise me?'

'I promise you.'

'No, I'm ashamed to say, my beautiful girl, I'm phoning to pick that encyclopaedic brain of yours.'

He glanced over his shoulder. The man half in army uniform still waited, arms folded in impatience.

'I've just seen an object of particular beauty, which seems not to belong in the place it's ended up,' said the fat man to Kara. 'Or at least, not the object itself, only a replica. The original, I gather, has been lost. Its origins may be near here, but it might equally have found its way here from anywhere in someone's suitcase. I want to ask you what you know about it.'

'Try me.'

'It's a bull, an ebony bull, decorated with gold. A small piece, but very fine; probably Minoan. Found and lost again, a couple of decades ago. Does it ring any bells?'

Kara didn't hesitate.

'Now I know exactly where you are,' she said. 'Hermes, you're in Mithros, aren't you?'

He laughed.

'No secrets from you,' he said. 'So, *kouklara,* tell me everything you can about Mithros's bull.'

She told him what she knew, and they said a lengthy goodbye. The fat man hung up the phone.

'So sorry to have kept you waiting,' he said to Manolis, and gave a small bow as he left him to use the phone.

Dusk brought little coolness, only relief from the sun's glare. Overhead, the swallows swooped after insects, cutting low between the *kafenion*'s awning and the heads of its clientele. At a table near the water, Loskas Vergas, the bank clerk, joined a man already there.

'*Yassou*, Loskas,' said Spiros. Out of his coastguard's uniform, he had no more of an air of authority than the men around him, though his cheeks were more carefully shaven, and the crease ironed into his slacks was very sharp. His shirt was a jaunty yellow, and his sandals were recently polished; he had applied both hair oil and cologne. 'Sit.'

'How are you, Spiros?' asked Loskas, pulling out a chair. He nodded a greeting to three men intent on a game of *tavli*, one there only to offer advice to the losing player, who glared each time his helper opened his mouth. The bank clerk's face was flushed; the heat was troubling him. He pulled a cotton handkerchief from his shorts pocket, dabbed the sweat from his forehead and wiped the back of his neck, then ran the handkerchief over his bald spot. 'It's too hot.' He settled into the chair and crossed one foot over his knee. 'I ate pasta for dinner, and it was a mistake.'

'You shouldn't eat such heavy food in the heat,' said Spiros. 'Fruit, and raw vegetables. I had a little salad, a little feta, and look at me, I'm fine. At our age, we have to be careful what we eat.' He ran his hands over his reasonably smooth belly, and cast a glance at the tight belt on Loskas's shorts, and the small mound of fat piled over it.

'You sound like a government announcement,' said Loskas, sourly. He turned towards the *kafenion* doorway, where a youth stood with a tray under one arm, his eyes on two bored-looking Danish girls drinking beer.

Loskas called out to the youth.

'Bring me a *frappé*, medium sweet with milk. And put your tongue back in your mouth before someone treads on it.'

The youth went inside; the Danish girls continued to look bored. The player losing at *tavli* shouted his objection to the way the dice had fallen. Seeing the game as hopeless, his helper walked away.

'I'm glad I found you,' said Loskas.

'Where else should I be?'

'I wanted to talk to you.'

Loskas looked around. The youth was bringing out his *frappé*. He placed it on the table alongside a glass of water; ice cubes chinked in the glasses.

'I'll have an ice-cream, too,' said Loskas to the youth. 'Do you have any of those strawberry and chocolate, mixed?' The youth nodded. 'One of those. And don't forget the spoon.'

Spiros glanced again at Loskas's midriff, and his eyebrows lifted.

'It's so hot,' said Loskas, defensively. 'I need to cool down.' He sipped his coffee through a pink straw. 'Now listen carefully. I'm going to say what I've got to say quietly.' He leaned towards Spiros. 'Someone came in the bank today. Someone I think we know.'

Spiros stirred the remains of his own coffee with his straw, and relaxed back into his chair.

'Don't say any more.' He raised a hand to a passing fisherman, and in a gesture which might or might not have been ironic, the fisherman deferentially touched the peak of his cap. Spiros pointed to the outer corner of his eye, and at the fisherman, letting the fisherman know he was being watched. 'I saw him too. He came into my office.'

'You agree with me that it's him?'

'Him, or his twin brother.'

'I wasn't so sure.' Loskas sipped again at his coffee. 'It's a long time ago. People change. And we didn't know him well.'

'You know it's him, or you wouldn't have mentioned it to me,' said Spiros. 'Why should you doubt it?'

'Because if it's him, he wouldn't be stupid enough to be here.'

'But he isn't here voluntarily. I had it from Captain Fanis that his shipmates tipped him overboard for cheating at cards.'

'That would make sense,' said Loskas. 'He came to me for money. He wanted me to bypass the system, take his word for who he was and give him access to his account.'

'What name did he give?'

'He gave no name. He told me to forget it.'

'He told me they call him Chiotis, Manolis Chiotis.'

'Is that the name he went under before? I don't remember. It's so long ago. The only one of us who might remember, is here no more.'

'Ah, but that's not true, is it?'

For a moment, Loskas looked puzzled.

'I see,' he said. 'The question is, what should we do?'

'The man is very anxious to be on his way,' said Spiros. 'Which is hardly surprising, is it? But you, of course, hold all the cards.'

'What cards?'

'He can't leave without money to buy himself a ticket. You control the money. You won't give him money without his papers, and he doesn't have his papers.'

'What if he finds a boatman to take him? If he promises enough money, someone will take him off here. Maybe he'll get a lift to rejoin his colleagues, wherever they've gone, and then we've lost him.'

'That's easily handled,' said Spiros. 'I'll put the word round no one's to take him, no matter what he offers. Anyone who takes him can look forward to my wrath, and needn't come to me for renewal of any fishing permits. And you can cast aspersions on his credit-worthiness. Let it be known he's got no money in the bank. Give out some story of him running from his creditors. Between us we can ensure if he tries to leave, he'll be up against a wall.'

The youth brought Loskas's ice-cream. Loskas dipped in his spoon, and took a mouthful of strawberry.

'So you think we could stop him going?' he asked Spiros.

'Oh yes,' said Spiros. 'We could stop him all right. But the question is, should we?'

'That's what I was thinking,' said Loskas. 'It's going to cause trouble, if certain people find out he's here. And is trouble what we want?'

'If certain people find out we knew, and didn't stop him, it might cause more trouble still. You and I are in a difficult position.'

'It's hard to know what to do for the best.'

'So what do you suggest?'

Loskas's ice-cream was melting quickly; the spoonful of chocolate he put in his mouth was almost liquid.

'I don't want trouble,' he said. 'But I don't want to give offence to certain people. So perhaps we should just tell what we know, and have no more to do with it. When he comes to me with the right papers, I'll give him his money, and he can go. All by the book.'

'But by the book takes time,' said Spiros. 'I say we let certain people know we've seen him, and leave it at that. Let matters take their course. Then it's not our funeral. Agreed?'

'Agreed,' said Loskas, and gave his full attention to his ice-cream.

Six

From the prow deck where he was relaxing with his copy of Herodotus, the fat man heard the rattle of a bucket, and the trickle of water running from a squeezed mop; he heard the slap of the mop on the deck, and the lazy slide of its head across the boards.

Silently, he rose from his recliner, and made his way to the corner of the cabins, from where he could see down to the stern. Ilias was barefoot, and not yet properly dressed; the buttons were all unfastened on his crewman's shirt, and instead of his white trousers, he wore a pair of rumpled shorts. As the fat man watched, Ilias yawned, and leaned, eyes closed, on to the handle of his mop, as if he might be going to fall asleep.

'*Kali mera.*'

At the fat man's words, Ilias fell into a brief enthusiasm for his task, before plunging the mop-head into the bucket, and turning with a small bow to the fat man.

'*Kyrie, kali mera,*' he said. 'I didn't realise you were awake.'

'Apparently not,' said the fat man, walking back to the stern. 'I awoke very early this morning. Where is Enrico?'

'He's in the galley, *kyrie,* brewing your coffee.'

'You look tired, Ilias. Did you not sleep well last night?'

'It's been so hot, *kyrie*. And if I turn up the air-conditioning, I get too cold.'

'As I've said to you before, you're welcome to sleep on deck, if you can persuade yourself from the softness of your bed,' said the fat man. 'You'd find the temperature out here almost perfect. When you've done the decks, get some coffee, and rouse yourself. What's the news on our repair? Did Enrico get the parts you need, yesterday?'

Ilias shook his head.

'They didn't have them in stock,' he said. 'They ordered them, and promised they'd be here on a boat this evening.'

'Not until then?'

'I'm afraid not.'

'It comes as no surprise. As I expected, we shall have to amuse ourselves here another day.' He looked across at the harbour, and at the Governor's Villa high on the headland. 'I shall take a walk, and maybe have a closer look at that beautiful house. As for you two, please make reasonably good use of your leisure time. By which I mean, I'm charging you to make sure Enrico does nothing to embarrass us.'

On the harbour-front, the fat man stopped before the window of the *zaharoplasteio*, where an assistant was putting out a fresh tray of *bougatsa* – crisp filo pastry thickly filled with vanilla cream, and dusted with icing sugar and cinnamon. It had not been long since breakfast, and the fat man was going to walk away; but the scent of warm cinnamon and vanilla was, in the end, a temptation he saw no reason to resist, and so he went inside, and bought two generous pieces to carry him through to lunch.

He strolled in a direction he had not yet taken, towards the peninsula at the harbour's end; but rather than taking an upwards path which would take him towards the Governor's

Villa, he stayed close to the waterside, following a route which led him away from the last harbour houses. In a few hundred metres, the path began to rise as it followed the contours of the rocky shore and skirted the base of the promontory, until he rounded a corner, and saw at the hilltop, beyond all the other buildings, the high walls surrounding the villa.

The path forked. The right fork rose to the hillside houses in a series of steps and twists, and seemed the obvious route for him to follow; yet after a moment's deliberation, he instead chose the left – a dirt path, leading to the sea.

The path led downwards through scrub to a small pebble beach, where a young woman crouched at the water's edge. She had left her slip-on shoes on the pebbles, and was in the shallows up to her ankles, with the skirt of her dress bunched in her lap to stop the hem trailing in the water. She had with her four empty water bottles, one of which she was filling from the sea. When she heard the fat man's footfall, she turned; she was no beauty – her eyes too small, her thighs too plump, her hair uncombed and wiry – but her smile, though shy, was warm.

The fat man took a seat on a bench, and watched her. When her first bottle was full, she screwed on the cap, and tossed the full bottle up the beach, out of the sea's reach. She took the next empty bottle from her lap, unscrewed its cap, and filled that bottle too, and so she went on until all four bottles were filled, when she left the water, straightening her dress. She put the filled bottles into a bag made from flowered fabric which might have been intended to upholster a chair, and headed up the beach in the fat man's direction.

He called out to her.

'*Kali mera, koritsi.*'

'*Kalos tou.*'

She was going to pass him by, but he stopped her with a question.

'Will you forgive me for asking,' he said, 'but I am by nature curious. Might I ask why you're taking water from the sea?'

'Medicinal purposes,' she said.

'Ah, I see. My guess was, you were going to use the water for boiling lobsters.'

She laughed – a light laugh which softened her flaws, and made her face attractive.

'We can't afford lobsters where I live,' she said. 'If I were boiling anything, it'd be chickpeas.'

'I should introduce myself. They call me Hermes.'

'Olympia.'

'*Chairo poli, Despina* Olympia.'

His formality amused her.

'Where're you from, *kalé*?' she asked. In her island accent, she ran all her words together, in contrast to his careful enunciation.

'Not here,' he said, 'and that's why I've lost my way. I was trying to get to the big house, up there.' He pointed to the hillside above them. 'But I think I've taken a wrong turn.'

'You have,' she said. 'Do you want me to show you the way? The house I'm staying in is just below it.'

'That would be very kind,' said the fat man. 'But I was just going to enjoy my *bougatsa*, here in the peace and quiet with the view. As it happens, I have two pieces. Can I persuade you to join me, and then we'll walk together?'

He produced the pink-and-white striped box from the *zaharoplasteio*, and slipped off the string tied round it. The pastries' buttery oils had seeped through the paper lining, and made dark blotches on the box's cardboard.

'I love *bougatsa*,' said Olympia. 'But I can't be long.'

As she sat down next to him on the bench, he offered to take her bag.

'Let me help you with that,' he said. 'It must be very heavy.'

'It's nothing to me,' she said, placing the bag of bottles under the seat. 'Look.' She flexed her arm to show its impressive muscles. 'You have to be strong, in my line of work.'

'And what is your line of work?'

'I'm a nurse.'

She bit into a piece of *bougatsa*, scattering crumbs on her dress and scooping up a squirt of vanilla cream with her finger.

She spoke with her mouth full.

'So what's your interest in the Governor's Villa?'

'I think I'd like to buy it,' said the fat man.

As she chewed, she laughed.

'You'd need to be a rich man to do that,' she said. 'You could buy a lot of lobsters, with the kind of money you'd need to pay for that house. But it's not for sale.'

'Is it not?' asked the fat man, biting off the corner of his pastry. 'Most things are for sale, if the price is right.'

'That place isn't,' she insisted. 'Uncle Vasso'll never sell. He says he's going to die there.'

'Uncle Vasso,' said the fat man, thoughtfully, as if racking his brain. 'I know that name. I saw his portrait in the museum.'

'Did you?' asked Olympia. 'I've never been there. Why's he got his portrait in the museum?'

'The curator says, because Uncle Vasso does the island so much good.'

'Maybe he does,' she said. 'I hadn't thought about it.'

She took another large bite of her pastry.

'This is very good,' she said. 'If you wanted to buy that house, you should have come here twenty years ago. Before he bought it, the place was a ruin. We used to play up there, when I was small. When the Italian governor lived there, they used to have lots of parties. My grandmother says the King of Greece came once, and they filled all the rooms with white roses, so many that you could smell their perfume right across the island. Do you believe that?'

The fat man smiled. 'Maybe.'

'But the house got damaged in the war. No one wanted a house that size, anyway. It was sad to see it – the glass all broken in the windows, the plaster all off the ceilings. There were cracks in the walls you could put your fist through. And the staircase was a death-trap – someone took the banisters for firewood, and you had to know which of the treads were rotten. And the gardens! All overgrown, and full of snakes and cats. My sister took a fancy to some kittens once – they used to nest amongst the weeds – and thought she'd take them home and tame them. *Panayeia*, did she get bitten! Those kittens were like tiger-cubs! It was me who put perox- ide on her cuts. That was the first bit of nursing I ever did, and my sister said I was better at it than our mother. That sowed a seed for me. From a little incident like that, a whole life's direction grew.'

'You're right,' said the fat man. 'It's extraordinary how the Fates will take a hand.'

'I suppose we thought the place would just fall down, it being so well on its way. But then Uncle Vasso came back from wherever it was he'd been, and he bought it.'

'And where was it that he'd been?'

'I don't know. Africa somewhere. All I know is, he came back rich enough to pay cash for the villa, and cash to all the contractors who worked on it. Who knows how many millions he must have spent? And everything was the best! He checked on the work constantly, and never left the builders alone. If they weren't working fast enough, or to his standard, he fired them, and got in a new team. They say it's like a palace, inside. They say there are gold-plated taps in the bathroom. Do you think that's true?'

'Maybe. So he was a man who went away and came back as rich as Croesus?'

'He came back a different man from when he left, that's what they say. I can't even have been born when he went. But he came back a cut above his old roots, and put his relatives' noses out of joint. They offered him bed and board, as of course they would, but he turned up his nose, and took a room at a hotel. He lived there until the house was finished, and that was the best part of a year. So you can see, he's a man with money to burn.'

'It certainly sounds like it,' said the fat man. 'And he fell out with his relatives, did he?'

She laughed again.

'Not permanently,' she said. 'They're not stupid, after all. He's got to leave his money somewhere, and he's no wife or children. As soon as the villa was finished, they paid a visit, a social call. Even then, they say he turned them away at the door. He doesn't like visitors, doesn't Uncle Vasso.'

'He's an unsociable man, then? He didn't strike me that way. I believe it was him I saw in the taverna last night, and he seemed very sociable.'

'Oh, he's sociable, on his own terms. He's generous too, when he's out and about. That's what he said to his relatives, that he'd buy them drinks and dinner, if they ever cared to join him. But his house is his castle, and he likes to keep it to himself. He locks it up like a fortress, and leaves all the lights on, all night. But he was always like that, from the beginning. After the robbery, though, it made him worse.'

'He was robbed, then?'

'Some years ago, now. I was still only a girl, but I remember the people talking. They tortured him to get what they were after. They burned his hands, holding them over a candle flame.'

'Really?' said the fat man. 'How extraordinarily cruel! Is that then why he wears gloves?'

'I've never seen him without them.' She put the last of her pastry in her mouth, and wiped the stickiness from her hands on the skirt of her dress. 'They say his hands are hideous, but it wouldn't bother me. In my job, you see all kinds of nasty things.'

'I'm sure you do,' said the fat man. He flattened the box that had held the pastries and slipped it into a front pocket of his hold-all for later disposal. 'What was it that they wanted from him that they were prepared to go to such lengths?'

She shrugged.

'Who knows? Money, I suppose. Some say gold. They say he has a chest full of it up there. Or did have, until they came and took it.'

'And did these robbers rob anyone else?'

'No. I suppose they didn't need to. They robbed him, ran back down to their boat and made their getaway.'

The fat man looked up towards the promontory's summit.

'Then they must have had him very much in mind as their target,' he said. 'There's no logic otherwise in their robbing the house furthest from their means of escape. Who were these men?'

'They were never caught,' said Olympia. 'Which is no surprise, given our police force. The one man who tried to stop them, they ran down with their boat as they were leaving. Socrates, they called him, Socrates Rokos. He's at the bottom of the sea still. If you listen to the old women, they'll tell you he can be heard wailing, at night when the moon is full.'

'You don't believe in that tale?'

'No, I don't. Dead is dead, in my book.' She glanced at her wristwatch, and tapped its face to make sure it was working. 'I must go back to my charge.'

Olympia picked up her water bottles, the fat man his hold-all, and they walked together along the upward path.

'Do you work at the clinic?' asked the fat man.

'I used to. Now I take on private clients.'

'I suppose the pay is better.'

She shook her head.

'Sometimes I get no pay at all.'

'So why do you do it?'

They were passing a garden, and she pulled a leaf from a rose bush, then absently let it fall.

'I used to work in Crete. I had a job in the hospital there, but it didn't suit me. It seemed less about nursing and caring for the patients than it was about forcing them back on to their feet and out of the door as soon as possible. Then I got word from home that a neighbour of ours was ill. She was very elderly, poor soul; she had one son, but he'd died before her, and she had no one to care for her in her final days. When you get to the end of life, no one wants you. They all want you gone and out of the way. So I came back to nurse her, and when her time came I held her hand. I intended going back to Crete, but someone else asked for me, a woman very ill, with no close family. So I nursed her too. And then there was another, and another. Sometimes they get well; mostly they don't. If they can pay me, they do, or sometimes I just get room and board. Sometimes they give me something – a ring, or a necklace – and tell me to sell it to pay their fees, but there's never been anything of any value, so I keep what they give me as souvenirs. Something to remind the world they were once here.'

'That is thoughtful of you. The world is too quick to forget those who have lit no fires at Posterity's altar. As for the gifts your charges give you – who knows? If you appreciate what is given you that has little value, maybe one day someone will be more generous.'

She stopped outside a house where the whitewash was cracked and long unpainted, but the shutters and the windows were open to let in air and light.

'This is where I'm staying,' she said. 'Keep going straight up until you reach a path leading to the left. Follow that, bear left, and take the first left again. That'll take you to the villa.'

'Thank you for your company, Olympia.'

'Thank you for the *bougatsa*.'

She went into the courtyard, and shut the door. He waited until he heard her go inside the house; but instead of following her directions up to the Governor's Villa, he took the path back down the way they'd come.

Lillis bolted back into place the part he'd tinkered with for days, and reconnected the wiring. He called out to Gounaris, who sat stripped to the waist in the driver's seat of the Jeep, drumming the rhythm of the song in his head on the hot steering-wheel.

'Ready!'

Gounaris leaned forward, and carelessly turned the key in the ignition.

The engine fired. Its rhythm was faltering, and it sputtered and shuddered, and blew black smoke from the exhaust. But Lillis held his breath and prayed, and Gounaris held his hands up in amazement, and somehow, the engine kept going. Outside the guardhouse, the captain looked up from his newspaper; Kastellanos opened his eyes from his doze.

Skafidis came running from the kitchen, and gave a cheer. Manolis – who had changed back into his shorts and was lying on his back in the shallows, staring up at the sky – made no discernible reaction at all.

In the ears of the men on the beach, the Jeep's engine drowned the noise of the fast boat approaching round the headland. But the water carried its sound to Manolis, and hearing it, he slipped on to his front, and watched the boat approach.

All the soldiers were moving towards the Jeep.

Gounaris climbed out of the driver's seat, and clapped Lillis on the back.

'Bravo, *malaka*,' he said. 'At last.'

The Jeep's engine died. Kastellanos and Skafidis jeered, and turned to walk away.

'It's out of fuel!' protested Lillis. 'Believe me, it's fixed!'

Gounaris shook his head, and followed the others towards the guardhouse.

In the new quiet, the boat's approach was loud. As it closed in on the beach, its driver cut the engine, and glided competently alongside the jetty.

Manolis began to swim lazily towards the beach. The driver of the boat – a red-hulled Donzi speedboat, with white trim and ivory upholstery – jumped ashore. As he tied up, the captain called out to him.

'*Yassou*, Spiros! How are you doing?'

The coastguard officer – not in his usual immaculate uniform, but wearing smart shorts and a well-ironed T-shirt – checked his fenders, and raised a hand to the captain as he came up the beach.

'*Yassou*, Captain Fanis,' he said.

He took a seat at the table, across from the captain.

'Gounaris!' shouted the captain. 'Coffee!'

Manolis walked slowly towards the guardhouse.

'What brings you here?' the captain asked Spiros. 'Have you just come to rub my face in it, with that pretty boat of yours? I still don't get how you afforded it, on your salary. Maybe I'm in the wrong job.'

Spiros shrugged.

'I got it for a good price,' he said. 'I told you, it was second-hand.'

'Even so,' said the captain. 'It's a beautiful toy. Come on, tell us – did you win the lottery?'

Spiros laughed.

'If I'd won the lottery, you'd have heard me shouting from here to the harbour. My shift doesn't start until four, so I thought I'd give her a run out. I came to see how you're getting on with our friend.'

'He's still here, if that's what you mean.'

'I suppose it is,' said Spiros. 'As long as he hasn't slipped away in the night. Just keep him sweet for another day or so, that's all I ask. When we've found out for certain who he is, he'll be out of your hair.'

'If I must,' said the captain. 'But you owe me for this one, my friend.'

'*Yassas*,' said Spiros, politely, as Manolis joined them. 'How're things?'

'Tedious,' said Manolis, taking a seat uninvited at the table. 'I hope you've come to tell me I'm free to go.'

Spiros laughed.

'You talk as if someone had put you under house arrest,' he said. 'The checks we're making are routine, no more than that. Unless you tell me we should be thinking otherwise.'

Manolis sighed.

'How much longer, then?'

'That depends,' said Spiros. 'Your friends are proving hard to find. They seem to have vanished without trace.'

'I told you, they're not my friends,' said Manolis. 'I never met them before. It was a business arrangement.'

'We expected they'd have put in somewhere by now, for supplies and fuel,' said Spiros. 'Only they don't seem to have done so. Not on Greek soil, anyway.'

'I can't help you,' said Manolis. 'They didn't leave me a chart of where they were heading.'

'Alexandria, you said.'

'That's what they told me.'

Gounaris brought out two coffees. He put one in front of the captain, and handed the other to Spiros. As he left them, Manolis called him back.

'Hey, son,' he said. 'Can you bring me one of those?'

Gounaris was about to object, but a warning in the captain's eye kept him silent.

'Go ahead, Gounaris,' said the captain. 'Make our guest a coffee.'

'Yes, Captain,' said Gounaris. 'If you say so.'

'So,' said Captain Fanis, 'tell us what's new in the harbour. Here in our isolation, we've no idea what's going on.'

Spiros tasted his coffee.

'Your boy there makes a good cup,' he said. 'There was some excitement today, as it turns out. There's another film crew arrived, doing a news story on the bull. They sent that reporter from ANT1, the blonde. She's a good-looking woman in the flesh, I'll tell you. If you like, I'll see if I can put in a word.'

'If she's here, no doubt the local Lotharios are out in droves,' said the captain. 'But is she journalist enough to make news out of our old story?'

Spiros turned to Manolis.

'You know the story of our bull, I suppose?'

'Yes, I know the story,' said Manolis.

'Shall I tell you what I think?' said Spiros. 'I think it's only a matter of time until it's found. Don't you agree, Fanis?'

The captain gave a snort of laughter.

'If that's what you say.'

'Think about it,' said Spiros. 'Why is there a news crew here? They say they've had a tip-off. I think someone wants to stir up interest in the bull, so when it's found, there'll be more bidders. Push the price up. Makes sense, doesn't it?'

Again, the captain laughed.

'What would you do with that kind of money, eh, friend?' Spiros asked Manolis, giving him a nudge. 'If you found that bull, you could just name your price. What would a collector pay for such a treasure? There's some Onassis out there who'd pay millions, tens of millions. All your life's problems'd be over, if you found that bull. You wouldn't be needing money for a boat-ticket then, would you? You wouldn't need a boat-ticket, because you could buy the whole shipping line.'

Gounaris brought out Manolis's coffee. Most of it was spilled in the saucer.

'If I had that kind of money, imagine how it would be,' went on Spiros. 'Women like that reporter would be falling at my feet.' He smoothed his T-shirt, and ran his hand over his hair. 'What do you think, eh? How could she resist a body like this, and a wallet full of cash? What do you think?'

The captain smiled.

'What I think is, sometimes you talk absolutely no sense at all,' he said.

When the day's heat diminished and became bearable, Olympia carried a cane-bottomed chair outside, and set it at the centre of the courtyard. In the bedroom, she helped the frail woman into a cotton robe, and supported her in the slow, short walk from bed to chair. The woman – all bones, wasted and weak – leaned her meagre weight on Olympia's arm, and concentrated on every harrowing step.

'Take your time, *theia*,' said Olympia. 'There's no rush.'

The woman squeezed her skeletal hand on Olympia's forearm.

'Time is what I don't have,' she said. 'This might be the last time.'

'No,' said Olympia, guiding her through the doorway, bending down to lift her feet for her over the stoop. 'You'll have many more times, yet.'

On the far side of the doorway, they stopped to rest. The woman winced.

'Are you in pain?' asked Olympia.

'A little,' said the woman. 'The sun will ease it.'

They reached the chair, at last. Olympia placed the woman's hands on its back.

'Hold on to that,' she said, 'whilst I take off your robe.'

She lifted the robe from the woman's shoulders, and taking the woman's hands one at a time from the chair-back, slipped it down her arms to leave her naked. The loose skin of her back and buttocks was a mess of lesions: fresh sores which wept clear liquid, and others part-healed and crusted with golden scabs, around which more liquid bled.

Olympia ran her eyes over the sores.

'Your skin's looking better,' she lied; the lesions were spreading further every day. 'Let's sit you down.'

She helped the naked woman on to the chair. The woman closed her eyes, and sat half-smiling in the light. The bottles Olympia had filled at the beach had been standing in the sun; she unscrewed the cap of one and poured water over her fingertips, finding it a little warmer than tepid. As the spilt water splashed on the stones, the woman opened her eyes.

'If you can't go to the sea, then the sea must come to you,' said Olympia. 'Are you ready?'

The woman smiled.

'Ready,' she said.

Slowly, Olympia poured warm seawater over the woman's shoulders, and let it run down her arms and back. She dribbled it over her thighs, and let it run down her calves, and poured the last of the bottle over her feet. The woman wriggled her toes. Putting aside the empty bottle, Olympia opened the second, concentrating as she poured it on the worst sores. Water ran down the chair-legs and dripped from the struts, and the air smelled of the water, and very faintly, of the ozone of the sea.

'The salt'll really help your skin,' Olympia lied.

'I love the sea. The sea is good for everything,' said the woman. 'Every single day in summer, my sister and I used to swim. Like mermaids we were, in love with the water. Those were good days.'

'We could phone your sister, later, if you'd like,' said Olympia. 'She'll want to know how you're getting on. You can tell her you've been bathing in the sea.'

'Yes,' said the woman, dreamily. 'We'll phone her, later on.'

In the same way, Olympia poured the third bottle, and the fourth.

'That's it,' she said, shaking the last drops from the last bottle. 'That's all there is for today.'

'Wonderful,' said the woman. Her pale skin glistened wet, and on her shins, salt crystals were drying white.

'Shall I fetch a towel?' asked Olympia.

'No, no towel,' said the woman. 'I want to dry out here.'

'Shall I leave you a few minutes, then?' asked Olympia. 'I could go and change your sheets whilst you relax.'

'Yes,' said the woman. She looked squinting up at the sky. 'Yes, you can leave me a few minutes.'

'I won't be far away,' said Olympia. 'You call me if you need me. Are you in pain?'

The woman shook her head.

'The pain is better,' she said. 'And I shan't be needing anything, *kori mou*. Let me just sit here, and have a talk with my friend, the sun. I've everything I need, for a while.'

Seven

Captain Fanis was hungry. The rota showed Lillis as the evening's cook, but Lillis had gone to take a shower half an hour ago, and hadn't yet returned. In the kitchen, Gounaris was making iced coffee. Spills of milk and sugar were unwiped on the table; the empty wrapper from a packet of biscuits lay on the floor.

'Clear that up,' said the captain. He opened the fridge, and was relieved to find Lillis had remembered to defrost the chickens. 'And tell Lillis to get in here, double quick. I need him as my sous-chef. I'm taking over as cook, for tonight.'

Behind the bunkhouse, the captain hauled the barbecue out from under the junk that had been piled on it since its last use, and carried it to a piece of level ground close to the kitchen. He tipped in charcoal from a sack – charcoal still in its olive-wood form, in the knots and twists of its sawn branches, but as light, piece by piece, as a handful of the leaves it once bore, and pure carbon, with not an atom's deviation from black. He lit it with a sprinkling of lighter-fuel and a dropped-on match; there was the whoomph of a small explosion, and the kindling under the charcoal began to burn. Quickly it set light to the charcoal, which tinkled as it sent up stinging sparks like tiny firecrackers; and when the charcoal was red at its heart, the glow spread slowly outwards, and the fuel began to transform into ash, caught by the breeze to rise in powdery dust. The captain raked the charcoal through and placed the clumsily butchered chickens on the rack; the dripping oils and fats sizzled on the heat, and gave off the appetising smell of roasting flesh.

When the chicken was almost cooked, Manolis came up the beach. He carried an octopus, soapy with slapping on the jetty to make it tender. He held it up, the slimy tentacles draped around his wrist.

'I brought an offering,' he said. 'A contribution to the feast.'

'Well caught,' said the captain. He moved some of the chicken from grill to plate, and made room for the octopus. Laid out on the rack, its body hissed and steamed. 'The lads will enjoy that.'

'Regard it as a thank you,' said Manolis. 'The very least I could do.'

The soldiers ate, cleared away the remains of the meal, and returned to their places at the table. The captain sat amongst them, indulgent of their banter. Manolis kept silent, sipping on warm lemonade, his eyes on the blackness of the night sea, on the lookout for the lights of approaching boats.

'I'll fetch the cards,' said Skafidis.

Kastellanos yawned, stretching his arms over his head.

'Count me out, *pedia*,' he said. 'Bedtime for me. I didn't get to sleep a single hour last night in that damned hammock.'

Skafidis slid the battered cards from their fragile box.

'You're crazy,' said Lillis. 'You'll never sleep in that bunk-house. It's hot enough to toast your balls. Might as well stay out here, and play.'

Kastellanos wagged a finger in his direction.

'Spoken like a sore loser,' he said. 'You'll be thinking that the thousand I won off you last night's coming back in your direction. Forget it. It's gone, spent. I'm going to bed.'

He stood up from the table, and as he passed behind their chairs, rubbed Lillis's and Gounaris's shaved heads, making them duck away. They cursed him as he wandered off to the bunkhouse.

As Skafidis shuffled the deck, Manolis's attention moved from the sea to the sticky cards as they dropped between Skafidis's hairless fingers.

'Who's in?' asked Skafidis. 'Lillis, how about it?'

Lillis dug in his pocket, and brought out a handful of money. There was no more than a couple of thousand, most of it change.

'Count me in,' he said. 'I'm good for a hand or two.'

Gounaris produced somewhat less.

'I'm feeling lucky,' he said. 'Deal me in.'

'What about you, Captain?' asked Skafidis. 'You want to lose some cash?'

The captain smiled.

'OK,' he said. 'Why not?'

Manolis was once again looking out to sea.

'How about you, friend?' asked Skafidis. 'You fancy a hand of cards?'

Manolis seemed startled to be spoken to.

'I'm sorry,' he said, 'what did you say?'

'Do you want a hand of cards?'

'Sure,' said Manolis. 'Why not?' But then he shook his head. 'I'm being stupid, aren't I? Count me out, son. I've got no money.'

The soldiers looked uncomfortable. Manolis saw their disinclination to make him a loan, and turned sulkily away.

'I'll tell you what,' said the captain. 'Forget cash. We'll use chips. Gounaris, go and find something we can use.'

Gounaris came back from the kitchen with a packet of dried butterbeans, and emptied it into the middle of the table.

Manolis laughed.

'Not exactly Vegas, is it?' he asked, moving closer to the group, pulling up a chair amongst them. 'Not exactly a man's game.'

'You're the one with no money,' said the captain.

'My credit's good,' said Manolis.

'We don't know that,' said Lillis.

'Believe me, it's good,' said Manolis. 'Come on, *pedia*, let's make it interesting. I've got money coming in a couple of days. Anyway, I'm not planning on losing.'

'None of us ever plan on losing,' said Skafidis.

'How about we play for fifty drachma a bean?' said Gounaris. 'That would make it interesting.'

'Not interesting enough for me,' said Manolis. 'My usual minimum's a thousand.'

'And look where that got you,' said the captain. 'Man overboard. We're soldiers on soldiers' pay. Besides, big stakes lead to bad feeling. One bean, fifty drachmas. Take it or leave it.'

'But who's the banker?' asked Skafidis. 'Who'll cash us in, when we win?'

'I'll keep the cash over here, and pay out when we're done,' said the captain.

'But what about him?' asked Gounaris, looking at Manolis. 'How will we collect what he owes us?'

'I told you,' said Manolis. 'I don't intend to lose.'

'And how many is he starting with?'

'We'll give him fifteen hundred drachma credit,' said the captain. 'And I'll make sure he pays his debts before he leaves. Fifty drachmas a bean. Lillis, hand them out.'

'I've got eighteen hundred drachmas,' said Gounaris. 'How many beans is that?'

There was silence around the table. Manolis smiled.

'How should I know?' said Lillis. 'I'm just handing them out.'

'Thirty-six,' said Manolis. 'Give him thirty-six.'

'He's right,' said the captain, at last. 'Gounaris, give him thirty-six beans.'

Lillis began to count, and made a pile of Gounaris's beans.

'There aren't going to be enough,' said Skafidis. 'Not at this rate.'

'So double the value,' said Manolis. 'Come on, lads. Let's play a man's game.'

Lillis studied him.

'OK,' he said. 'Let's do it your way.'

'Seems to me,' said the captain, 'that the one who wants to play for high stakes is the one who's got nothing to put in the pot. If you lose, friend, all you lose is a handful of beans. My boys here, they're going to lose their beer-money for the next week.'

Manolis looked around the table.

'Then they'd better not lose, had they? Come on, lads – take me on! Is that the only deck you've got?'

Whilst Lillis counted the beans, Manolis held out his hand, and Skafidis gave him the cards. Manolis slid a couple between his fingers, and feeling their tackiness, pulled a face. He riffled through a few more, fanned the pack, then gave it a couple of hand-to-hand shuffles, but fumbled it. A scattering of cards fluttered to the floor.

'They're lousy,' he said, bending to pick up the cards he'd dropped. 'Is this the best pack you've got? How're we supposed to play with cards like these?'

With the dropped cards retrieved, he knocked the pack back square and returned it to Skafidis.

'You dealing? Here you go.'

He looked expectantly at Skafidis.

And Skafidis dealt.

The moon was high, and a path of its soft light fell on the water. On *Aphrodite*'s deck, the fat man was reading a newspaper's obituaries. As he read, he dipped into a bowl of salted sunflower seeds, discarding the cracked shells on to a white plate. The ice in the wine-cooler was almost melted; the wine itself – a Malagousia, from a small Attican vineyard – was almost drunk.

Dressed in his uniform but barefoot, Enrico came up from below decks. In the heat, he had unbuttoned his shirt down to the waist, and untucked his undershirt from his trousers. The fat man appeared not to notice he was there. Enrico gave a light cough to announce himself.

The fat man looked round at Enrico, who stood by his shoulder.

'I was wondering if there was anything else you needed, *kyrie*,' he said.

He lifted the wine from the ice-bucket to check the level, and poured what remained in the bottle into the fat man's glass.

'I shall be fine, thank you,' said the fat man. 'You can go to your bed. I was just reading this piece in the paper – an obituary of Isaakios Nanos, the philosopher. You remember him, I'm sure. We came across him in our travels, several years ago. I found him very dry, and rather pompous – he took himself and his flawed ideas extremely seriously. He was capable of thinking only in absolutes; everything to him was black or white, right or wrong. Reading this description of him, you wouldn't know it was the same man. Perhaps he changed after we left him, though I had little hope of that at the time.'

'I remember him,' said Enrico, leaning forward to get a better view of the philosopher's grainy photograph. 'He wore spectacles he didn't need to make himself look intelligent. See, he's wearing them in that picture.'

'That's the man,' said the fat man. 'Still. We shouldn't speak ill of the dead. By the way, where is Ilias?'

'Already sleeping, I wouldn't doubt.'

'Well, wake him, and send him to me. I have a job I want him to do. Tell him to bring the eucalyptus-wood box from the drawer in my study. You know the box I mean?'

Enrico smiled.

'Oh yes, *kyrie*. I know the box. And by the way, may I ask if you have plans for tomorrow?'

The fat man looked at him closely.

'Should I have?' he asked.

'I learned as I was buying vegetables that there's a name-day service tomorrow morning, over at the hamlet of Kolona. It's a deserted village, but I gather the church might be of interest. It's a very old one.'

'Ah, Kolona. The place was mentioned to me, today. And who is the saint being honoured?'

'St Nikodemos, I believe.'

'Another philosopher, then. I wonder whether he was less dry than our friend here in the paper. I suspect not; and a holy man who was also a philosopher would not, I feel, make very cheerful company at dinner. Still, I should like to see if there's anything of interest within the church, so we shall go. No doubt they will start early, and so shall we. What is our best route to get there?'

'There'll be trucks, if you wanted to hitch a ride. I gather the road is not fit for taxis, or regular cars. Or we might take the dinghy. The hamlet is by the sea.'

'Why did you not say so in the first place? By boat it is. Have breakfast ready at seven.'

An hour passed at the card table, and the game was amicable, with no winners and no losers. The beans went to the centre of the table, and were won by Lillis, or Gounaris; another hand was played, and they transferred to the captain, or Skafidis, or Manolis. Manolis's play was amateurish, and matched the soldiers. From time to time a cigarette was lit, and smoke drifted over the table, slow to disperse in the still, hot night.

But as the moon grew close to its height, the game underwent a change. Manolis seemed to have a run of luck. Within fifteen minutes, Lillis and Skafidis were out, and most of the butterbeans were piled in front of Manolis.

'You're doing very well,' remarked the captain, throwing his cards back on to the table. Manolis reached out, and raked the beans staked on that hand towards him.

'Just luck,' said Manolis. 'Your deal, Captain.'

'Let's see how this one goes,' said the captain. 'Because it would seem unnatural to me, if your luck holds again.'

But hold it did. Two more hands were played; Manolis won them both. The second hand took the captain out of the game.

Manolis looked down the table at Gounaris.

'It's just you and me, son. You want to go on?'

Gounaris considered the pile of beans in front of Manolis, and the five remaining to himself. Skafidis left his chair, and bent down to his comrade's ear.

'You can take him,' he said. 'Take him, and we'll have a party on the proceeds.'

'I can't afford to risk it,' objected Gounaris. 'If I lose, I've no money left for a week.'

'You won't lose,' said Skafidis. 'How can he win again? No man has that kind of luck. Take him on.'

The captain watched Manolis.

'Can't afford to take me on, son?' asked Manolis. 'Is that lack of money, or lack of balls?'

'I've got the balls, *malaka*,' said Gounaris. 'But obviously I can't match your stakes.'

'I think you can.' Manolis touched his neck. 'That's a beautiful chain you have there.' And so it was; Gounaris's chain was diamond-cut gold, of good weight and high value. 'You can use that.'

'Gounaris, stop,' said the captain. 'It would break your mother's heart, and yours, if you lost that. It's late, *pedia*. Time to turn in.'

But the soldiers were considering the odds.

'He can't keep winning,' said Skafidis. 'His luck has to change. Take him on.'

Gounaris hesitated; then he reached up to his neck, and unclasped his chain.

'Come on then, friend,' he said to Manolis. 'Let's see who's got balls.'

He laid the gold in front of him, next to his little pile of beans.

Manolis passed him the cards.

'You deal,' he said.

Gounaris dealt. Manolis picked up his cards.

Play went on, and on, until all of Manolis's beans, and Gounaris's beans and his chain formed one pot in the middle of the table.

Behind Gounaris's chair, Skafidis struggled to keep triumph from his face.

Manolis leaned down and scratched his ankle.

'Damned mosquitoes,' he said, and studied his cards. 'I'll see you.'

Grinning, Gounaris laid down his cards: four fours, and the two of hearts. 'Four of a kind. Beat that,' he said, and reached out to draw the pile of wealth towards him.

But Manolis's smile was wider.

'I think I can,' he said, and laid down his cards: the six to the ten of clubs in a straight flush.

Gounaris's face fell. Skafidis banged his fist on the table.

'*Malaka!*' he shouted. 'Cheat! How can you have those cards? The ten was played five minutes ago! How can it be in your hand?'

'I think you're mistaken,' said Manolis, unconcerned. 'How can it have been played, when it's here? And I don't appreciate being called a cheat.' He took Gounaris's chain from the pile, and held it up to the lamplight. 'Very nice.' He looked at the captain. 'Looks like I won myself a ticket out of here. I'd appreciate a ride to the harbour, tomorrow.'

Gounaris left his chair. In a quick step around the table, he reached Manolis and delivered a hard punch into his face. His fist found the scabbed-over cut inflicted by the Albanian mate; the cut split open, and blood began to flow.

Dazed, and eyes squeezed shut against the pain, Manolis covered the side of his face with his hand. He opened his eyes slowly, and looked at Gounaris, who stood over him, breathing heavily and keen to land another blow; and if he chose to do so, it appeared neither the captain nor the soldiers would move to stop him.

Manolis wiped a dribble of blood from his chin, and looked at his red-smeared fingers. His jaw was taut with rage.

He looked up at Gounaris.

'Under normal circumstances,' he said, 'I'd give you a good hiding for hitting me. A little piece of shit like you should know better, and if you don't know better, someone should teach you. But I see the odds are stacked against me. A man could vanish in this place and this company, and never be seen again. So I'm going to let it go. But don't cross my path again, son. You'll regret it, if you do.'

The captain rose from the table.

'Don't you ever speak to my boys like that again,' he said, quietly. 'Tomorrow, you go. For now, get out of my sight.'

Manolis stood, and gave him a mocking smile and a salute.

'Whatever you say, Captain.'

In two fast paces, the captain stood nose-to-nose with him. With white knuckles, he grabbed the neck of Manolis's T-shirt, and twisted it.

'This is my base,' he said, through clenched teeth, 'and I make the rules here, including for civilians. So I'm ordering you to go to your quarters, now, and to stay there until I tell you you can come out.'

Manolis was still smiling.

'*Amessos*, Captain,' he said. The captain let him go. Manolis touched his knuckle to his lip; it was still bleeding. In his other hand, he clutched Gounaris's chain. He held it up to taunt them. 'Well, it's been a real pleasure, but it's getting late, so I think I'll take my winnings and turn in. I wish you all *kali nichta*.'

He left them, walking unhurriedly away into the dark, in the direction of the stores.

'*Malaka!*' Gounaris called after him. His eyes were filled with tears. '*Koproskilo!*'

'Enough!' said Captain Fanis. 'You brought that on yourself, Gounaris.'

'What about my chain? How will I get it back?'

'It's gone, son, lost. Say goodbye to it. But let that be a lesson to all of you. In life, never, ever bet more than you can afford to lose.'

* * *

125

Milto carried a storm-lantern to the stable, where it cast barely enough light to see. The stable door was propped open with a woodworm-peppered plank. The tethered mule snorted, and pricked its ears.

A cat – a worn-out female, with drooping teats from many seasons of hungry kittens – came yowling from behind the hay stacked along the wall. Milto bent down and touched her head.

'*Yassou, agapi mou,*' he said. He unwrapped a foil parcel of table scraps – a thigh-bone with a little chicken-meat left on it, a few pieces of fatty skin from the same bird – and dropped them on the ground. 'Not much tonight. Maybe we'll do better tomorrow.'

The stable was hot, though the flies which bothered the mule in daylight hours had dispersed. Milto placed the storm-lantern on the stone floor, and held out a piece of carrot on the palm of his hand, smiling at the tickle of the animal's lips as it took it. He stroked its muzzle and patted its neck.

'*Kali nichta*, then, old man,' he said. 'I'll leave the door open a crack, give you some air.'

Milto removed the plank, and the door swung to. On its back hung a cobwebbed rifle case, and his violin case, which Milto reached up to, as if to take it down.

The mule, crunching on its carrot, turned its head to him, and again pricked its ears.

Milto took his hands from the violin case.

'No, not tonight,' he said. 'We've work early tomorrow. Sweet dreams, old man.' He patted the mule on its rump. 'See you in the morning.'

Skafidis, on watch, settled into the hammock. On the captain's orders, Lillis had left the generator running, and the lights from the terrace shone in his eyes. That didn't bother Lillis; he came from a family of eight, and had learned early in life to shut out distractions, and sleep whenever and wherever the opportunity arose.

He might have dozed, but he was suddenly awake, alert. Something had disturbed him. He listened, though his hearing was impaired by the hammock's sheeting; but there was nothing but the sea, and the slight movement of the branches over his head.

When he opened his eyes, the terrace lights were blinding; but as his vision returned, he was sure of one thing: in the darkness behind the bunkhouse, someone or something moved.

Eight

The fat man rose from his bed just after dawn, and stretched – arms high, then from the waist to left and right – before touching his toes a dozen times. Lifting his elbows, he pulled them back to stretch his chest and, satisfied with his own suppleness, he slapped his generous belly with both hands and stepped into the shower.

In the bathroom, he dried himself and wrapped a white towel around his waist. Using a badger-hair brush, he spread shaving cream over his face, and shaved with a silver-handled razor. From a bottle of his favourite cologne (the creation of a renowned French *parfumier*: a blend of bitter-orange neroli, the honey notes of immortelle and the earthy tang of vetiver), he splashed a few drops into his palms and patted it on to his cheeks. With a fingerful of pomade from a small jar, he smoothed his damp curls, then cleaned his teeth with powder flavoured with cloves and wintergreen, ran the tip of a steel file behind his fingernails and polished each one with a chamois buffer.

Somewhere below decks, he heard hammering and the whine of a drill.

From the bedroom closet, he picked out a mint-green polo shirt and a suit in pewter linen. He chose a belt from his collection and threaded it through the trouser waist-loops, leaving himself plenty of breathing room when he fastened the buckle. Then he sat down on the bed and took a bottle of shoe-whitener from his hold-all.

He gave both tennis shoes a full coat of whitener, paying particular attention to the rubber toecaps and heels, and holding the shoes up to the porthole's light as he worked to check no spot was missed. As he finished, a knock came at the door, and Enrico entered, carrying a tray with a cup of Greek coffee and a glass of chilled juice. He gave a slight bow of the head, and placed the tray on the bedside cabinet.

'*Kali mera, kyrie*,' he said. 'I trust you slept well.'

'Excellently, thank you, Enrico,' said the fat man. 'I can hear some activity in the engine-room. What's going on?'

'Ilias has already started on the repairs,' said Enrico. 'I encouraged him to get up early this morning.'

'And how did you do that?'

Enrico smiled his wicked smile.

'Yesterday I found a little shop which sold water-pistols,' he said. 'A single shot, ice-cold from the fridge, seemed to do the trick.'

'Simple, but effective,' said the fat man. 'Usually the best way. I shall be ready for breakfast in ten minutes.'

Reveille was, for once, on time; the captain made sure of it. When the first small boats arrived bringing the priest – a gaunt man, said to live on wild greens and potato soup – and the earliest, most pious celebrants for St Nikodemos's name day, all the soldiers were ready in full uniform. The captain put the conscripts through a perfunctory inspection. Skafidis had cut himself shaving, and had a piece of bloody tissue stuck on his jaw; Gounaris had no green socks, and was barefoot inside his polished boots.

Manolis, unshaved and untidy in his loaned T-shirt and

trousers, sat at the guardhouse table, his feet on a chair in front of him. The captain watched him watch another boat approach. As the conscripts set off in the direction of the church, the captain called Kastellanos over, and nodded in Manolis's direction.

'Go and ask our friend to join us,' he said.

'What?'

'Go and ask him to join us,' said the captain. 'With all these boats coming and going, and trucks backwards and forwards on the road, he'll disappear if we don't keep an eye on him, and then our friends from the coastguard will take it out on me. So be persuasive. Look sincere. Remind him there'll be alcohol, and women. Say whatever you have to say, but get him to come with us.'

'No disrespect, sir, but why do *I* have to ask him?' asked Kastellanos.

The captain smiled, and patted him on the shoulder.

'Because I'm in charge, and I told you to,' he said.

Persuaded as much by his own boredom as by Kastellanos's coaxing, Manolis followed the soldiers to the church, where the growing gathering was preparing for the service. A stout woman whose widow's black had grown too tight for her was arranging bottles on a trestle table.

'Can I get you a drink, *kalé*?' she asked. 'What'll you have?'

'Ouzo,' said Manolis.

She reached under the table, and pulled out a stack of plastic cups.

'Tell you what,' he said, 'give me half a dozen of those, and I'll take the bottle round my friends over there.'

He waved a vague hand towards the company.

Without demur, she handed him a full bottle, and the cups.

* * *

Manolis left the plastic cups in the kitchen, and carried the bottle, a glass and a jug of water outside. He sat down in front of the guardhouse, and poured himself a tall measure of ouzo; he added water, and the ouzo turned the pale blue-white of moonstones. He took a long drink, and closed his eyes against the sun.

'May I join you, friend?'

The newcomer had not come up the beach; perhaps he had followed Manolis from the church. He waited for no answer to his question, but took a chair, and crossed a foot over his thigh. From the pocket of his shirt, he took out cigarettes, and offered them to Manolis.

'Smoke?'

Manolis looked at him, as if only now noticing he had company.

He jerked his chin upward to signify no.

The newcomer lit himself a cigarette, and laid the pack and his lighter on the table, implying he might stay long enough to smoke a second, or even a third.

Manolis's eyes moved back to the sea. He squinted at a distant tanker, then brought his focus back to his cloudy drink, from which he took a swallow.

'You're an ouzo man, eh?' asked the newcomer.

Manolis looked at him again, with little interest.

'Help yourself,' he said. 'You'll have to find a glass.'

The newcomer laughed.

'Not me, friend,' he said. 'I never touch it. You're not from here, I know. You passing through?'

'Something like that.'

'I'm Mithros born and bred,' said the newcomer. He flicked ash from the end of his cigarette, and brushed grey flecks from his trousers. The cicadas in the olive trees behind them fell simultaneously silent, then a moment later intensified their clamour. 'I know every stone of this island. I know it better than anyone, I'd venture to say.'

He waited for Manolis to respond, but Manolis said nothing.

'No, you'll not find anyone who knows this place better than me,' went on the newcomer. 'I could tell you stories. I've seen things. Heard things. But you know the difference between me, and most folks here?' He leaned forward, and pointed to his mouth. 'I know how to keep this shut.'

Manolis drank more ouzo, and watched a tall-masted yacht as it crept across the bay's end.

The newcomer picked up his cigarette packet and began to play with it, dropping it on to its four sides, one by one, like a broken wheel.

'You know about our bull, I suppose?' he asked, watching the packet as it turned, until it seemed to bore him, and he pushed it away. He took a last draw on his burned-down cigarette and ground it out under his boot.

'Oh yes,' said Manolis. 'Everyone talks about your bull.'

He drained his glass, and uncapped the bottle to pour more ouzo.

The newcomer lit himself a fresh cigarette. At a distance behind the olive trees, the church bell rang briefly, rhythmic and clanging. With his cigarette burning between his knuckles, the newcomer described three crosses over his heart.

The fat man sat at the prow of *Aphrodite*'s dinghy, his hold-all between his feet. Enrico reversed from the yacht's stern, and motored away from the mooring.

As the port disappeared behind them, the beach at Kolona bay came into view – a broad crescent of salt-bleached pebbles, with several boats already moored at the jetty. At the beach's centre was a group of utilitarian buildings, all single-storey and little better than sheds, and a flagpole with a drooping blue and white flag.

Behind the jetty, on posts hammered secure amongst the stones, a red-lettered sign forbade landing.

'This is military property,' said the fat man, as Enrico cut the engine almost to an idle and let the dinghy drift in towards the shore. 'Shall we be welcome here?'

Enrico shrugged, and waved his arm towards the boats already moored – bright-painted fishing boats, a couple of small cruisers, a compact launch in the navy-grey livery of the coastguard. He manoeuvred alongside one of the fishing boats, and leaning out to grasp the rope of a fender, pulled the dinghy close.

'Are you going to join me?' asked the fat man.

Enrico craned his neck, in case anything of the gathering were visible, but the buildings blocked any view.

'These church affairs aren't good hunting grounds for me,' he said. 'All the women are married, or devout. I'll stay close by, so whistle when you want me. If I go back to *Aphrodite*, Ilias'll have me elbow-deep in engine-oil.'

The fat man stepped on to the fishing boat, and across it on to the jetty. From there, he made his way up the beach, following the sound of a priest singing dirges, somewhere behind the trees at the head of the beach. Wary of trespassing, he left a respectful distance between himself and the guardhouse, where a man he took to be a sentry sat with a civilian at a table. But as he drew closer, the fat man saw that, apart from a pair of camouflage trousers and a khaki T-shirt, there was nothing of the military about the supposed soldier: his hair was not close cut, nor was he young enough to be a conscript. His face, though, was one the fat man had seen before, even though he couldn't place it at that moment. As the fat man drew close, the second at the table stooped down, and his face was hidden. The fat man raised his hand, and called out *kali mera*, but the man in khaki only looked at him, and took a long drink from his glass.

The fat man went on. Beyond the buildings was a path; where it forked into a track which was almost a road, trucks that had brought name-day celebrants from the port were parked under trees, their windows wound down fully to let in air. The dirges stopped, and a bell rang out, clear and sharp.

He followed the path away from the beach, across a stretch of bare earth which marked the canvas of his shoes terracotta. When he reached the well, he saw that the bucket – fashioned from a feta tin – was on the wall, and after checking it was securely tied, he dropped it into the shaft, letting the thin rope run through his hands. As it fell, he heard the bucket knock on stone-lined walls; but as it reached the depths, the sound was lost. The rope went slack at last. The fat man flicked his wrist to tip and fill the bucket, and hauled it up hand over hand, weighty with water, until it reappeared.

He stood the bucket on the wall, and looked into it. The water it held was clear, sparkling with the reflected aluminium. He bent to sniff the water's clean smell of stone and rain, and dipped in a cupped hand, and drank. The water was cool, and sweet. When his thirst was slaked, he filled a depression in the stone for insects to drink, and left the part-filled bucket on the wall.

'What would you say if I told you the bull's not such a mystery as folks think?' asked the newcomer.

Manolis lowered his glass from his mouth, and looked at the newcomer over the rim. The newcomer blew out smoke, and peered across the water at a passing fishing boat. He knew its owner, and raised a hand. Despite his distance from shore, the boat's captain was watching his watcher, and raised his hand in return.

'Go on,' said Manolis, cynically. 'Tell me you know where it went.'

The newcomer shook his head.

'I wouldn't waste your time, friend,' he said, apparently offended. 'I'll keep what I know to myself.'

For a few minutes, neither man spoke. Manolis drank. The thump of the fishing boat's old engine grew distant, and faded from hearing. Small waves broke on the shingle. The newcomer seemed content to watch the scene; but his silence needled Manolis, who glanced over at him, once or twice, waiting for his next words.

'Come on, then,' said Manolis, at last. 'I'm interested. Truly. Tell me what you know.'

'I've said as much as I know,' said the newcomer. He glanced up at the sun to judge the time. 'I've work to do. I thank you for your company.'

He half-rose from his chair, but Manolis grasped his forearm to stop him leaving.

'What do they say?' he asked. He leaned low over the table. The alcohol on his breath was strong, and sweet with aniseed.

'They say nothing,' said the newcomer, looking Manolis directly in the eye. 'They say nothing, because they know nothing. What knowledge there is, is mine alone.'

Manolis released the forearm, and gave a spluttering laugh.

'You're playing me on your line,' he said. 'But I'll take the bait. Come on, what do you know?'

'Something I've seen that I've told no one, not even my own brother. The bull never left Mithros. It was only moved

135

to another hiding place. When it was stolen, the man who stole it, hid it. But he never went back for it.'

'Why not?'

'Circumstances overtook him. That's all I can say.'

'So if you know where it is, why haven't you retrieved it, and sold it?' Manolis's speech was beginning to slur. 'Forgive me, friend, but if it's made you wealthy, you're hiding it very well.'

'Like I said, I'm Mithros born and bred. How should a man such as me know where to go, what to do with a treasure like that? I need a partner, but not someone from here. Here, they're all mouth and talk; they couldn't keep a secret if their own child's life depended on it. And it needs two men to fetch it out. One might do it alone, but it's risky. But I'm in no rush. It's safe enough where it is, until I find the right partner.'

He lapsed again into silence. The mad chorus of the cicadas rose, and fell.

'What do you think, then?' asked Manolis. 'Do you think I might be your partner?'

The newcomer picked up his cigarettes, and slipped them into his shirt pocket.

'You and I are new acquaintances,' he said. 'I need someone I can trust.'

'You can trust me. I have connections, good connections. If you've got the bull, I guarantee I can find the right buyer. But I'd need some cash up front. Expenses.'

'I could give you cash. I've got cash at my house. But how do I know you'd be discreet?'

'I'll be as discreet as you like. Give me the bull, and I'll get top price, and bring you your share. Fifty-fifty.'

'Seventy-thirty.'

'Whatever you say. And you can say what you like, until

I've seen the beast. Thirty per cent of nothing is the same as fifty.'

'You doubt me, but it's there all right,' said the newcomer. 'The two of us together could prise it out. But it's a tricky spot. It hasn't kept hidden all these years on public view.'

'So how come you found it?'

'Luck, pure and simple; a shaft of sunlight at an angle, at the right time of day, at the right time of year. I know it's there, though I've not yet managed to reach it. It is there.'

'You talk a good story,' said Manolis. 'Is it far?'

'Not far, no.'

Manolis hauled himself to his feet.

'So what are we waiting for?' he said. 'Let's prove the truth of it, here and now. Lead me, and I'll follow. Why shouldn't we be the ones to solve the mystery? Lead the way, friend, and let's see if we can find this precious bull.'

On the far side of the orchard, the fat man reached the church of St Nikodemos. At the base of the ox-blood rendered campanile, a black-clothed old woman was tolling one of the bells, pink-faced and fierce with effort. As the fat man approached, she squinted him into focus, and realising, as he drew close, that he was a stranger, took his appearance as her signal to stop ringing. He stood close to her, and looked up at the structure towering over him, as she – very much shorter than he was – stared up at him unabashed. He took in the campanile's grandiosity, and its neglected condition (one of the bells, he noticed, was cracked), then looked down on her, and smiled.

'*Kali mera sas*,' he said.

'*Kalos tou, kalos tou*. Go in, *kalé*, go in.' She shooed him towards the gate. 'They're bringing the saint out shortly, and you won't want to miss that.'

The gate was open; the fat man passed through it into the dry meadow, and looked across with interest at the church. Built at the centre of the field, it was of classical more than ecclesiastical design and so more temple than church, appropriate to an *agora* but a poor fit with the Baroque-inspired campanile. Its design had the simplicity of the ancient, but the church was as neglected as the campanile, and peeling paint of mottled ochre and blue evoked a quiet decay.

The celebrants were gathered around the church, where the wardens had laid out benches and mismatched chairs, and trestle tables spread with white cloths where the loaves of communion bread were ready to be blessed. The men were keeping their distance; the women were inside listening to the priest's guttural dirges, or waiting by the door for his emergence with the icon, whilst the children ran wild, shouting as they chased each other in circles, or poked sticks into ants' nests, or built wax towers from dripping candles.

The fat man followed the path between gate and church, to the point where Captain Fanis was talking with four others.

'Gentlemen, *kali mera sas, kai to chronou*,' said the fat man.

'*Kai to chronou*,' they all echoed.

'I was a little nervous, walking so close to your camp,' he said to the captain. 'Happily, there seemed to be no sentry there to challenge me. Forgive me; I haven't introduced myself. Hermes Diaktoros, of Athens.' He held out his hand, and the captain shook it. 'The name comes from my father's sense of humour. He prides himself on his knowledge of mythology.'

The men all looked blank.

'Captain Fanis Andreadis,' said the captain. 'And you're right about the sentry. My lads, as you'll see, are all here.' He indicated a bench up by the church, where the soldiers were seated with a prime view of the unmarried girls as they went in and out. 'I thought we were safe to gamble, and assume the Turkish invasion won't start before lunch.'

'I think your assumption is reasonable,' said the fat man. 'Unless the men drinking in front of your guardhouse are invading Turks?'

'One man, surely.' The captain looked across at Spiros, who stood arrogantly in an immaculately white uniform. 'Our friend. He's not in a very sociable frame of mind. He walked over here, blagged himself a bottle of ouzo, and left.'

'He was making good progress on the bottle when I saw him,' said the fat man.

He held out his hand to the coastguard officer, and Spiros took it.

'Spiros Tavoularis,' he said, and gestured in turn to the three others. 'Vassilis Eliadis, Loskas Vergas and Makis Theonas.'

The men all nodded in acknowledgement of their names. Loskas, the bank clerk, had made no gesture to the day's celebration, and was conventionally dressed for work in the branch. Makis, the butcher, had made some effort with hair oil and cologne, but carried a smear of blood on the seat of his trousers.

The fat man knew Vassilis from the taverna; he recognised the seersucker blazer, matched today with polished brogues and a violet shirt, and on his hands, cream kidskin gloves.

'Are you by any chance the man they call Uncle Vasso?' asked the fat man.

'I am.'

'I've been hearing about you, from the curator at the museum. You are something of a philanthropist, I gather.'

'I'm a Mithros man, by birth,' said Uncle Vasso. 'No

matter how far anyone travels in this world, we all have a duty to our place of origin. I do what I can.'

Makis had a habit of blinking hard from time to time, as if he suffered with his nerves. He blinked now.

'We're all Mithros men,' he said. 'I was born here in Kolona, in one of those ruins over there.' He pointed in the direction of the abandoned houses. 'Some of these gentlemen, too, are from here. It broke our hearts to leave. We pride ourselves on being a rare breed, the last generation from Kolona. Tavoularis, Theonas, Loskas and Rokos – our great-grandfathers and great-great-grandfathers scratched a living from these soils. They reckon there were men living here in ancient times, two thousand years ago, maybe more. And we were the last of their lines.'

'And which of you is of the Rokos line?'

'There's no one here today,' said Uncle Vasso. 'We're here in part to remember Socrates of that family, and to light candles in his name. He died in tragic circumstances, not far from here. I personally owe him a great debt. May his memory be eternal.'

'May his memory be eternal,' echoed the others.

'So if life was so idyllic here, why did you leave?' asked the fat man.

'We ran out of the one thing we couldn't live without,' said Spiros. 'The well ran dry.'

'There's water again now,' said Captain Fanis, with some pride. 'That's down to army efficiency, and hard labour.'

'It was hard labour here then,' said Spiros. 'I remember my father breaking his back, raising crops to maturity, and having no water in those last crucial days. That broke his heart, watching what he worked for wither when the heat was at its worst.'

'Those were good days,' said Makis. 'We knew what life

140

was about. We struggled, and we grafted, but we were free. We had no debts to anyone.'

'Surely, *pedi mou*, your debts don't make you unhappy,' said Uncle Vasso. 'Your creditors never press you for payment. And anyway, no man is ever free of debt, even if he owes not a single penny of currency.'

'That's a profound observation,' said the fat man. 'I agree, it's a rare man who owes no debt at all of obligation, or gratitude, or honour. What business are you in, if I might ask?'

'I've a butcher's shop,' said Makis. 'But I'd move back here tomorrow, if I could. I'd give up the business, and come back here, and hunt and fish to feed ourselves.'

But the others laughed. Makis blinked, as if alarmed now at his temerity in speaking.

'You'd be here without your wife,' said the captain. 'She's the last one who'd settle for the simple life.'

'It couldn't be done,' said Loskas. His arms were folded to challenge any contradiction; there was a pen-pusher's callous on his right middle finger. 'Now the army's moved in, there'd never be enough water for them, and your crops. You'd still need money for clothes, and money to pay for fuel for your boat. And I can't see your wife firing up that old bread-oven every morning, or scouring the beach for driftwood, either, if it comes to that.' He clapped the sullen Makis on the back. 'You should count your blessings, my friend.'

'You'd have company, anyway,' said the fat man, nodding towards the captain.

'Only me, for any length of time,' said Captain Fanis. 'My lads here are conscripts; they come and go. Seven, eight months I have to make soldiers of them. As soon as they start shaping up, away they go again. I'm like a mother to them, all that time, and they leave me without a backward glance. They find it dull here, as you can imagine.'

'Except for your recent arrival,' said Uncle Vasso. 'I've heard he's added some colour to your days.'

'The sooner he's gone, the better,' said the captain. He turned to the fat man. 'They mean the man you saw when you arrived. He was thrown overboard by his shipmates. Sharp practices at the card table, and bad company, Albanians, he says. They tipped him in and left him with us. No papers, nothing.'

'He can't leave until he's got money,' said Loskas, 'and that won't be until he's got papers. Another day or two, at least.'

'But he could get himself money now,' said the captain. 'He caused a bad stink last night, and took Gounaris's gold chain off him at poker. I don't want to see him going anywhere until Gounaris has had a fair chance to win it back, or there'll be blood spilt.'

'You didn't tell me this,' said Spiros. 'I don't want to see him leave until he's proved to my satisfaction who he is.'

'Or who he isn't,' said Loskas.

The bell-ringer began a steady tolling.

'Is that the cue for the parading of the icon?' asked the fat man. 'If you'll excuse me, I shall make my way over there and see what's going on. No doubt we shall all speak again.'

'I need to take a leak,' said Uncle Vasso, as the fat man headed away, towards the church. 'At my age, you always need to take a leak.'

He left them, going in the direction of the derelict houses. The captain began to tell the tale of how Gounaris lost his chain, but before he finished, Uncle Vasso returned, panting with the effort of almost running.

With his gloved hand, he grasped the captain's arm.

'There's someone up there!' he said, and pointed up to the hills behind the village. 'Up in the rocks, he was watching

142

me! I caught the flash of something – binoculars! And when he saw I'd spotted him, he ducked down. He had a rifle on his back, Fanis! He could pick us off, one by one!'

But the captain shook his head.

'Someone hunting,' he said. 'The only thing he'll be picking off is partridge.'

But Uncle Vasso gripped his arm tighter.

'Please, go and see,' he said. 'He could have his sights on any one of us, right now! I think we should put a wall between us and him, and move everyone inside the church. Please, Fanis, go and see what he's about. Isn't that what you're here for, to keep strangers off these shores? I'm telling you, there's someone up there who shouldn't be!'

He released the captain's arm and moved behind him, making the captain a shield between himself and the rocks.

'I think you should probably take a look, Fanis,' said Spiros, looking anxiously in that direction. 'There are women and children here who need your protection.'

'It's bound to be someone hunting,' said the captain. 'Who else could it possibly be? Surely you don't think the Turks are invading? For God's sake!'

'What about our friend, over there?' said Spiros, turning in the direction of the army camp. 'What if his friends have come back for him? They might be here to take him away, or they might just finish him with a single head shot. Albanians with guns, Fanis! It'll look bad for you if they start shooting, and you did nothing to stop it.'

'If they've come in by sea, that's your remit,' objected the captain.

'If he's on land, it's your jurisdiction,' said Spiros. 'Really, I think you should go and see who's there.'

The captain sighed. He put two fingers in his mouth, and gave a sharp whistle, so all the people gathered at the church turned to look. Lillis was refilling the soldiers' cups from a wine bottle. When the captain beckoned them down, they came reluctantly.

'What's going on?' asked Skafidis.

'There's someone up there, in the rocks,' said Uncle Vasso, still careful to keep the captain between himself and the hillside. 'I saw him when I went to relieve myself. He was watching me through his binoculars. He's got a gun.'

'What kind of gun?' asked Kastellanos.

'It looked like a rifle to me,' said Uncle Vasso. 'But from this distance, I couldn't be sure.'

'Don't worry, lads,' said the captain. 'It'll just be someone after partridge.'

'I heard something, last night,' put in Skafidis. 'When I was on watch, I heard somebody moving about.'

'*Panayeia mou!* I told you so!' Uncle Vasso crossed himself, and moved a step closer to the captain.

Captain Fanis frowned.

'And you raised the alarm, did you, Skafidis? When you heard someone moving on the camp, what did you do about it?'

Skafidis went red.

'I didn't think it was worth mentioning,' he said. 'Everybody was sleeping.'

'Don't you think you should take a weapon of some kind?' asked Uncle Vasso.

The captain looked at him.

'A gun,' said Uncle Vasso. 'Don't you think you should take a gun?'

'We won't be needing any weapons,' said the captain, as he led the soldiers away. 'Do you have any idea how much paperwork would be involved, if we discharged a weapon this close to civilians?'

* * *

144

The fat man didn't go directly to the church, but left the path and crossed to the field's eastern corner, where the wall was overhung by black mulberry. Tethered to one of the branches was a grey mule wearing a wooden saddle. It seemed that the mule had been left in the mulberry's shade, but as the sun had risen higher, the shade had vanished, and left the animal in full sun.

The fat man stroked the mule's nose, and laid the flat of his hand on its neck. The skin was hot to the touch. Untying the lead-rein, he led the mule a few paces along the wall, back into the tree's shade, and re-tethered it to a branch. Obscured by the deeper shade of the wall-corner was a memorial, a rustic cross of olive wood entwined with wooden leaves, and a wooden frame in the same style set around a marble stone. Though the woodcarving was well preserved, the marble's inscription was badly weathered, and over-grown with lichens, but by leaning close, the fat man could make out a name – Socrates Rokos.

He patted the mule's neck, and left it sniffing at the sparse, dry grass. At the church, the white-garbed, gold-surpliced priest was carrying round the icon of St Nikodemos, droning as he led the faithful in their short walk. The smoke from rattling censers was fragrant with rose incense; behind the priest, the churchwarden scattered bergamot-scented holy water on the congregation. At the fat man's approach, the people made space around the doorway to let him enter the church and pay his respects to the saint; but the fat man smiled politely, and instead found himself a seat on one of the benches, beside a heavily pregnant young woman and her mother, who warned him with an expression of disapproval against making any advances to her daughter.

The priest finished his recital, and carried the unsmiling saint back inside the church. The great loaves of aniseed-flavoured communion bread were blessed, cut and offered round in baskets, and the women brought weak coffee and glasses of sweet wine. Children scrambled for warm *loukoumades* – honey-soaked, cinnamon-sprinkled doughnuts – and the pregnant girl and her mother wandered away, leaving the fat man alone on his bench, nibbling on a hard-baked *koulouri*.

'Can I offer you one of these?'

Olympia held out a plate of foil-wrapped cakes, where only three remained. Though tied back in a ribbon, somehow her hair was still disordered; her dated shade of lipstick had been applied without a mirror.

The fat man smiled up at her.

'*Yassou, koritsi*,' he said. 'If they're chocolate, you certainly may offer me one. Thank you.'

'I'd save it for later, if I were you.' She sat down beside him with the plate on her lap. 'They've got too warm, and you don't want melted chocolate on your suit.'

'Sound advice,' said the fat man. 'You're looking very pretty, if I may say so. Are you here with your patient?'

Olympia shook her head.

'This excursion is far beyond her. A neighbour's sitting with her for me. Sometimes I need to leave the sickroom, just to see what else is happening in the world. I think there's going to be dancing, if they can find someone to play. Do you dance?'

A boy approached with whisky on a tray, and the fat man took a glass. A young man greeted them on his way to smoke a cigarette outside the gate; he was handsome in his festival clothes, but Olympia showed no interest as he passed.

'The last time I danced was at my cousin's wedding,' said the fat man, 'and that's some years ago, now. Are you married, *kori mou*?'

She held up her right hand to show her empty ring finger.

146

'I had a gift from one of my charges, her wedding head-dresses. Since the day she'd married, she'd kept them in a box, but she knew when she was gone, they'd be thrown out with the rubbish. So she gave them to me as a blessing, a token of good luck, in the hopes they'd bring me a treasure of a husband, like the one she had. But so far, no luck.'

'Surely you have suitors?'

She blushed.

'Not the right suitor.'

The fat man drained his whisky.

'A gift of good wishes is always welcome,' he said, 'but sometimes a charm needs time to take effect. And sometimes one who seems wrong in the beginning may turn out to be the right choice in the end. You should give it time, *kori mou*. That's my advice to you. And speaking of time, I have kept my man waiting long enough.' He stood, and held out his hand, so she gave him hers; but instead of shaking it, he bent his shoulders in a short bow, and touched it very lightly with his lips. '*Despina*, it has been a real pleasure talking to you. Please forgive me, but I really must go.'

The bell-ringer had abandoned the campanile, and the men the fat man had been speaking to had dispersed. A flash of movement caught his eye: a line of khaki-clad figures amongst the scrub and rocks up on the hillside, their leader waving his arm over his head in a signal to the others to spread out. For a minute or two, the fat man watched them; then he set off in the same direction, towards the village ruins.

He found a place of gradual dilapidation: the unheard slipping of stone from stone, the damage caused by determined plants and undermining roots, the destructiveness of goats and their pressings on unstable walls. He wandered through the houses, in and out of their melancholy rooms. Through a one-hinged door, he entered what had once been someone's *salone*, where the slabbed floor was no longer level and no roof remained except the timbers. A homely chair, now seatless, was upturned in a corner. Beside the fireplace, a collapsing ladder led up to the *moussandra*, the wooden platform where a family once slept; its balustrade – a craftsman's piece of ornate turning – was still intact.

He went in every house, in every building, and covered every metre of the overgrown paths which led between them. On the hillside, he heard a whistle from a soldier, and a shout from another in return. Here, amongst the old houses, were a thousand hiding places; but if anything, or anyone, was hidden there, whatever, or whoever it was, was hidden well.

Nine

The captain led the soldiers in a sweep of the hillside, heading up through the gullies of dry stream beds, scrambling across slopes of scree and through sharp-thorned thickets. His target was a trio of walnut trees, from where there was a view of the whole of Kolona. The trek was lengthy, the sun was hot, and when they reached the trees, he raised no objections to the soldiers slumping down around their roots. Overhead, an eagle floated high on rising thermals; below them, the rocky hillside seemed empty. The captain shielded his eyes to block the sun, and scanned to left and right, but nothing moved.

They tramped back down to the church, where the women were pleased to welcome them.

'Here, *kamari mou*,' said one, offering Gounaris more *loukoumades*. 'You see how good they are? I made them myself.'

A second gave Skafidis a plate of mullet, fished from a fire-blackened pan of oil. Skafidis took the plate, and from her apron pocket she gave him bread. As he took it, she patted his boyish cheek.

'*Kouklos!*' she said, and called out smiling to the other

women. 'Aren't they all handsome? Eh, Sofia – if we were twenty years younger . . .'

'Twenty years ago, I could still have been his grandmother!' said Sofia, a woman without teeth. 'But you'd have wanted me once!' She laughed at Skafidis, and scooped up her sagging breasts, and lifted them to where they would have been when she was a girl, and twisted her hips, and turned the circle of a dance. 'I'd have shown you a thing or two, back in those days!'

The people laughed; Skafidis tried to smile, and blushed deep red. The women poured more wine, and served more food, and even the priest broke off a crust from a blessed loaf, and chewed. The company was convivial, and the wine was good. The men drank more than they ought to; cigarettes were smoked, and tales were told: tales most of them already knew, embellished and embroidered to be more humourous, or shocking, or remarkable, as each one deserved. The priest put away his holy-day garments, and sweated in his grey robes, and lifted his hat from time to time to scratch his itching scalp; and when the wine was gone and the day had reached its hottest hour, the people drifted away, clambering into the boats and trucks that had brought them, and were carried away with their shouts of '*To chronou*' echoing on the blistering air.

At the camp, there was an ouzo bottle and a glass on the terrace table. Of Manolis, there was no sign.

'Where's our friend?' asked Lillis.

'He'll be sleeping off that ouzo,' said the captain from the kitchen. He lifted the lids on the water barrels. The levels were getting low. 'Lillis, Skafidis, you're on water detail. Get the buckets, and get over to the well. Let's make sure there's water for my coffee, after siesta.'

The soldiers went unwillingly, each carrying two empty buckets. They took the path they had only recently walked, back in the direction of the deserted village.

Skafidis yawned. The wine and heat together had made him dozy, and he wanted his bed.

'The captain's just picking on us,' he said. 'This would have waited until later. It makes no sense to send us now, whilst it's still hot.'

'Nothing in the army makes any sense,' said Lillis. 'But if we fetch it now, he won't be hammering on the door after siesta.'

They reached the well. The well bucket lay on its side in the dirt, its long rope on the ground beside it. Lillis picked it up, and brushed the dust from it as best he could.

'The wind must have blown it off the wall,' he said.

'What wind?' Skafidis looked over to the orchard, where the branches of the old trees barely stirred. 'There's been no wind. If there was wind, it wouldn't be hot as hell now.'

'Goats, then, looking for water. We should haul up a bucket for them before we go.' Lillis dropped the bucket into the well's opening. 'I hate the army. I can't wait to get home, where life is civilised.' He let the rope run over his palm, and through the fist of the other hand. 'Where I come from, they've invented something called a mains water supply. You turn on a tap, and out comes . . .'

With only a metre or two of rope run out, the bucket stopped falling. Puzzled, Lillis lifted the rope slightly, assuming it was stuck on some stony ledge, and dropped it again. The bucket fell a few centimetres, and halted.

'What's up?' asked Skafidis. 'Come on, *malaka*, stop messing about. At this rate, by the time I get my head down, he'll be making us get up again.'

'It's blocked,' said Lillis. 'The bucket won't drop.'

'You've got it lodged,' said Skafidis. 'You haven't dropped it straight. Here, let me.' He snatched the rope, and hauled the bucket back up; with a twist of his wrist, he sent the bucket speeding down the well. But the result was the same. After only a couple of metres, the bucket dropped no further.

He hauled the bucket back up, and peered down into the blackness.

'Something's blocking it,' he said. 'But I can't see what.'

'Maybe it's collapsed,' said Lillis. 'With it being so dry, maybe the sides have caved in.'

'But it's rock, surely?' said Skafidis, uncertainly. 'And it's been here hundreds of years. Why should it collapse now?'

'How should I know? We need lights to see what's going on down there. Go and get a torch, and tell the captain.'

'Why me, *malaka*? You go.'

Lillis sighed, and swore, and went. Skafidis sat down on the well-rim, and listened. The flies were many, and bothersome. In the orchard, the cicadas sang.

In no hurry, Lillis sauntered back to the camp, taking the time to smoke a cigarette as he went.

Captain Fanis was already half-asleep.

Lillis called to him through the closed door to his quarters.

'What do you want?' shouted the captain. 'Come back at four o'clock. And when you come back, bring coffee.'

'Captain,' said Lillis, 'we can't get water. The well's blocked.'

'For Christ's sake.' The captain left his bed, and opened the door. He wore nothing but a pair of undershorts. 'Can't I trust any of you to do anything? What's the problem now?'

'We can't get to the water. The bucket won't go down the well.'

'What the hell are you talking about? Where's Skafidis?'

'I left him there. We need a torch to see what's down there. Skafidis says it's a collapse.'

'What do you mean, a collapse?'

'He thinks the sides have fallen in.'

'*Panayeia mou!* Is there no hope for any of you? I send you for water, you come back to ask me to hold your hands. Get a torch, and let's go. Tell Gounaris and Kastellanos to come too. If there's been a rock-fall, it's you four who'll be shifting it.'

Gathered around the well-head, they all looked over the rim. Around them, flies buzzed. The captain wafted them away.

'Give me the torch,' he said, and Lillis handed it to him. The captain leaned over the wall, and directed the torch-beam downwards.

'*Theé mou.*' His voice was muffled by the stones.

He straightened up, and handed the torch back to Lillis.

'Have a look down there, and tell me what you can see.'

Lillis did so; as his eyes focused, he gave a womanish scream.

'Feet! It's a pair of feet!'

He leaped back from the well-head; the others peered down, in silence.

'Those are army boots,' said the captain, 'so I should say this is our friend. Kastellanos, fetch a rope, and let's see if we can get him out.'

Ten

Evening brought the people out into the cool of falling darkness, on to balconies and into courtyards whose doors stood open so as not to obstruct views of comings and goings, or impede conversation between the houses – the banalities women called to each other as if they were in the same room, rather than across the street.

As the fat man passed, they fell into silence, and covertly watched him, ready to remark and speculate when he was gone from sight; but the fat man, unconcerned by their curiosity, looked up at the balconies and in at the doors as he passed, and wished each family – grandmothers and mothers, aunts, cousins, children – *kali spera*.

'Where are you going, *kalé*? Have you lost your way?'

The woman who called out to him received a nudge of remonstration from the woman seated by her, who, judging by the similarity in features – the peasant nose, the widow's peak, the long limbs and lean build – might have been her sister.

The fat man stopped.

'I don't believe I'm lost,' he said, politely, 'but you ladies might save me the trouble of becoming so. I'm looking for the professor's house – I believe you know him as such? I mean the museum's curator.'

Intrigued by his way of speaking, the woman studied him.

'Where're you from, *kalé*?' she asked. 'You're not from anywhere round here.'

'I come from Athens,' he said.

'Athens.' She nodded, in apparent wonder. 'I suppose it's very hot, in Athens?'

'I suppose it is,' he said. 'It's been some time since I was there.'

'You're on the right path for the professor's house.' She eased herself from her chair, and stood beside him, very close, so he could smell fish on her breath. She put one hand on his forearm, and pointed in the direction he was already heading. 'Keep straight now, until you come to a house with dark-green shutters, a big house on a corner. Go right there, and then right again, then straight up. You can't miss it, *kalé*. You can't miss it.' She gripped his forearm tight, then seemed to feel she had taken too great a liberty, and released him and stood back a respectful distance.

The fat man eyed her, coolly.

'Thank you,' he said, with a slight bow of his head. 'Your instructions confirm the route I proposed to take. It's all too easy to get lost in these narrow lanes.'

'Especially in the dark,' said the seated sister, anxiously. 'Who knows who you'll run into, in the dark?'

'My sister's seen a stranger.' The woman moved back closer to him, fighting the urge to grasp his arm again. 'A strange man, going through these lanes. We don't see many strangers, up here. And one with no business with any of us, has no business being here. You should take care, *kalé*. My sister and I are taking extra care.'

'Indeed,' said the fat man, with a small smile. 'You are wise to be so cautious. Ladies, I wish you *kali spera*,' and he moved on.

* * *

155

The professor's house, when he found it, seemed so much quieter than those around it, that the fat man was not certain he had either the right house, or the right evening. In contrast to its neighbours, the courtyard door was firmly shut, and no noise, no music or chatter, came from behind it. But a light was shining at an upstairs window, and he thought he could perceive, too, the glow of a lamp in the courtyard; and so he stepped up to the door and knocked.

A solemn boy – a teenager of fifteen or sixteen – opened the door, and looked in silence at the fat man.

'*Kali spera*,' said the fat man. His own smile drew no response from the sullen face. 'Is this the professor's house?'

'Who wants him?' asked the boy.

But before the fat man could answer, his father appeared behind him, and putting his hands firmly on the boy's shoulders, steered him away from the door. The boy was then inclined to leave their company, and tried to break free of his father's grip; but the professor held him where he stood.

'*Kalos tou, kalos irthes*,' he said, smiling broadly and standing back to admit the fat man. 'Come in, come in. Tao, please welcome our guest in an appropriate manner. This is *Kyrie* Diaktoros. He comes to us all the way from Athens.'

The glowering boy said nothing.

The fat man extended his hand.

'*Yassou*, Tao,' he said. '*Chairo poli*.'

For a moment, the boy looked as if he might refuse to respond; but in the end he offered his own hand, though giving the fat man the merest touch of his fingertips.

'*Chairo poli*,' he said.

'Bravo,' said his father, releasing the boy and ruffling his hair. The boy scowled, and immediately reached up to smooth his short crop, making plain his objection to his father's affectionate gesture. 'Go and tell Mama our guest is here.'

The boy left them, and went into the house. The professor showed the fat man to a table at the corner of the courtyard. All around were objects of interest and some age – more amphorae, with the white scars of barnacles telling of time spent under the sea; several old-fashioned candle lamps; various sizes of goat-bells strung on dried-out leather. Candles burned in an antique brass candelabra, giving off the lemon scent of citronella as a deterrent to mosquitoes; but as the fat man took his seat, buzzing insects zinged. The professor slapped his forearm, looked down at it, and flicked away an insect's gangly corpse.

'Damned things,' he said. 'I do my best to keep them at bay – my son's allergic, he gets it from my wife – but this time of year, the job's impossible.'

'If your family's allergic, I may be able to help,' said the fat man. 'I myself use an oil I get from an acquaintance in the west. What he puts in it, I have no idea, but mosquitoes seem to hate it. I can't say it is the smell they dislike, as it is – to my nose at least – quite odourless. I would be happy to let you have some of my supply. I have a couple of bottles, I think, aboard the yacht.'

'That would be very kind,' said the professor. 'What can I get you to drink? There's wine, or beer. My wife makes an excellent lemonade, if you'd prefer a soft drink.'

'A glass of wine would be excellent. Red or white, I don't mind. I leave the choice to you.'

'*Amessos.*' The professor gave a small bow in the style of a waiter, and left the fat man alone.

In the kitchen, the professor took glasses from a cupboard. His wife was slicing bread, her face sour with bad temper.

'Why are you using those glasses?' she asked. 'Don't use those. Use the good glasses, our wedding glasses.'

'There's no need to get them out, surely,' said the professor, reasonably. 'These'll do perfectly well.'

'You're determined to embarrass me, aren't you?' There seemed the possibility of tears. 'Only a slut would put those glasses in front of a guest.'

He opened a drawer, and rattled cutlery.

'Where's the corkscrew?'

The woman sighed, and slammed down her knife.

'For heaven's sake,' she said. 'Can't you find anything?'

'It's usually in here,' he said. 'But it's not here now.'

She rummaged in the drawer and found the corkscrew, and held it up close to his face.

He took it from her, and began to peel the foil from a bottle of wine.

'Why are you opening that wine?'

'Why shouldn't I?' he asked. 'It's a very drinkable wine.'

She pointed to a bottle on the table.

'I got that bottle from Petros's. It's supposed to be very good.'

'Who said so?'

'Petros.'

'And what does Petros know about wine?'

'Why would he recommend something that was no good?'

'To get money out of your purse.'

'I see.' She snatched up the knife, and began to saw again at the loaf. 'So I paid a lot for it, and now you're not going to drink it. You invited him, and all the work falls on me.'

She turned her back on him. The silence between them grew. Her face was red, though not from the heat of cooking; the food was already prepared, and covered with cloths.

'OK,' he said. 'You win. Your glasses, your wine. Though I find it ridiculous that you're choosing the wine, when you don't even drink it.'

From a high cupboard he lifted down two crystal glasses, heavy and unwieldy. He put them on a tray, beside the bottle of wine she had chosen.

She watched him, arms folded.

'Don't forget to wipe those glasses, before you take them out there,' she said.

The fat man seemed good-humoured, as if he had heard nothing from the kitchen. The beginnings of a headache pulsed at the professor's temples. He unloaded glasses, wine and corkscrew on to the table, and propped the tray against its leg.

The fat man picked up one of the glasses, and held it up to the candlelight.

'What beautiful glasses,' he said, perhaps slightly louder than necessary. 'Excellent quality.'

As the professor twisted the corkscrew into the bottle, his wife carried out a basket of the bread she had sliced, and a dish of black olives, shiny with oil.

'My wife,' said the professor. The wine cork was dry; as he withdrew it from the bottle neck, it broke into pieces. 'Lukia.'

She was a fading woman, with winter-pale skin untouched by sunlight; scraped back into a knot, her tight-fastened hair made her features sharp. Without make-up, she had made no apparent effort for their company; her dress – a shapeless shift – was more suited to a woman twice her age.

The fat man got to his feet, and offered his hand; but when she had put down what she was carrying, she fussed a while over the table's arrangement, so his outstretched hand became awkward, and he let it drop.

'A delight,' he said, anyway, 'a pleasure to meet you. Hermes Diaktoros, of Athens. And let me thank you for welcoming me into your home. I travel a great deal, and it is a rare luxury for me to dine with a family. I've already met your charming son. I see now where he gets his manners.'

She spoke without looking him in the eye.

'It was my husband who invited you,' she said, shortly. 'You must thank him, not me.'

'It would be a poor guest who did not thank his hostess. I'm sure it was you, and not your husband, who has prepared the food we are about to enjoy.'

She glanced at him as if his reasonable words were worthless, and left them alone.

Professor Philipas poured the wine.

'You'll have to forgive my wife,' he said. 'She's not a sociable woman.'

'There are some men that would please. They live always doubting their woman's fidelity, and the slightest contact with any male sends them wild with jealousy. I suspect that is a problem you do not have.'

They tried the wine. A year or two before, it might have been excellent; now on the point of turning, it was tart and unpleasantly dry. The fat man politely drank more, whilst the professor offered no comment, but looked with some annoyance after his wife, then lowered his eyes and fell into silence before drinking down half the contents of his glass. Lukia brought out more food: aubergines baked with feta, in a tomato sauce flavoured with bay and a little honey; chicken braised with lemon and oregano; a rice pilaf with squid. She wished the men *kali orexi*, and turned to go.

'Aren't you joining us?' asked the fat man.

She gave a weary smile.

'The heat exhausts me,' she said, 'so I can't eat. You must excuse me. The time I've spent in that hot kitchen has given me a migraine. I shall try and sleep it off.'

Again, she left them.

'What about your son?' asked the fat man. 'All this food! Surely he will come and eat something?'

'He's learned his mother's habits,' said the professor, with some bitterness. 'He's not a boy who enjoys company. Please, help yourself.'

The fat man filled his plate, and tried the chicken.

'She is a good cook, at least,' he said. 'Tell me about the museum, how it came into being.'

'It was my father's project, originally,' said Professor Philipas, 'though only in a very small way. He collected curios, items of interest. The people here see little value in antiques, or any relics of the recent past. Some don't value our ancient heritage much more. My father started with what people were throwing out, items he saw beauty in that they didn't. He drove my mother mad; she suffered the shame of his hoarded rubbish, as she saw it. The neighbours thought he was deranged. But bit by bit, as his collection grew, people began to offer him things they might otherwise have thrown out. I used to go with him, all over this island, sometimes to others, if he got wind of something special. Sometimes he broke the rules, and removed pieces he perhaps shouldn't have done. But he took care of his collection, and treasured every piece. As I do now. After he died, I took on the collection myself. It caused some difficulties with my own wife, as you can imagine.'

'I can,' said the fat man.

'Happily, those problems were resolved when the collection found its benefactor, as I told you.'

'I remember,' said the fat man. 'I met the man today. I do wonder, though, at his motivation. A wish to improve the lot of one's fellow men is sadly not too common. What are his reasons for giving his wealth away? Most men who have made money tend to keep it in the family.'

'He has no family,' said the professor. 'At least, not close. The usual collection of aunts, and cousins, whom he does right by, though they see it as insulting that he would rather house a collection of antiques than be generous to them.'

'How sad for him not to have close family to share his good fortune with,' said the fat man. 'A man's family is his strength. Do you have brothers and sisters?'

The professor looked a little sad.

'Your question shames me somewhat,' he said. 'Yes, I have a brother, but it's been many years since we've spoken. We had a disagreement, a falling out, for which he's never forgiven me.'

'That is unfortunate,' said the fat man. 'As for this Vassilis Eliadis, I'm surprised that he's not married. A man with his assets usually has all kinds of matches thrown in his way, and finds it difficult to remain a bachelor.'

'Maybe he was too busy making his money,' said the professor. 'He's one of those men who has the Midas touch, a man who sees opportunity in everything. They're not a common breed in these islands, and certainly not in Mithros. He's a man of energy, even though he's not the man he was. He was the victim of a robbery some years ago, and the incident scarred him, physically and mentally, I think.'

'I heard about the robbery.' The fat man ate more of the aubergines. 'Was it ever thought it might have been connected in some way to the bull?'

Professor Philipas drained his glass, and poured more wine for them both, though the fat man's glass was still almost full.

'I don't know about that,' he said. 'Possibly. Can I tell you something? You've shown such interest in the bull and the museum, and I feel I can trust you.'

'Indeed you can,' said the fat man. 'If my trust is warranted, I would never betray it.'

'Something I would never have expected has happened. We had a break-in, last night. As far as I can tell, only one item was taken.'

'Which was?'

'The bull.'

'But the bull is a replica, surely?'

'You know it is. And it states quite clearly on the cabinet that it is so.'

Now the fat man drank more wine, but only a little.

'How curious,' he said. 'Why do you suppose anyone would go to the trouble of stealing a replica?'

'I don't know. It has some value on its own account, in its craftsmanship, and the gold work too, of course. But not enough value, I wouldn't have thought, to make it worth the risk of stealing. We've no crime at all here normally, as I'm sure you're aware, and I'd be surprised if there's any local involvement. This time of year, though, all kinds of people come and go. Who knows who's here, and what they're up to? But I admit I'm baffled. There's not much value in the gold hooves and horns, and if there are thieves in Mithros, it would seem more logical to set their sights on the jeweller's in the harbour.'

'It is curious, isn't it?' said the fat man. 'Intriguing.'

'It's left me troubled,' said Professor Philipas. 'I wonder if the thief might have seen what else is there, and come back a second time. I'm thinking especially of the antiquities, the coin collection and the arrowheads. They're worth a bit of money to collectors. I thought when we had eaten I'd go across there and make sure all's well. You'd be welcome to join me, if you'd like.'

'Gladly,' said the fat man.

The professor fetched the keys from a hook on the kitchen wall, and led the way the short distance to the museum, lighting the dark lane with a torch. He used the torch beam to find the keyhole in a new padlock, and opened it with a shiny steel key.

'I thought my precautions were sufficient,' he said. 'I didn't think we had anything here to attract thieves. It was a clean job, at least, the locks picked and no damage to anything. Even so, it makes me uneasy. I put this padlock on, but there's no reason it should stop someone any more than the other locks did last night.'

Inside the museum, the professor turned on the lights. He showed the unbroken display case, and the space where the bull used to be.

'You know, I shouldn't worry too much about the thief returning,' said the fat man. 'I think he knew what he wanted, and got it.'

'Since he went straight to it, and left with nothing else,' said the professor, 'I think you're right. I know the contents of these cases like the back of my hand, and nothing else has been touched.'

'I'll leave you to make the place secure. Please do thank your wife for an excellent dinner.' They shook hands. 'Might I return the compliment, and invite you to dine with me aboard my boat? I think you'd find *Aphrodite* comfortable, and Enrico is a passable cook. I expect to be here a couple more days at least; so why don't we say the day after tomorrow? If you come down to the harbour-side at seven, I'll send the launch over to collect you.'

Professor Philipas smiled his appreciation.

'Thank you,' he said. 'That's very kind.'

'Your wife is welcome to join us, of course.'

'I'll pass on your invitation, but I'm afraid she's unlikely to accept,' said the professor. 'As you'll have seen, she finds socialising stressful.'

'Well, in that case you must come alone.'

'I'll look forward to it.'

When the fat man had gone, the professor sat down at his desk, where he stayed for some time, looking at the phone, until at last he seemed to find some resolve, and picked up the receiver. He dialled a local number.

'It's me,' he said, when the call was answered. 'I had to speak to you. Can you talk?'

Enrico was waiting at the quayside. When he saw the fat man approaching, he stood up in the bows and leaned forward to hold the dinghy steady as the fat man stepped aboard.

The fat man gave the signal to depart, but Enrico didn't immediately start the engine.

'With respect, *kyrie*,' he said, 'before we go, there's something you should know. Whilst you were eating dinner, I learned there's been something of a drama which will interest you.'

The fat man's eyebrows lifted.

'A drama? Of what kind?'

'They've found a body,' said Enrico. 'They brought it round from Kolona, where we were this morning. They're keeping it in a fridge at the butcher's shop. I joined the crowd, of course, and went to see it for myself. I caught no more than a glimpse, but it wasn't pretty.'

'Whose body is it?'

'Not a local man, by all accounts. What I heard was, it's a man abandoned by his shipmates a day or two ago.'

'Really?' The fat man became thoughtful. 'I saw him myself, this morning, and he was very much alive. How did he die?'

'In the most bizarre fashion. They found him head-first down a well.'

'Did they? That must have been the well I myself drank from, earlier today. It's hard to imagine a man might fall down there accidentally. The opening is quite narrow. Did anyone have a theory as to what had happened?'

'They were speculating, of course. But people often speculate, and make very little sense.'

'The police were there, I presume.'

'The police, the army, the coastguard, all trying to push responsibility on to each other. The scene was chaotic, as you can imagine. They called a doctor to certify the death, but it was hardly necessary. A man can't be that black in the face, and still be alive. He made a grim corpse, what I saw of him. They're keeping him in the butcher's fridge until they find out who he is. And with him having drifted in here, there's some concern as to how they'll find the next of kin.'

The fat man glanced at the gold watch on his wrist.

'It's too late to do anything tonight,' he said. 'The butcher's will have closed some time ago. But we can assume the poor castaway won't be going anywhere before morning. We'll go back to *Aphrodite* now. Tomorrow will be soon enough to have a close look at the body, and ask some questions.'

Eleven

Ilias was yawning as he laid the table at the stern. Early for breakfast, the fat man wandered up to the prow. The deck was damp with mopping, and the smell of cedar wood and varnish mixed with the saltiness of the sea. The sky had not yet hardened into the day's absolute blue, but blended the pinks of sunrise with the landscape's dawn-pale greys. The sea was very calm, and within an hour or two would be tepid, even warm; but in this short time remaining before the sun's full blaze, the water gave off a welcome coolness.

The fat man leaned on the deck-rail and scanned the harbour-side. In the market square, a man was spreading the awning of his stall; a woman at one of the tourist shops fastened back shutters. At the *kafenion*, an early customer took a seat, and the proprietor rose wearily from his chair and limped inside to brew the day's first cup. Mounted on a wooden saddle, a rider kicked on his mule, disappearing down a lane. In civilian clothes, Spiros Tavoularis helped a woman and two children into his speedboat, and handed them picnic bags and beach towels from the quay.

Ilias brought out a glass of peach juice poured over crushed ice and announced breakfast, of which the fat man ate only lightly: sheep's yogurt sweetened with a swirl of honey; a croissant with soft almond paste at its centre.

'Tell Enrico I'm ready to go,' he said, as Ilias cleared his plates. 'And by the way, how are our repairs coming along?'

'All done,' said Ilias. 'I guarantee there'll be no more trouble there.'

'Only a fool would guarantee anything in this life, and I have never taken you for a fool,' said the fat man. 'But I accept you believe you have done the best you can, on this occasion. When Enrico returns, take *Aphrodite* and refuel her. When it's time to leave, I don't want any delays.'

When Enrico left the fat man at the quayside, the day's business was getting underway. The fat man made his way to a bus shelter – an unsound structure of corrugated sheeting and iron poles, with two damaged and dusty chairs in its shade. He lit a cigarette with his slim, gold lighter, and as he smoked, watched a white ferry move noiseless and noble towards its next port of call, an island which was a blur on the horizon. Up on the hillside, a church bell clanged its call to the devout. A young woman, slender-waisted and broad-hipped as a statue from Mesopotamia, passed by with a bag of bread loaves, and returned the fat man's greeting with a shy smile.

He finished his cigarette. A taxi motored by, its driver unshaven and red-eyed from lack of sleep. The fat man picked up his bag, and walked along the harbour-side to where a hawker was selling watermelons from the back of a truck. The hawker had split a melon with a machete, and was displaying it on the tailgate to show its quality, the glistening redness of its wet flesh and the glossy blackness of its seeds. As the fat man approached, a woman with her hands full of shopping was eyeing the fruit.

'I can't carry it,' she was saying, shaking her head. 'I'll send a boy down, later.'

But the hawker was too wise to risk losing a customer.

'Maybe I won't be here, later,' he said. 'If a ferry comes in, I'll be on it. And you're still a young woman. You look strong. Why don't you take half? Which one do you fancy? This one? This?' He pointed to one of the largest watermelons, and heaved it on to the pan of his scales, where the needle immediately settled past the end of its measured range. 'We'll call it ten,' he said, and named a fair price; then he placed the melon on the tailgate, pushed the point of the machete through its dark-green skin and sliced the melon through. He bagged both halves, and put one to one side; the other he held out to the woman, who was searching in her purse for change.

The fat man stepped up to the tailgate.

'I'll take the other half,' he said, handing over coins. 'Tie up the bag to keep the wasps off, and put it in the shade to keep it cool. I'll be back in a while to pick it up.' He turned to the woman. 'In the meantime, *kyria*, I have free time on my hands. Might I offer to be your beast of burden?'

'That's very gallant of you,' she said, 'but I don't want to take you out of your way. If you'd help me as far as Ayia Triander, I can leave the melon with my cousin, and collect it from there later.'

'Where exactly is it that you live?'

'I'm going to the Governor's Villa, up there on the promontory.'

'Then I shall be happy to accompany you the full distance,' said the fat man. 'It's a beautiful house, and I shall be glad to get a close look at it. And I'm used to walking. My shoes are well suited to it.' The woman glanced down at his tennis shoes. 'I call these my winged sandals. It's a little joke between my father and myself. He is a scholar of the classics, as is reflected in my name. Hermes Diaktoros, of Athens. Diaktoros is an ancient word for messenger. I'd offer you my hand, but with our bags, I think we would do better to dispose with any formal handshake.'

'Lemonia Bousali,' she said. '*Chairo poli.*'

They passed a yard where chickens scratched at hard-baked dirt, and a twitching dog slept on its side in the shade of the orange tree to which it was chained. She walked three steps ahead of him so there could be no eye contact between them, no suggestion of impropriety in their being together. She led him up a lane of steps, where a woman in rubber gloves sat on a milking stool, peeling the tough skins from a bowl of prickly pears.

'Lemonia, *kali mera*,' said the woman, ignoring the fat man as if she hadn't noticed him; but her malevolent eyes followed them both after they passed her by.

Lemonia walked steadily as a pack animal, her shopping stretching the muscles of her upper arms. Her gait was smooth, as in one accustomed to the climb and the heat, and beneath her dress, her hips moved like a younger woman's, with perhaps a little more sashay than if the fat man hadn't been following. She was disinclined to talk, and respecting the over-interest conversation might provoke in her neighbours, he too kept silent, until they reached the cobbled lane where the Governor's Villa was hidden behind its jasmine-draped wall. From the limp-leaved lower branches of a fig tree all the accessible fruit had been picked, though the lane was spattered with figs fallen from the higher branches, where the tree was laden with its developing crop, from lime-green buds to near-black, ripe orbs. At the arched doorway, she placed her shopping on the ground, and as she was hunting for her keys, thanked him for his help.

'You've been very kind,' she said.

'It was nothing.' He went a few steps to where the lane's far end dropped away down the hillside, giving a view of the glorious sea and the distant islands. 'And it is unforgivable of me to ask anything in return. But I have a yacht out on the bay, and now I appreciate the house's marvellous position, it seems to be the perfect vantage point from which to take some photographs of her at anchor. I'm sure you have wonderful views from your windows. Might I come in just for a moment and take some pictures? I have my camera here.' He held up his hold-all. 'It would only take a moment.'

'I'm afraid Vassilis doesn't like strangers in the house,' she said. 'He keeps himself very private.'

'I believe the house belongs to *Kyrie* Eliadis, does it not?' asked the fat man. 'I met him yesterday, so he and I are not strangers. Truly, I would take no time at all. A couple of snaps are all I want. I assume he's not at home?'

'No,' she said. 'He's not at home at this time.'

A silence fell between them which the fat man made no effort to fill, except by offering her a genial smile.

'All right,' she said, at last. 'But it stays between us. And you must be very quick.'

The courtyard was filled with roses, climbers which spread over the natural stone walls and bushes rooted in pots which were laid out with no regard to colour, so scarlet and ruby reds clashed with salmon pinks and peaches, and brash oranges and yellows clashed with them all. But whilst the display was unsettling to the eye, the scent of the blooms was sublime, sweet and heady, musky and seductive.

'What beautiful roses,' said the fat man. 'Quite breathtaking.'

'They're Vasso's pets,' said Lemonia. 'He chooses them for their scent rather than their colour, as you can see. His aim with this house is to honour the five senses. The roses are for the nose, and the views from here are feasts for the eyes. It's restful for the ears to enjoy the peace and quiet of the place. Most of the time, at least, we hear nothing but the wind.'

'That covers three of them,' said the fat man. 'What about taste?'

'He has me for that. I enjoy cooking, and I know what he likes.'

'And the fifth?'

She turned to him with a coquette's smile which lifted years from her face, and gave no answer.

They entered a spacious kitchen, where strings of garlic bulbs and red onions plaited by their papery stalks hung from the beams. On the walls was an array of steel and copper pans, and in a rack, a range of sharp French cook's knives. The shelves were filled with herbs and spices, some commonplace and others in quaint tins labelled in Arabic; there were bottles of oil with their flavourings still in them – whole chillies and peppercòrns, sprigs of herbs, and in the smallest one, several pincered beetles, drowned and pale. There were bottles, too, of orange-flower water and rose water, and jars of preserves – damson and quince jellies, marmalades of lemons and bitter oranges, and fuchsia-pink rose-petal syrup. A cast-iron pot on the stove gave off an appetising steam carrying cardamom, cumin and chilli in a combination unknown in Greek cuisine.

At the centre of the kitchen was a pine table large enough to seat eight, and on it was a ledger open to pages filled with columns of names, dates and figures. She closed the ledger and pushed it aside along with the ruler, pen and pencil someone had been using to make entries, and put her shopping in the space where the book had been. The fat man placed the watermelon next to her shopping, and bent down to his hold-all.

'I won't keep you,' he said, taking out an Olympus camera of very recent design. 'If you wouldn't mind showing me where I'd get the best shot, I'll do what I have to do and get out of your way.'

'Through here.'

She showed him into the *salone*, where the sun shone through the open balcony doors, highlighting the African memorabilia. Lemonia crossed straight to the balcony and stood there expectantly; but the fat man seemed to be taken with the collection. He looked closely at a lampshade made from the stitched-together skins of some small animal; then he examined the table the lamp stood on – an upended tribal drum with a warthog's hide stretched over a cane frame, all lashed together with knotted thongs. He studied a beaded ostrich egg, then stood over the zebra-skin rug.

'An extraordinary collection,' he said, looking round at the masks and the necklaces. 'Extraordinary. Though there seems to have been a lot of bloodshed to put it together. Do you know what animals are in the lampshade?'

'I believe they're some kind of shrew. Elephant shrews, I think.'

'I myself would find it disturbing, to have my nights lit through the skins of dead animals. Still, a different man, a different taste.'

'The best view is from here,' she said, and he joined her on the balcony, where a binocular case lay on the table alongside Uncle Vasso's Russian pistol.

The fat man picked it up.

'A Stechkin 9mm,' he said, turning it in his hand. 'Where on earth did he get this?'

'On his travels,' said Lemonia. 'He acquired many things on his travels.'

'This is quite a rare item, in this part of the world. It must be very hard to find ammunition for it. And it's a strange thing to have to hand, surely? Do you not feel threatened to have a weapon like this lying so casually about the house?'

'There's nothing casual about it,' she said. 'Only he and I are ever here, under normal circumstances. And it's quite safe, because you're right about the ammunition. He has no bullets left for it now. He used the last one very recently, doing someone a favour, as usual. Which is your boat?'

He pointed out *Aphrodite*, just beyond the harbour's end.

'She's splendid,' said Lemonia.

'She is,' agreed the fat man. 'But she's getting to be an old lady now, and so is becoming temperamental. That's why we're here in Mithros. We put in to make repairs.' He aimed the camera; the shutter whirred as it opened and closed. 'I appreciate your allowing me in here. The light at this moment is perfect, and the vantage point unique. It puts me in mind of Sophocles's poem.

> '"Here stretcheth by the sea
> A fair Eubœan shore, and o'er it creeps
> The vine of Bacchus, each day's growth complete.
> In morning brightness all the land is green
> With tendrils fair and spreading. Noontide comes,
> And then the unripe cluster forms apace:
> The day declines, and purple grow the grapes;
> At eve the whole bright vintage is brought in,
> And the mixed wine poured out."'

'That's beautiful.'

'Are you a lover of poetry?'

'I know very little about it,' said Lemonia. 'I used to have an interest in literature. I suppose I lost it, somewhere along the way.'

'You should revive it. Our interests – our true interests – are never lost. Sometimes they lie dormant for a while, but when the moment is right, they come back to us. As for poetry, a good poet will move you with his words, and a great poet will stir your very soul. But I suspect your soul is stirred enough, with a view like this to enjoy.'

'Vassilis enjoys this view alone, mostly,' she said. 'As he is entitled to do, this being his house. He spends much of his time alone. He was the victim of an attack, some years ago. It had a deep effect on him, and made him nervous of others. He finds it difficult to trust people.'

'Even you?'

'He trusts me more than most. And I've betrayed that trust by letting you in here. If you're finished, forgive me, but it would be better if you left.'

'Of course.' He put away his camera. 'I shall tell no one I was here. Yet it seems a tragedy for this house – which cries out to be filled with people – that he is too nervous to entertain anyone here. The attack on him must have been serious.'

'It was brutal, and unnecessary. Even now, I think he expects the robbers might come back at any moment. That night still casts a long shadow. But he escaped with only scars – his hands, if you could see them . . . Another man lost his life.'

'Socrates Rokos.'

'Yes, Socrates. He tried to stop them getting away. He left a family with no one to take care of them. Of course Vassilis has done his best for them. That's the kind of man he is.'

'I have heard of his reputation for generosity,' said the fat man. 'I was talking to Socrates's son, Milto. A talented musician, who I gather got his start in music with a gift from

Vassilis. That was an inspired choice. Milto told me the police investigation came to nothing.'

'When do their investigations ever come to anything?' said Lemonia. 'Vassilis expected nothing from them, and he wasn't disappointed.'

'Are you sure? In my experience, most people who haven't received justice are bitterly disappointed. They brood, and hatch devious, vengeful plots.'

'Not Vassilis. His view has always been to trust in God. God sees all and knows all, he says. He leaves it in His hands.'

'Sometimes we do well to give the Almighty a little help,' said the fat man. 'I take it he is cautious enough not to keep any valuables in the house, these days? In a small place like Mithros, rumours of hidden treasure grow wings, and fly to the ears of those who'd be better not to hear them.'

'As far as I know, there's nothing here. I take care of this house, and I believe I know every last corner. If there're treasures here, they're very well hidden.'

In the kitchen, the pot on the stove was hissing.

'I have outstayed any welcome,' said the fat man, 'and you will think me incorrigible, but before I go, do you think I might try what you are cooking? It smells unlike anything I have ever tasted.'

She smiled.

'Goat curry,' she said. 'A favourite of Vassilis's. I should warn you, it has a little kick to it. Not too much, but enough.'

She lifted the pot lid, and the steam rose in a symphony of spices. She gave him a spoon; he dipped it into the sauce, blew on it to cool it, and tasted.

'It's good,' he said. 'As you say, it has a little kick. You are a good cook, Lemonia. Maybe you could write down your recipe for me, and I'll see what my man makes of it.'

She laughed.

'If only I could,' she said. 'There is no recipe. I make it as I feel. I cook by principles, rather than by recipes.'

'You are an artist, then, a creator and improviser. And I see by your preserves you're industrious too.'

'Take some,' she said. 'I make too much, and there's no one to eat it.'

'If you're sure,' he said. 'A jar of the rose-petal syrup would be most welcome. I'm very partial to it.'

She gave him a jar. As he slipped it inside his hold-all, he said, 'I must return your favours. And a gift for a gift. I have a book of poetry I'd like you to have. I'll make sure it reaches you. *Yassas*.'

'*Yassas*.'

He turned towards the door. Lemonia began to unpack her bags of shopping.

The fat man glanced down at his feet. One of his shoelaces was undone.

'Forgive me,' he said. 'One moment.'

He crouched down, and spent a minute or two fastidiously retying his lace, making sure both loops and tail-ends were equal lengths.

Lemonia reached for the last bag of her shopping. It had come from a harbour cobbler's, and held a pair of shoes: the prettiest of shoes in soft pink leather, decorated with sequinned butterflies and in a size to suit a very young girl.

Twelve

Back at the harbour-side, the fat man asked the way to the butcher's, and was directed to a shop in the traditional style, a box of bare stone walls with brown-painted doors the whole width of the frontage. Yet despite its being peak business hours, the doors remained closed; only at one end was one a little ajar, with an open padlock hanging in a hasp.

The fat man put his face to the narrow opening. There was the buzz of flies, and the smell of flesh and dried blood, and faintly beneath that, of putridity.

'Butcher! Are you there?'

There was a short silence before a face appeared close to the fat man's own.

'I'm closed this morning,' said the butcher. 'Come back this evening. I might be open then.'

'It's you, Makis,' said the fat man, with apparent surprise. 'Hermes Diaktoros, of Athens. We met yesterday, at Kolona. I wonder if I can persuade you to open up, only briefly. I'll be quick in my choice, and I won't keep you.'

'I'm sorry,' said Makis. Still only his face was visible. 'I can't serve anyone this morning.'

'Does your reluctance have anything to do with the corpse you're storing in your fridge? Please, don't worry about him on my account. I'm well aware he's in there. On a small island like this, his presence could hardly be kept secret. I only want something from the freezer, and I'll be gone.'

Makis hesitated, then pulled back the door a fraction further.

The temperature inside the shop was markedly cooler than on the street outside. In the dim light, the fat man made out along one wall the boarded front of the refrigerator cabinets, which reached from floor to ceiling, solid-seeming as a safe. On the opposite wall was a glass-topped chest freezer; at the back of the shop, an old office desk held an antiquated till with round brass keys, a mincing-machine plugged into a high socket, and a pile of waxed paper printed with 'Makis Theonas, Best quality meats and frozen foods'. A cigarette burned in an ashtray; there was a cup with cold coffee in its saucer. At the centre of the floor was a butcher's block, a hefty slice of hardwood mounted on a pinewood trestle; the block was stained to a third of its depth with the blood and juices of raw meat, and its surface was crossed with hundreds of scars from the saw, knives and chopper which lay ready for use. Flies crawled on the block; beneath it, a cat licked at its extended leg.

Makis wore a red apron over his shirt and jeans. His fingernails and cuticles were foul with dried blood.

The fat man gave him a warm smile, and crossing over to the freezers, looked down through the glass on to the stock: imported chickens, skinny rabbits with opaque eyes, ice-glazed red mullet, milky-white squid. He slid back the glass, and shifted a few bags of vegetables – French beans and artichoke hearts, scattered with green rondels from a burst bag of peas.

'Well, well,' he said. 'Here's a guilty secret.'

Makis blinked. The fat man pointed to a tray of tiny birds, plucked and cellophane wrapped in pairs.

'Are these quail?' asked the fat man. 'I don't think they can be. Could they possibly be . . .?'

'*Ambelopoulia*,' said Makis. He snatched up the cigarette from the ashtray; there was a slight tremor in his fingers as he put it to his lips.

The fat man was leaning down for a closer look.

'What are they, finches? They can't be thrushes, surely. They're too small.'

'Don't ask me to sell you those,' said Makis. 'I don't know you. And it isn't me that traps them. I'm just the middleman.'

'I'm sure they fetch very good money, don't they, especially since the ban? I imagine they're almost worth their weight in gold. But it's a risky business, isn't it, these days?'

'It's the trapping that's illegal,' said Makis. 'That isn't down to me. It's a ridiculous law, anyway. They're just birds. If people want to eat them, let them.'

'So you let someone else take the risk, and you take the profit? That might be good business, except I think you're mistaken that the illegality is all in the trapping. I believe the trade in general has been outlawed. Still, let me put your mind at rest, on this score. I shan't report you for what you're keeping in your freezer.' He covered the songbirds with the vegetable packs, and slid closed the lid. 'Actually, my father is very partial to *ambelopoulia*, particularly to larks. He boasts he once ate fifty-four at a single sitting. I myself have no taste for them. The eating is too fiddly, and I think they're of more value on the wing, where they belong. And for my purposes, they're hardly adequate to serve my guests for dinner. Might you have mutton in stock, or goat? My man's a fair cook, and can do wonders with most cuts of mutton, but I'd favour the leg, if you have it.'

But the butcher jerked his chin up to signify no.

'I can only sell to you from the freezers today,' he said.

There was a blackness under his eyes which hadn't been there the previous day, and whereas he had been clean-shaven for the festival, now a dark shadow of stubble covered his face. He yawned a yawn he didn't trouble to cover. The tobacco on his breath mingled with the yeasts of alcohol.

'There's squid, but its frozen form is so inferior to the fresh,' went on the fat man. 'Did your wife enjoy the festival yesterday, by the way?'

'My wife? My wife didn't go. Someone had to stay and mind the shop.'

'Ah. You're an unusual couple, then. I've always found women much keener on those festivities than men are.' He peered again into the freezer. 'I suppose there's always chicken, but that's such an unadventurous choice. Look, Makis, I realise you're reluctant to open up the fridge. But you must have a quantity of meat in there which will, quite frankly, very soon be unfit for anything but cat food.'

The butcher shook his head.

'You're wasting your breath,' he said. 'That fridge stays closed, until they come to take him away.'

'It would take you only a few moments. Cut me a leg of mutton, and we're done. Better that, surely, than to throw it out. You're losing a morning's business already, and no doubt you lost a good deal more last night. I'll go away a satisfied customer, and you'll have made a sale.'

'I don't want the sale, with him in there,' said Makis. 'Come back this evening. They've promised me he'll be gone by then. I'll be scrubbing the fridges from top to bottom, after they've taken him away.'

'Forgive me, but you're very squeamish for a butcher,' said the fat man. 'I would have thought you'd be hardened to dead flesh, whatever its species. Surely a man's carcass isn't so dissimilar to a cow's or sheep's?'

'His is,' said the butcher. He went to the ashtray, and stubbed out the burned-down cigarette, then took a fresh one from the pack and lit it, inhaling deeply on the smoke. 'He's about as ugly a corpse as you could make. The sooner they take him away, the better. Though he's done me plenty of damage already. I'll be lucky ever to see my customers in here again. I thought there was some hope of keeping it quiet, but that was only wishful thinking.'

'Why did you let them bring him here, if you were so against it?'

'It was an act of Christian charity,' said Makis. He drew again on his cigarette, and flicked a short length of ash into the ashtray. 'Who else has a fridge he might go in? Left in the open air, he'd have been stinking by the day's end. As it turns out, he isn't so fresh now. He was down that well too long.'

'The nature of his death interests me greatly,' said the fat man. 'How on earth do you suppose he ended up down the well?'

The butcher shrugged.

'Drunk, most probably.' He inhaled again on his cigarette, and stubbed it out, hardly smoked. 'My wife's beside herself, worrying about the business. She thinks we'll have to change our line of work. If there's one job I never saw myself in, it was undertaking. We're lucky no one's put a name to him, or we'd have the next of kin down here lighting candles.'

'Has no one put a name to him, then? You've no idea who he is?'

'They're trying to find out,' said the butcher. 'Seems to me the only way is to track down that boat he came in on.'

'You will perhaps think me morbid for asking,' said the fat man hesitantly, 'but I have something of a professional interest in these matters – accidental death, and such. I'd be very interested to see the body, if you wouldn't mind.'

'I would mind,' said Makis. 'If you see him, I have to see him.'

'Avert your eyes,' said the fat man.

'I can avert my eyes, but I can't avert my nostrils, can I? Once you open that fridge, he'll stink the place out again, and my business'll be done for the day.'

'I could make recompense for that,' said the fat man. 'I wouldn't want you to lose trade, on account of me. What should we say? Three thousand? Four? Five?'

The butcher sighed.

'On your head, then,' he said. 'But Christ knows, he isn't pretty. His own mother wouldn't know him. Be warned, he'll turn your stomach.'

'It would take a great deal to turn my stomach,' said the fat man. 'Believe me, I am used to unpleasant sights.'

Makis opened the refrigerator doors. There was a rush of chilled air, and the iron smell of cold blood, and bad meat. Dangling on hooks were hacked and sliced carcasses – a sheep, almost intact, the remains of a pig hooked by a vertebra, the ribs and foreleg of a cow – and on a shelf, the pig's head and its feet, alongside several sheeps' heads ranged like trophies, and a large bowl containing bloody livers, hearts and lungs.

On the refrigerator floor, under the hanging carcasses, a white sheet covered an object laid lengthways. The fat man crouched, and peeled back the sheet.

As the butcher had warned, the corpse bore little resemblance to how Manolis had been in life. His face was black and bloated, his upper torso was dark with pooled blood, whilst the rest of his body from feet to chest was ghastly parchment yellow. On his upper arms were deep grazes, the skin scraped away as he had slipped down the shaft; his army trousers were ripped at the knees from his struggling to move himself either up, or down. His cheeks bulged; his lips and eyelids were peculiarly swollen, his lips engorged enough almost to hide the cut where both Gounaris and Manolis's crewmate had landed punches. A dark trickle from lobe to left temple showed where his ear had bled.

The fat man reached out and lifted an eyelid. The eyeball was dark red, and swollen with blood.

'He's certainly not pretty, is he, poor fellow,' he said. 'But why were his arms by his sides? Why didn't he put out his hands to save himself?'

Drawn to do so, Makis looked down at the corpse, and shuddered.

'He'll haunt my dreams for years to come,' he said. 'Ugly bastard. Still, now you've got the fridge open, I suppose I might as well cut your meat. If you don't mind what it's been keeping company with.'

'I don't mind, no,' said the fat man, glancing up at the animal flesh. 'Mutton, then, if you will.'

The butcher stepped around him, hauled out the headless sheep and dropped it on to the block.

The fat man leaned closer over Manolis's body, and sniffed. The odour of decay was distinct, and now the corpse was uncovered, the flies gathered on and around it.

The fat man did his best to waft them away.

'He waited a while to be found, I think. And there's no doubt, I'm afraid, that he suffered badly. Most people who fall down wells go feet first, finding disused wells by accident. Head first is far more unpleasant, and much harder to survive. I knew of a man in Zakynthos who came to a similar end. He was repairing a bakery chimney, and leaned too far down the stack. Hidden from view as he was, and his shouts muffled by the thickness of the stone, by the time they found him, it was too late. When they pulled him out his face was black, and they took it to be soot. But when they washed him, the black remained; it was the blood pooled in his head. Did you know hanging upside down has often been used as a form of torture? The suffering it causes was exploited by the Romans, who tended to invert their prisoners for crucifixion.'

'I don't see why,' said Makis, examining the sheep carcass for the best cut. 'How can a man die from being upside down?'

'It's all to do with gravity,' said the fat man. 'When you're standing upright, the lungs expand naturally within the rib cage. But when you're upside down, your organs – your liver and your intestines – press on to the lungs. It's a long, slow death from suffocation. Death is far from instantaneous. The inversion induces blindness, too. The vessels in the eyes become engorged quite early on, and burst as has happened here. And this trickle of blood from his ear suggests more internal bleeding. I imagine he would have been in considerable pain.'

Makis picked up a steel, and began to sharpen a boning knife.

'Let me tell you something, friend,' he said. 'No disrespect to the dead, but it seems to me anyone who falls down a well has only themselves to blame. I grew up around that well, fetched water from it from being four years old, and never once managed to fall into it. So it seems to me if he did, it was through his own stupidity. He was drinking. We all saw him take the bottle. Drink'll do that to you. Makes you stupid.'

'You're correct on that point,' said the fat man. 'But even so, why should he have fallen in?'

'Leaning too far over the rim, surely.'

'Yes, but why would he be leaning over the rim? Do you think he might have been looking for something?'

'Like what? What's down there but water? You don't need to look for the water to draw it. And anyway, you can't see to the bottom. The army bored it deep. It goes halfway to the centre of the earth.'

'I wasn't thinking of water. Might he have been looking for something else? Something like your famous bull?'

The butcher was silent for a moment, then he let out a laugh.

'Looking for the bull down that well? Then that would make him stupid!'

He lay down the steel, and shifted the sheep's corpse to expose the best of its legs.

'Did you ever see the famous bull?' asked the fat man.

'No, I never did.'

'Did you see the replica?'

'What replica? We've ten thousand replicas in Mithros.'

'I mean the one at the museum. The one with hooves and horns of gold.'

'Is there such a thing? That's news to me.'

'It will be news to you also, then, that the replica has been stolen.'

'Why would anyone steal a replica?'

'Why, indeed?'

The fat man touched Manolis's swollen cheek, and pressing gently with his fingers, found it hard. Prising open the mouth, he looked inside, then reached in and pulled an object from the cavity.

'Now this is very interesting,' he said. 'Look what we have here.'

He held up a round, smooth pebble. The butcher poked the tip of the knife into the sheep's hip joint.

'A gag,' said the fat man. 'That's why no one heard him shout. This pebble was put in his mouth to stop him

186

shouting. It's too big for him to have spat it out. Whoever put him down that well, intended that he shouldn't be found, or not found quickly, at least. Someone wanted him to suffer. And suffer he did.'

The butcher was slicing expertly into the sheep, separating the leg at the joint.

'You think someone put him down there? Sounds a bit far-fetched to me,' he said. 'But if he'd been keeping bad company, who knows?'

'Am I the first to notice he'd been gagged?' asked the fat man. With great care, he replaced the pebble in the mouth. 'Surely the police and the coastguard have had a good look at him?'

'I suppose they didn't look as closely as you're doing. They've called the coroner, but the coroner's at his summer place and isn't rushing back. And dead is dead. Cause of death isn't their responsibility.'

'It is if he met his end at someone's hands. He's been punched, too. Look, here on the lip.'

'I don't want to see,' said the butcher. 'But if someone killed him, it's obvious who it was.'

'Enlighten me.'

'There was a stranger in the hills, yesterday. He had a rifle. The captain took his men to look for him. Maybe it was one of his shipmates, come back to settle a score. A quick shove in the back, and down he'd go. If that's how it was, it was a score settled, well and truly.'

'If his shipmates were involved in his death, then that boat shouldn't be too far away.'

'I said the same to Spiros. He's been on to his coastguard colleagues. They're all out looking.'

'So there are people who know what this boat looks like?'

'The soldiers at Kolona. They saw it come and go when he

first arrived. They saw the argument, and him being thrown overboard. They're witnesses to the bad feeling between him and the crew.'

'No doubt that might be useful, when it comes to proving the case. Though when it comes to witnesses, I'm always mindful of the proverb: one witness, one liar; more witnesses, all liars. But a man with a rifle would surely shoot a man, rather than going to the trouble of forcing him down a well.'

'Not if he wanted to make no noise,' said Makis. 'Which plainly he didn't, since the man is gagged, as you say. There were a lot of people at Kolona yesterday. If someone had shot him, it would have been heard.'

The fat man looked at him.

'You're right, of course,' he said. 'It had to be done without too much noise.'

The butcher brought the chopper down on the mutton. The first blow split the bone; the second cut it clean through.

'I wish you'd cover him up,' he said. 'He gives me the horrors. And that fridge needs to be closed. It's hot, and the meat'll spoil. Not that anyone would buy it now, anyway.'

'You mean no one but me,' said the fat man. 'But even I hope the necessary steps have been taken to make sure he doesn't leak?'

'We've stopped him up, if that's what you mean,' said the butcher, placing a sheet of waxed paper on the scale before he weighed the mutton leg. 'A piece of string for his manhood, and a cork at the other end. The doctor did it yesterday, before we put him in there. With luck, that should hold him until he's claimed.'

'But what if no one does claim him?'

'An unmarked grave, I suppose. And if that's how it's going to be, the sooner, the better.'

'You'll forgive me for saying, but you seem to have little

sympathy with a man who's died such a gruesome death.'

The fat man drew the sheet back over the corpse's face, and stood up. The butcher wrapped the mutton in the waxed paper, and put it in a carrier bag.

'Five thousand five hundred,' he said. 'Sympathy or not, it's not the first bad death at Kolona. Drowning's a nasty death too, by all accounts.'

The fat man drew out his wallet, and handed over money.

'There's something extra there for your trouble, as we discussed,' he said. 'So you have unhappy associations with Kolona, yet you talked yesterday as if you'd like to go back there.'

'I've always wanted to go back,' said the butcher, as he opened the till. 'Beholden to no one, living off the land. In the meantime, like a fool I borrowed money, and set up this shop.'

He tucked the banknotes into the drawer, and pushed it shut.

'You borrowed money for this enterprise, did you?' asked the fat man. 'But I expect a butcher's shop must be very profitable, isn't it?'

'I'd be doing all right if it weren't for the wife. I save money, and she spends it. It was a mistake, looking back, to borrow from an acquaintance. She'd take our debts more seriously if we'd borrowed from the bank. It costs me a fortune in meat to keep the man sweet when she's spent what I've put aside. Prime cuts, and a whole lamb at Easter – she doesn't understand it comes out of my profits. When you add it all up, it's double what I'd pay him in cash.'

'So your loan was on an unofficial footing, was it? In my experience, such favours often turn sour. I knew a man once who borrowed money at the age of twenty, and at sixty still hadn't managed to pay it back. Fortunately for him, his creditor then died; but the poor man had spent his working life enslaved to his creditor. There was no favour this man could refuse him, or the debt would have been called in, and unable as he was to pay, he'd have been disgraced. What looked like a favour became a yoke the poor man bore most of his life. Why did you not go to the bank?'

'Because the bank wouldn't look at me. What could I offer as security? The family plot? That's just a few trees on a piece of near-barren land. Banks are for rich men.'

Makis carried the remains of the sheep carcass to the fridge, and was spiking it back on its hook when a voice called out from the door.

'Butcher! Eh, Makis, where are you, *malaka*?'

Tavros, the taverna owner, squeezed through the door's narrow opening. Makis slammed the refrigerator door closed.

'So you are here, *malaka*! Where's my order?' demanded Tavros.

'Tavros,' said the butcher, deferentially. '*Kali mera, kali mera*.'

Tavros only glanced at the fat man; he offered him no greeting.

'Where's my order, *malaka*?' he said. 'Why hasn't it been delivered? I've a cook over there picking his nose and reading the newspaper, and when I ask him why, he points the finger at you. For Christ's sake, I've got lunches to serve in two hours! Give the order to me, and I'll take it with me.'

But Makis spread his hands in apology.

'It isn't ready yet. Be reasonable, Tavros. You know the drama I've had here. You can hardly expect business as usual. I didn't get an hour's sleep last night.'

But reminded of the corpse, Tavros wasn't listening.

'Where is he?' he asked. 'Is he in there?'

He threw open the refrigerator door, and seeing the sheeted

form on its floor, crouched down, and uncovered it. Shocked by the blackened, bloated face, he blanched, and dropped back the sheet.

'Christ,' he said, and stood up. 'He makes an ugly corpse, doesn't he?' He crossed himself. 'Christ.'

'You should close the fridge,' said Makis. 'I think it's more respectful to leave him be. Spiros promised me they'll be coming for him soon.'

'Spiros?' Tavros gave a snort of disdain. 'I can't be waiting for those *malakas* to sort themselves out.' Keeping his eyes off the body, he turned back to the fridge and, hauling out the beef carcass, pressed it on to Makis. 'Let's start with this.'

'I don't know, Tavros,' said the butcher. 'I'm not sure people will want to eat this, now it's shared room with him.'

'If no one tells them, people won't know, will they?' said Tavros. 'Now, let's get to it. You might have time to stand around wringing your hands, but in my business, time's money.'

The fat man searched out a *periptero* – a kiosk. The vendor there sat low in a plastic chair, his legs stretched out before him, his arms folded over his chest, a baseball cap pulled down over his eyes, sharing a canopy's shade with displays of chewing gum and biscuits, of guidebooks and postcards, of salted almonds and pistachios in their shells. There was chilled beer and Coca-Cola, fruit juices and chocolate; the ice-cream was hidden by ripped-up cardboard providing extra insulation against the heat. Fastened to the kiosk with four rusty drawing pins was a handwritten sign which said 'Fresh Fish'.

The harbour-side was lively with summer's bustle – with wandering tourists, with women shopping and men lingering. In the midst of it all, the kiosk vendor appeared to be sleeping; but when the fat man stood before him, he immediately reached up and pushed the cap's peak from his eyes.

'*Kalos tou*,' he said, but without yet sitting up from his slouch. He had the leathery skin of an outdoor man, with sun-ingrained wrinkles in his face; as he looked up from his chair, his expression was cheerful. 'What can I do for you?'

'*Yassas*,' said the fat man. 'I'm looking for a particular brand of cigarettes. I'm hoping you might have them in stock.' From his pocket, he brought out a near-empty pack, and held it up for the vendor to see.

The owner squinted up at the starlet's picture, and smiled.

'Now do you know,' he said, 'I believe I might.' He got up from his chair, removed his hat and dropped it back on the seat. His head was shorn bald, a fresh cut only a day or two old. 'I think you might be in luck, friend. You just might be in luck.'

He disappeared through the kiosk's back door, and reappeared at its small hatch.

'You'll have to give me a minute,' he said. He turned his back to the fat man, and began to search amongst the stock piled against the rear wall. 'I used to have a regular customer who smoked those,' he said, opening boxes and closing them again. 'I used to get them in specially for him. Since he died, no one's ever asked for them. It was only yesterday I was thinking I should throw them out. I won't lie to you, I've had them a while. They might be stale, or got at by damp – it's damp like you wouldn't believe down here by the water, come winter. But I said to myself, just wait a while, you never know when someone might happen along. So I kept them, and now here you are.' There were sounds of cartons being lifted and dropped, of paper rustling. 'Here we are!'

Triumphant, he slammed a box of the fat man's cigarettes on the counter.

'Do you just have the one pack?' asked the fat man.

'Oh dear Lord no,' said the vendor, cheerfully. 'I've half a dozen.'

'Then I'll take them all. They are increasingly hard to find. And I'll take a box of matches to go with them.'

The owner put both cigarettes and matches in a bag.

'Like I told you, they're old stock,' he said. 'The quality may not be as good as it should be. If you're not happy with them, bring them back, and I'll give you your money back.'

'Really? That's a rare offer indeed. How much do I owe you?'

'Let's call it seventeen hundred, for cash,' said the vendor. 'You've done me something of a favour, taking them off my hands.'

'I see from your sign there you sell fish,' said the fat man. He handed over his money, leaving little cash remaining in his wallet.

'I do when I have any to sell.'

'Is there any chance you could get me any for tomorrow? Something of premium quality. I'm having dinner guests.'

'Well, that's in the lap of the gods,' said the vendor. 'I was thinking of going out in the morning, if the wife will let me. She gets sick of fish, you know. Thirty years we've been married, and many of those days we've eaten fish. I suppose you might get sick of it, though I never have.'

'I have a suggestion for you, then,' said the fat man. 'My preference would be to serve fish, but I have a leg of mutton here as my contingency. If you catch anything suitable, what do you say to you and I doing a trade? You can have my leg of mutton for your wife; I get fresh fish for my guests.'

The vendor offered his hand through the hatch.

'Done,' he said. 'I'll do my best for you. But I offer no guarantees. Maybe the gods will be kind.'

'Maybe they will. And if they are, come and find me or my crew. I'm on the *Aphrodite*, over there. They call me Hermes. You should ask for me.'

'Nondas is my name. So she's yours, is she? She's a beautiful craft. I've been admiring her. Wish me luck with the nets, then, and if I get anything worthwhile, I'll bring it over.'

The fat man found a waste-bin stencilled with the initials of the Municipality of Mithros, where wasps crawled on the stickiness of melted ice-cream.

He reached into the bag from the *periptero* and took out the matchbox. Sliding off the cover, he tipped out all the matches, which fell tinkling to the bottom of the waste-bin. He replaced the lid on the empty box, dropped it back in with the cigarettes and tucked them away in the front pocket of his hold-all.

Thirteen

In no hurry, the fat man walked in the direction of his rendezvous with Enrico. When he reached the bank, he saw that the door stood open, and behind the counter, counting out notes to a middle-aged woman, was Loskas Vergas.

Recalling he had been low on cash when he paid for his cigarettes, the fat man went inside.

Loskas's customer was gathering up her passbook, tucking the money she had withdrawn inside its pages.

'It doesn't seem like much interest to me,' she was saying, tartly. 'I think I'd be better off with some stocks and shares.'

'That's up to you,' Loskas replied. 'But then you're gambling, aren't you? You might make a little more, or you might lose it all. Personally, I'd never take such a risk. And you'd have to pay someone to invest it for you, and those fees mount up. It's not what I would do. But it's up to you, Maria. That's all I can say to you – it's up to you.'

'It'd be less of a worry kept under the mattress,' she said. 'That's all my mother ever did. She never had all this worry about making returns.'

She turned from the counter and came face to face with the fat man, whom she hadn't noticed enter the bank.

'Oh!' She looked him up and down, admiring his tailored

clothes and his shoes, and her belligerence evaporated. 'Please, excuse me,' she said, and called out a polite *Yassas* as she went out the door.

The fat man stepped up to the counter, and gave Loskas a smile. Through the glass between them, the cashier looked tired. A disorder of slips and dockets was spread before him, and his half-moon spectacles were pushed back on his head, dishevelling his hair.

'*Kali mera*,' said the fat man, laying his hold-all at his feet and the leg of mutton on the counter. 'You and I have already met, if you remember. At Kolona.'

'I remember. What can I do for you?'

'Let me see if I can recall – I think your name is Loskas. Loskas Vergis.'

'Vergas.'

'Vergas, that's right. I never forget a name,' said the fat man. 'It was so interesting to hear of your families' histories yesterday. Between you, you have an impressive heritage. And I found it touching you have all remained so close. You, Makis, Spiros – you are good friends still, it seemed to me, and you seem so proud of your bond. I want to withdraw some cash, if I may.' From a trouser pocket, he produced a passbook for a savings account, and pushed it under the glass to the bank clerk.

Loskas moved aside the slips and dockets to clear space on the counter, and found a withdrawal form in the rack behind his pencil pot. His hands were slight and almost feminine, with one of his little fingernails kept long as a sign of his clerical status.

'You'll forgive me for saying so,' said the fat man, 'but your filing system seems a little haphazard.'

Loskas shook his head, and sighed.

'There's a discrepancy, from yesterday,' he said. 'I never

have discrepancies. I've been through these papers a dozen times, and I still can't get the books to balance. Every time I have someone stand in for me, it ends the same. No one takes the same care I do. But I'll find it. No discrepancy's been reported from this branch, in all the time I've run it. I'll need to see your ID.'

'If someone else has made an error, you should fetch them in to put it right,' said the fat man.

'It was my wife,' said Loskas. 'I don't want to upset her.'

The fat man handed over his ID card from his wallet.

'I seem to remember one of you saying there were four families at Kolona when the well ran dry,' he said. 'But I recall being introduced to representatives of only three. Was there no one there from the fourth? I know how people are on these small islands, and I would hate to hear there has since been a falling out between the clans.'

'No, no,' said Loskas. He pulled his glasses forward on to his nose, and studied the fat man's ID, reading even the smallest print. He looked up at the fat man's face, checking for a match with the photograph, then checked the name with the name on the passbook. 'Our contemporary was poor Socrates, who we so tragically lost. He and I were friends from childhood. He's the reason I go to St Nikodemos every year – to honour his memory. The saint has plenty of folk to remember him. Socrates has only us. His son was there yesterday. How much do you want?'

'Fifty thousand,' said the fat man. 'In fives, if you would.'

Loskas opened the passbook. The bottom-line balance was high, and had been so since the account was opened, with generous deposits outpacing the modest withdrawals.

'Whatever the gentleman wants,' he said. He slotted the withdrawal form into the printer beside him and dextrously keyed numbers on a keyboard. The form fed through the printer; when it emerged, Loskas removed it, and pushed it under the glass to the fat man. 'Sign, please.'

The fat man did so, and pushed the withdrawal form back to Loskas, who checked the signature with the specimen in the passbook.

'You're a good customer of ours, I see,' he said.

'I've been a customer for many years,' said the fat man. 'Happily, I'm in the fortunate position of being a depositor rather than a borrower. I appreciate that it is not the same for everyone.'

'No, it certainly isn't,' said Loskas. He folded back the pages of the passbook, slotted it into the printer and hit a single button on his keyboard. When the printer had made its updates, he removed the book, and made a mental check of the recorded entries. 'The majority are otherwise. They come to borrow money, not to make deposits. I have a policy of saying yes, if I can. With some of them it's impossible, of course. I know before they open their mouths what they're worth, by and large, and with those plain dirt-poor or already mired in debt, I'd be mad to give them money. But I try to be sympathetic. I'm a man with three daughters, and I paid for three dowry houses. Believe me, I know what it means to worry about money.'

He laid the passbook on the counter and, opening the cash drawer, took out a wad of notes bound by a paper band.

'And surrounded by it, as you are,' said the fat man, 'no one could help but sympathise with a man in your position. Three daughters, and a drawer full of cash . . .'

Loskas slipped the paper band from the banknotes.

'It takes courage to be a thief,' he said, 'and I've never been a very courageous man. I've always played by the rules, except where the rules didn't matter.'

'That's an interesting concept. Who is it who decides when

the rules don't matter? Surely only those who made the rules in the first place can decide to suspend them? Or are you saying that no rules matter? And something else I've often pondered – when is a rule bent, and when is it broken? Do you think bending is any different from breaking?'

Frowning, Loskas counted out ten of the banknotes, and knocked what remained in his hand back into shape before replacing the paper band.

'You sound like a philosopher,' he said, putting the notes back in the drawer. 'I'm not much of a philosopher myself.'

'But my point's a simple one,' said the fat man. 'Let me give you an example. The rules – the company rules – state that this branch closes at a certain time. Two o'clock, would it be?' Loskas nodded agreement. 'But on a winter's day, when the wind's howling and the rain's pouring and you've had no customers for over an hour, have you never closed up a few minutes early?' Loskas shrugged. 'Of course you have. Why should you stick it out, when common sense tells you it's a waste of your time? And yet the rule is, 2 pm. Now, is that rule bent, or broken?'

'What difference does it make?' asked Loskas. He pushed the fat man's passbook and cash under the glass. 'No one's harmed.'

'Ah, but you can never know that, can you? You'll never know if, on that winter's day when you close up early, some poor desperate soul comes banging on the door at the last moment, and finds you already gone.'

'It isn't likely, is it?'

'Many things that happen in life are not likely. Some even appear to be impossible. Tell me about your daughters. Are they all married now?'

'The last one married this year, only a few months after the second. I married them off in order, as I should have done, oldest to youngest. We were lucky enough to find suitors for the two youngest close together.'

'But the expense! You now, I knew a man once who had seven children, and all seven were girls. And without wanting to be unkind, they were not great beauties. There was no queue of men at the door to claim their hands. So this unfortunate fellow had seven houses to find, and seven portions of land to go with them. Of course he couldn't afford it. It would be a rare man that could. So he solved his dilemma in a unique way.'

He stopped speaking, and seemed to become absorbed in putting away his passbook and his cash.

'How, then?' prompted Loskas. 'How did he do it?'

The fat man smiled.

'Ah, now. No doubt you're wishing you had met me before you spent your money. How did you solve this problem yourself?'

Loskas shrugged.

'For the first, I borrowed from the bank, a loan I'm still paying back now and won't be saying goodbye to anytime soon. As an employee, there's no way for me to increase my income and pay it off. A fisherman may catch more fish and a carpenter may sell more doors, but my salary stays the same, more or less, from year to year. Happily I have a good friend who helped me out with the other two. It's not everyone who has such friends.'

'No, indeed,' said the fat man. 'Your friend was generous, I'm sure. Though no doubt you'll be paying him back for years to come, too.'

'But he isn't one to worry too much if I miss a payment,' said Loskas. 'Especially since I'm able to do him a favour in return.'

'That's fortunate,' said the fat man. He craned his head to

see to the back of the office, where the stuffed owl perched under its glass dome. It was a pretty bird, with cream and taupe feathers and large eyes of green glass. 'Is that an Athena's owl I see back there?'

'It is. And not just any owl. She was my pet for several years. I found her as a fledgling, and raised her by hand. She used to sit on my shoulder whilst I worked. When she died, I preserved her, and here she is.'

'I think I saw some of your other work, at the museum.'

'I've given them a number of my pieces,' said Loskas. 'Mostly birds. I keep an aviary at home. Most of the birds I give to the museum have come from there.'

'The Athena's owl reminds me of home,' said the fat man. 'In ancient times, they lived in great numbers on top of the Acropolis. They've long been a symbol of wisdom, of course. Was your owl wise, in life?'

Loskas smiled.

'Maybe not wise, but clever,' he said. 'She knew which customers would pet her, and which to stay away from. My friend, the one I mentioned, she never went near. He's one of those who thinks all animals should be useful.'

'Does he use you, then? Or have you only used him, to bail you out of your financial predicament?'

'Of course he doesn't use me,' said Loskas, offended. 'He scratched my back, I'm happy to scratch his. That isn't using each other. It's what friends do.'

'A favour in return for a favour.'

'Exactly so.'

'And because you're friends, the size and scope of the favours wouldn't matter. Which is just as well, since it would be hard for any man – especially one such as yourself, on a limited salary – to match the favour of a generous loan. I myself would feel the weight of the inequality of our positions. With nothing comparable to offer, I would feel I was the poor relation. But you, no doubt, were better than I would be at swallowing your pride.'

'I've no need to swallow my pride,' said Loskas, indignantly. 'My friend's grateful for what I can do for him. A bank has facilities you don't find in other places, and my friend has assets he wants to keep safe.'

'Is that so?' asked the fat man. 'I assume when you say facilities, you mean the vault?'

'It doesn't hurt, does it? You talked about bending rules, and of course by the rules we're not allowed to use the vault for anything but the bank's business. But my friend was robbed a number of years ago, and that's made him very nervous. He's a self-made man who's done very well for himself – he made a lot of money in the coffee trade – and of course those with money tend to have all kinds of valuables. It's easy enough for me to keep them here. And in return, when the time came for my daughters to marry, he was happy to help out.'

'Your friend being Vassilis Eliadis, of course.'

'Yes. And I'm proud to call him my friend. He's a man of importance, here in Mithros.'

'But what are you keeping safe for him that couldn't be kept safe by other means? Why doesn't he open an account with you, and deposit his funds like other people?'

'It isn't funds, it's a box,' said Loskas. 'And don't ask me what's in it, because I haven't asked, and I haven't looked. I couldn't look if I wanted to without him knowing. The box is bound. It'd take a week to unwrap it.'

'How intriguing,' said the fat man. 'If it were me, I'd be eaten with curiosity to know what is in it. Plainly he doesn't want you to know, good friends though you might be. But I didn't finish telling you about the man with seven daughters.

His first step was the same as yours: he took a loan from the bank, as much as they would give him. Then he sat down, made his calculations, and worked out how much that would be for each daughter, and divided up the money into seven portions, plus one remaining. I don't need to tell you, it wasn't much: nowhere near enough to give each girl a house, and land. So instead, he wrote a letter, to a cousin of his mother's in Australia. He took her advice, and gained her agreement to his plan. As each girl came of age, he paid for a whole wardrobe of new clothes, a visit to the hairdresser's, perfume and jewellery: he spent a good amount to make her look the very best she could. Then he bought a boat ticket, a one-way ticket from here to Australia, and sent the girls off, one by one. He didn't send them steerage, but put them in first class, and had them spoiled and cared for to make them appear much wealthier than they were. And do you know, in the length of time it took to make the journey, all but two of those girls had won themselves suitors – men from a Greek background, setting out to make a new life for themselves – and free of the constraints and conventions of our dowry system, they made themselves a match. The remaining two were taken in by the cousin, who enjoyed herself playing matchmaker to find them husbands amongst the Australian-Greek community. And when word reached the man his daughters were all settled, he sold the property he had used to secure the debt, paid it back and used the last portion of the loan to buy tickets for himself and his wife to go and visit his girls. For some years, he and his wife lived happily, moving from one daughter to the next, a month or two here, a month or two there. I had letters from him, once in a while; and when he felt the old country call him home, he got over his homesickness by seeing how happy and settled his daughters were. He died a happy man, without a penny of debt, surrounded by family. They brought his ashes back here, and scattered them on the sea.'

'A happy man indeed,' nodded the clerk. 'Why didn't I think of that?'

'People are not creative thinkers, generally. They look for no solutions beyond the obvious. Also, this man didn't insist on being stuck like a limpet in one place, with his family stuck on the rock beside him. He understood life is short, and if we have to endure some discomfort – in his case, inter-mittent homesickness – it cannot be for long, as life itself is so brief. What are forty years, or fifty, after all? Take it from me, they are gone in the blink of an eye.'

The fat man picked up the leg of mutton from the counter.

'I must go,' he said. 'I'm afraid your friend Makis's trade is very slow this morning. People are understandably reluc-tant to buy meat from a makeshift morgue. I persuaded him to let me see the corpse, and it is rather shocking. I suspect the wretched man went through a great deal of pain before he died. Have you seen him?'

Loskas was going through his pencil jar, trying to find a pen which worked. He scribbled the tip of a biro on a blank paying-in slip.

'No, I haven't,' he said. 'What's it to me, a stranger dead?'

'You didn't know him, then? I believe he's the man I saw at the army barracks at Kolona, yesterday. It's a sobering thought that perhaps even whilst we were together, talking and laughing, he was suffering down that well. Do you think he shouted? I'm sure he would have done, if he were able.'

'I suppose over the music and dancing, no one heard him.'

'Do you think not? Even those who passed the well when they were leaving? How did you get there and back yourself?'

'I had a ride in the coastguard launch.'

'Are they allowed to carry civilians, then, in the launch? Or was that another rule being justifiably bent?'

'It's another of those rules that makes no sense,' said Loskas, defensively. 'It's paid for with public money. And if we're all going to the same place, why shouldn't we travel together? The launch is fast. It takes much longer in a fishing boat.'

'Were you in a hurry, then, to leave?'

'No. Why should I have been?'

'I don't know. But I'm still wondering about that poor soul down the well, and why no one heard him shout.'

Loskas chose a different pen. When it didn't work, he put it back in the pot and tried a third.

'Obviously, because he wasn't there. Clearly, he fell in after we were all gone.'

'Do you think that's the obvious answer? It is *an* obvious answer, I grant you. But in fact, it isn't right. No, the reason no one heard him shout was because he was silenced before he was put in there.'

Loskas stopped scribbling and looked at the fat man.

'What do you mean, put in there?'

'Unless he put a stone in his own mouth to gag himself, and tipped himself over the rim with his hands by his sides, someone forced that unfortunate man down that well.'

'My God.' Loskas put a hand over his cheek. 'So old Vasso was right. There *was* someone there.'

'Tell me.'

'I didn't give it much credence at the time. He tends to paranoia. Since he was robbed, he jumps at every shadow. He went off to attend to a call of nature, and when he came back, he swore he'd seen someone on the hillside. Seems now he was probably right.'

'But if there was someone there, who could it have been?'

'How should I know? You must excuse me, I have to sort out this discrepancy.'

'Did you know the dead man, Loskas? Apart from yesterday, had you seen him before?'

'Yes, I had. He came in here for money, two, three days ago. Said he had an account. Of course I couldn't give him money without proof of identity. That's the rule.'

'I'm sure it is,' said the fat man. He turned to go; but as he did so, he caught sight of a piece of paper, wedged behind the leg of a chair. He picked up the paper, and studied it.

'You might want this,' he said. 'A withdrawal slip, in the sum of twenty-two thousand drachma. I suppose the wind caught it, and blew it off your counter. Will it help to balance your books?'

'Thank you,' said Loskas, as the fat man slid it to him under the glass partition. 'Yes, that will solve my problem very nicely.'

'So now you've balanced your books, I shall be doing the same with mine,' said the fat man. 'You and I are in the same business, in a manner of speaking. We're both balancers of books. We'll talk again, maybe. In the meantime, I wish you *kali mera*.'

Outside the town hall, a TV crew was conducting an interview. In a glare of white lights, the blonde reporter spoke into a microphone; the man beside her was nervous, sweating in a formal black suit.

The fat man collected his watermelon from the hawker and went to find Enrico, who was sitting at a waterside table, his chair a little too close to a woman of thirty or so, with bronzed skin and a white cotton dress.

When the fat man joined him, Enrico took his eyes away from her with reluctance.

'I'm in love,' he said, turning his head to gaze again at the woman. 'But she's hard-hearted. She won't even speak to me. Not a word, not a smile.'

'You should take that as a no, then,' said the fat man. 'And good for her. You're much too old for her.'

'Many men have happy relationships with women much younger than themselves,' said Enrico. 'With respect, *kyrie*, you yourself are one of them. And your father is noted for it.'

'My father is a special case,' said the fat man, 'and patently I have more charm than you can muster. Leave the poor creature alone. I think you're frightening her. I've decided that after siesta, it would be a good idea to return to Kolona. I've seen the corpse, and it throws up some interesting questions. But now, I think it's time for lunch.'

'Maybe we could eat here, *kyrie*?' suggested Enrico, glancing across at the woman. 'It's pleasant enough, here under the canopy.'

'I think better not.' The fat man rose from his seat, and waved away the *patron*, who was approaching the table. 'We'll lunch aboard *Aphrodite*. Then a siesta, and some thinking time. When it's cooler, I'll take a walk over the hills, and have another look at Kolona.'

Fourteen

The fat man found the Kolona road quite easily. Leading between houses set in generous gardens, it began as a concreted lane barely wide enough for a vehicle to pass between the badly parked cars and motorcycles. As he walked, the distances from one house to the next increased, until at a stream bed where bulrushes poked through the drying mud, he crossed a bridge of heavy boards, and came into open countryside.

In a field of thigh-high grasses, a farmer scythed rhythmically at the stalks; the fallen hay lay behind him, marking the track he had taken across the meadow, from west to east. The sky was alive with calling swallows feeding on insects flying up from the grass; dust and pollen drifted on the still, warm air.

The fat man stopped at the field gate, and noticing him, the farmer paused in his work, and looked towards him, shielding his eyes from the low sun. The fat man raised his hand, and called out, '*Kali spera!*'

With an excuse to take a break, the farmer began to amble towards the fat man, rubbing the sweat from his palms on the legs of his trousers, which were bound with string around his boot-tops to protect him against snake bites; his shirt was fastened with a single button to allow air to his torso whilst protecting him against biting insects.

'It's hot work, making hay,' he said as he reached the fat man, wiping his shirtsleeve over his brow. 'I'm getting too old for this business.'

'I agree it has been particularly hot today,' said the fat man. 'I thought an evening walk would be refreshing.'

'So where are you walking to?'

'To Kolona, if I get that far.'

The farmer pulled a face, to show his doubt at the wisdom of such a choice.

'There's nothing there but a bunch of dozy soldiers,' he said. 'But if you're going, take plenty of water. You wouldn't want to be drinking from their well.'

'Really? Why not?'

The farmer shook his head.

'A man died there, yesterday,' he said. 'Down the well. You wouldn't want to be drinking from a well a man's drowned in.'

'I've heard the story,' said the fat man. 'But I don't believe he drowned.'

'Drowned or not, it isn't healthy. They'll be asking the priest to bless it to remove the contagion.'

'No doubt,' said the fat man. 'But how did he come to be in there? It's not a common occurrence for a man to fall down a well.'

'Who says he fell down?' The farmer spat, aiming his spittle at a fly settled on a rock, and coming close enough to disturb it. 'As you say, that's not a common thing. So maybe he had a helping hand.'

A swallow swooped low over their heads, so low the farmer flinched.

'Whose helping hand?' asked the fat man.

'Like I say. There's no one over there but a bunch of soldiers.'

'You think one of them might be involved?'

'I'm saying nothing, for certain. But things happen on those camps. All living on top of each other, in this heat, things get said. Tempers fray. Young men have fiery tempers.'

'I hadn't heard the man down the well was a soldier.'

'Oh, he was no soldier. He was too old to be a soldier.'

'So what was he doing there, in this place where there are only soldiers?'

'I only know what I've heard,' said the farmer. 'I can't vouch for the truth of it. But what I was told was that he fell out with his shipmates, and they tipped him overboard. Which I don't find hard to believe. He caused trouble when he was here before.'

The fat man looked at him sharply.

'What do you mean, when he was here before?'

'It's a long time ago now. It was a bad business, that was.'

He looked off into the distance, as if remembering; then he seemed to come back to himself, and finding the scythe in his hands, recalled the job of mowing the meadow.

'I must get on,' he said. 'There's only a couple more hours of light.'

The fat man reached into the pocket of his linen jacket, and took out a small tin, decorated with Turkish writing and dainty pictures of desert camels.

'Do you take snuff?' he asked.

'Well, I'll be damned!' said the farmer. 'I reckon that's the brand I was using thirty years ago! Are they still making it, then?'

'Don't be fooled by the packaging,' said the fat man, prising off the lid. 'It's an old tin I've had for some time, and the snuff is from my father. He grows a little tobacco on some of his land, and himself prefers snuff to cigarettes. He claims it's healthier, though whether that's true or not, I couldn't say. I myself am not a regular user. I take it as a treat, now and then, though he takes it in large quantities, and swears it keeps him young. He claims it's a powerful aid to memory, but that may be invention on his part.' He offered the brown powder to the farmer. 'Try some.'

'You're a gentleman,' said the farmer. He took a generous pinch of snuff, and dropping it in a mound on the back of his thumb, blocked first his left nostril, then his right, and expertly snorted the powder. He sniffed loudly, several times. '*Panayeia*, that clears the head!' he said. 'That brightens the spirits!'

'My father's very proud of it.'

'Maybe I should start growing tobacco,' said the farmer. 'That's marvellous stuff, is that!'

'You were saying that the man who fell down the well had been to Mithros before.'

'No doubt of it, in my mind. Though it's fifteen or twenty years ago, easily.'

'Mithros is full of strangers every summer, and there have been thousands of visitors to the island in that time. Why do you think you remember him so particularly?'

'I remember him because he was one of them,' said the farmer. 'I never forget a face, and I'd certainly never forget that one. I saw him with the army captain in the harbour, and I knew him straight away. He was one of them that set on old Vasso. They hung around Mithros for a few days, maybe a week. They came and went without anybody much noticing them, and I suppose that's how they planned it. But I noticed them. I had cause to notice them.'

'Why was that?'

'I suppose you wouldn't offer me a pinch more of that snuff, friend?'

'Gladly,' said the fat man. 'Shall we sit down for a moment? It's too warm to be standing in the road.'

Kicking at the dried weeds to disturb any sleeping snakes, the farmer found a section of collapsing wall where the stones were relatively flat, and sat down with his scythe resting against his thigh. The fat man sat down next to him, and offered the open snuff-tin to the farmer, who helped himself to another generous pinch.

'Wonderful stuff!' he said, sniffing. 'Your father wants to go into business with that.'

'My father has plenty of irons in the fire already,' said the fat man. 'You were telling me why you particularly remembered the man down the well.'

'I had a chandler's shop at that time,' said the farmer, reflecting. 'He came in the shop two or three times in the space of a few days, alone or with his friends. The last time was to buy rope. Of course I didn't think anything of it, at the time. But afterwards I realised it was me who'd sold him the rope old Vasso was tied up with.'

'I've heard the story of that robbery,' said the fat man. 'It was an ugly business. But there was a hero in that hour, wasn't there? Socrates Rokos, who put himself in the way of their departing boat. Undoubtedly a remarkable act of bravery.'

The farmer eyed him with amusement.

'Do you think so?' he said. 'That's not how others see it. Ask yourself, friend, how did he come to be in the vicinity to give chase? And *why* did he give chase? Out of heroics? Out of a wish to avenge poor old Vasso?' He shook his head. 'No, young Socrates was in on it. It was him who led them to Vasso's door in the first place. Once they'd got what they wanted, in their rush to get away they forgot all about him. They were going to leave him behind, and unpaid – without his pieces of silver for his betrayal. He went after them because they hadn't given him his due. It's true he borrowed a boat, and raced after them to Kolona, and it's true he drove the boat in front of them to stop them. What did he care for that boat? It wasn't his. But he didn't know what he was dealing with. They were ruthless men, and they ran him down. Old Dinos who lent him the boat is still sore at the loss of his old tub. Every year that goes by, his lost boat gets more wonderful and more valuable.'

'Are you saying, then, that people don't think well of Socrates? His friends spoke very highly of him, yesterday.'

'Was his son there? Milto, they call him.'

'I know Milto. He wasn't there that I saw, no.'

'He wouldn't have been far away, at St Nikodemos's festival. They play the part for his benefit. They let him think his father was a hero. It was a hard thing, to be at the scene of his father's death.'

'He was there?'

'Oh yes, he was there. And that's tough for anyone, let alone a young boy, to see your Papa go down and not come up again.'

'Did they never find the body?'

'They never did. The water's deep there. No, he's down there still. Milto plays the fiddle for him, some nights. If you're going over there to Kolona, you might hear him. Gives you the chills, it does, that sad music playing in the dark.'

'The nature of that robbery puzzles me. It was an act of gross brutality, to burn a man's hands to get what they wanted. Who is it who would do that to such a good-hearted man?'

'If it had to do with Vasso, no doubt at all it had to do with money,' said the farmer.

'I'm told he's very generous with his money.'

'He's generous enough, but at a price. I borrowed from him, some years ago. Not much – I had a fire, and lost my hay crop and my tools, so he lent me enough to cover my losses set against the value of my land. And you know, somehow, I still haven't paid it back. Now, he's got enough that it doesn't bother him, and I let him have a gallon of oil from time to time, and when I make *raki*, he has a couple of bottles of that. But I suppose you might say this land's as much his as mine, so it's my good fortune he's never called in the loan.'

'Do you know where he made his money?' asked the fat man. 'Was it in coffee, or in cotton? Egypt, or the Congo?'

'Neither, that I've been told. Though for certain it was in Africa, somewhere. They say his house is full of souvenirs, all voodoo masks and shrunken heads. But I always thought his interests were in mining – copper, I seem to recall. Nigeria, or Namibia. Or was it Cameroon?'

'No one seems very certain,' said the fat man.

'If it interests you, maybe you should ask the man himself.'

'Maybe I should.' The fat man stood up from the wall. 'I must go on, or by the time I get to Kolona, it will be too dark to see the road. It has been a pleasure talking to you. And since you enjoyed my father's snuff so much, perhaps you would like to keep the tin?'

The farmer smiled broadly.

'I would.'

The fat man held it out to him.

'I must caution you to use it wisely, though,' he said. 'Three pinches a day is quite enough to use as a tonic. Any more, and you'll find its effects are detrimental. Too much can cause prolonged sleeplessness.'

'I won't waste it,' said the farmer. 'It's wonderful stuff, and I'll make it last.'

The fat man turned to go, but then turned back.

'Something I should ask you,' he said. 'If you were so sure the dead man was one of those who set on Vassilis, why did you not tell the police?'

The farmer spat again on the ground.

'Those fools?' he said. 'Why should I waste my time with them? After the robbery, I took myself down to the police station, and gave them a full description of the men. Not just this one who's come back, but all of them. Every day for two weeks I went down there, offering to identify anyone they might have brought in. But they never brought anyone in. I doubt they ever left the office. There was bad feeling between old Vasso and the police chief at that time. The chief of police had a brother, Thodoris. Thodoris called himself a builder, idle and incompetent though he was. When he was restoring his villa, old Vasso fired him from the site, and Thodoris and the chief didn't like it. They weren't interested in what I had to say then, and I see no reason any of them would be interested now.'

'But even so, perhaps it wasn't wise to keep such information to yourself.'

'Who says I did?' asked the farmer.

Within a kilometre, the road to Kolona deteriorated. Winter rains had exploited its weaknesses until its surface cracked, broke up and washed away, leaving only irregular sections of the cement intact, so now it was passable only by the most rugged of vehicles, or on foot. The fat man saw no traffic. For a while, the road followed the line and contours of the coast, before turning inland and climbing, taking a route which connected several farmsteads, where stocks of firewood were piled up in the yards and nets lay in the olive groves ready for the autumn's harvest. It led then back to the coast, above stretches of inaccessible rock and isolated beaches surrounded by scrub, until at the top of a steep descent, he glimpsed the campanile of St Nikodemos, and a stretch of sea which must be part of Kolona's bay.

His pace was surprisingly quick, and by the time he reached this point, there was still another hour of evening sunlight. He found himself a seat on a tree root, and in its shade took a small vacuum flask from his hold-all, poured water into the cup which was its cap, and drank it down. He looked down at his shoes, and frowned; they were grey with dust from the road. He put away the flask. Above him in the tree branches, cicadas called; an aeroplane was passing high overhead. From the direction of Kolona, there were voices, and laughter.

A light breeze was reaching him off the sea. He picked up his hold-all, and followed the road its remaining distance down to Kolona.

'*Kali spera sas.*'

The fat man had appeared unobserved and unheard on the guardhouse terrace, and the startled captain turned abruptly in his chair, jarring the table in front of him with his knee and spilling water from his glass. He glared at the fat man.

The fat man raised a hand in a conciliatory gesture.

'Please, forgive my trespassing, Captain,' he said. 'We met briefly yesterday. Hermes Diaktoros, of Athens. I wouldn't intrude on military property, under normal circumstances, but I need to refill my flask before I walk back to Mithros, and – it may sound foolish and squeamish, I realise – but I cannot bring myself to drink from the well where that poor man died. It seems both unseemly and insanitary. So I was wondering if you would be kind enough to ask one of your men if they would fill it for me from your supplies, and I'll get out of your way.'

The captain looked at him for a long moment, then gestured at the sea, where the four soldiers were playing volleyball. From midriff-deep water, Gounaris leaped energetically sideways for the ball, punching it to Skafidis before going under.

'My men, as you see, are doing their physical fitness training. Take a seat, if you like, until they're finished.'

'Thank you,' said the fat man, and did so.

They watched Lillis mis-hit the volleyball, sending it flying high over Skafidis's head. As Skafidis set off swimming after it, Gounaris and Kastellanos jeered and laughed at Lillis's lack of skill.

'Your men look so fit, don't they?' said the fat man. 'Absolutely in the prime of life, and all muscle where some of us are becoming rather soft.' He patted his belly, and shook his head. 'It might make older men like us wish to turn back the clock, if our wiser heads didn't know of youth's shortcomings. And they have such energy! You do well to keep them under control. That energy might easily become aggression if not properly channelled.'

'Hence the water sports,' said Captain Fanis. 'With luck, they'll come out of there exhausted, and be docile this evening. They like to play cards – there's not much else for them to do here, after all – but if they're lively and raring to go, the card games descend into shouting matches and even, occasionally, into fist fights.'

'Your job is a responsible one, a guiding hand between the apron-strings and the full autonomy of adulthood. I presume you practise your skills on your own children?'

'I have no children. I'm not married.'

'Really? You surprise me, greatly,' said the fat man. 'A handsome man such as yourself – I speak as would a father, or an uncle – must surely have had plenty of choice in that direction?'

The captain shook his head.

'I'm a confirmed bachelor,' he said. 'There was a woman, once, but she preferred someone else to me. And as for children – well . . .' He indicated the young men in the sea. 'To borrow your expression, I stand as father or uncle – or mother, often – to so many of them. They have no interest in soldiering, for the most part. Occasionally, when I get them, they're close to middle age, having dodged the National Service draft for many years, and with them, it's hard to build a rapport. They resent being here, they resent me and they resent my orders. But most are like these boys here, wet behind the ears and never been away from home. I do what I can with them, which in this place is limited to instilling a little self-discipline, and teaching them the rudiments of teamwork. Then I send them on their way. The problem I have now is that I am myself not far off being middle-aged, and it's hard to command respect when even the least of them can outrun and outswim me, or in fact beat me hollow at almost anything they care to try. My strategy up to now has been not to compete with them. I stay on the sidelines, as I am doing now. And I can still outshoot most of them, except those who've grown up with a hunting rifle in their hands. But the truth is, my days in this outpost are numbered. The top dog in this pack is only top dog as long as he can beat all challengers, and I rely too much these days on my wits. I've an old dog's wiliness, but this job needs a young dog's strength, and I don't have that. That's not what the army's about. These lads aren't far off being my last recruits.'

'So what will you do?'

'I'm crossing my fingers for a desk job somewhere. It won't be here. That much is certain.'

'But don't you have family, here in Mithros?'

The captain looked down the beach. The approaching dusk made it difficult to make out the young men. One of them leaped, a silhouette, from the water, and slammed the ball down hard on to its surface, spraying the others and drawing shouts of laughing protest.

'Gounaris,' said the captain. 'He gets the best of the others, every time. He's a natural soldier, but his interests lie in other directions. He says he wants to be an architect.'

'An admirable ambition,' said the fat man. 'Were you not saying yesterday that Gounaris lost something of value to that poor fellow who died?'

'He lost a chain to him, yes,' said the captain, guardedly. 'Why do you ask?'

The fat man smiled.

'You are protective of your brood, Captain, and suspicious of my question, so perhaps I should explain. I am, by profession, an investigator.'

'A policeman?'

The fat man laughed.

'No,' he said. 'There is no police force in the land which would employ me. I work for a higher authority. Their interests are wide-ranging, and they would want me to take an interest in that man's death. His name and origins seem to be in doubt, and there is no one, at present at least, who seems to mourn him. But I myself saw him fit and healthy yesterday – at least I believe I did so, though there was some distance between us – and now he's died a bizarre and gruesome death. It is in my nature and my remit to look into the facts of the matter, and see if I can ascertain what has happened here.'

'What does that have to do with Gounaris?'

'To be honest, I don't know. Maybe nothing. But when I saw the corpse this morning, it wore no chain. Now, it is my understanding you and your men found the body. If you tell me he was wearing the chain when you pulled him from the well, and that you took the chain from the corpse and returned it to Gounaris, then the mystery is solved.'

The captain shook his head.

'He wasn't wearing any chain,' he said.

'And did you check the body at all? Search the pockets, anything like that?'

'No, I didn't. It didn't occur to me to do so. What for, after all? I knew who he was.'

'Or who he said he was.'

'Or who he said he was, yes. I expected Spiros to do all that. Spiros Tavoularis, the coastguard officer.'

'Then I'm sure he will have done. But just to be certain on the point – you haven't found the chain in any drawer, or anywhere in the room where this man slept?'

'He left nothing in that room. He had nothing to leave.'

'Except Gounaris's chain.'

'Except for that, I suppose.'

'What did he call himself, by the way?'

'He called himself Manolis, Manolis Chiotis. I have to say I was never sure that was his name. Such a famous name – it seemed to me he might have grasped it out of the air. But he came with nothing but a pair of shorts he was wearing when they threw him overboard.'

'Hmm.' The fat man became thoughtful. 'Tell me about that incident.'

'There's little enough to tell. The boat he was on put in here, the men aboard played cards. They argued, the argument escalated, and his shipmates dropped him in the sea. I think he fully expected them to come back for him, but they never did.'

'Not so far, at least.'

'I suppose someone will come for his body,' said the captain. 'For his sake, I hope that they do. He should be taken home and buried with family. No doubt the coastguard have put the word out, and a description.'

'No doubt they have. I wonder if I might ask you whether it has struck you as in any way unusual that it should be here, particularly, that this drama has played out.'

Again, the captain looked at him.

'What do you mean?'

'Only that such a quiet place as this should attract such drama, not once, but twice.'

'Twice?'

'Did not a man drown here, some years ago, in the aftermath of a robbery – a robbery which was itself highly unusual for this part of the world?'

The captain considered.

'You mean Socrates,' he said. He looked out across the blue water where the young men laughed and shouted, and a shadow crossed his face. 'He's still down there, somewhere. I don't like to think of it.'

'Did you know him?'

'Yes, I knew him. He and I were close contemporaries. He was the same age as my brother.'

'What did you think of him?'

The captain gave an apologetic smile.

'That's difficult for me to answer,' he said. 'His memory should be respected.'

'Please, be truthful with me, Captain,' said the fat man. 'There's at least one connection between Socrates and Manolis: they both died in this place. I might go further, and point out that not only did they both die here, they both died at the hands of others.'

The captain's face showed doubt.

'Really? Why do you say that about Manolis?'

'Do you really believe he fell down that well all by himself?' asked the fat man. 'Tell me, then. In all the time you've been sending soldiers to that well for water, have any of them ever fallen down it? Or even come close?'

'No. No, they haven't.'

'There is something else too, which I will tell you in confidence, and only to persuade you of the circumstances of Manolis's death. Then I hope you will be honest with me about Socrates. When I heard about Manolis's death, what troubled me about it more than anything was why no one had heard him shouting. I'm afraid he must have taken some hours to die – at least two, and probably more. There were a good number of people around that day – far more than is usual, here at Kolona – and yet nobody heard him cry for help. I don't believe there's any question he would have shouted for help if he were able. When I looked at the body, I saw no sign of any blow to the head which would have rendered him unconscious. And so I drew the inevitable conclusion – something stopped him shouting. When I looked inside his mouth, the object responsible was still there – a pebble, large enough to hold his tongue down, and too large to swallow.'

The captain seemed shocked.

'That's horrible,' he said. 'Horrible, and . . .'

'Horrible, and ingenious, I would say,' said the fat man. 'You didn't notice it when you got him out?'

The captain shook his head.

'I didn't look too closely at him,' he said. 'He wasn't pretty to look at, as you no doubt know.'

'How did you get him out?'

'We lowered Lillis down by his legs, and he tied a rope around the feet. Even then, it wasn't easy. The poor bastard was well wedged in there.'

'With his arms by his sides.'

'Yes, they were. How did you know that?'

'Easily, from the abrasions on his upper arms. Yet anyone falling accidently, puts their hands out to save themselves, do they not?'

The captain nodded, thoughtfully.

'So, if you understand why I say his death was no accident, will you now give me your opinion of Socrates?'

'I didn't like him,' said the captain. 'He was cocky, full of himself. But I wouldn't wish that death on anyone.'

'Who do you mean?' asked the fat man, with a half-smile. 'Socrates, or Manolis?'

The captain shrugged.

'In truth, either, or both. You think there's definitely some connection between them, then?'

'I'm almost certain of it.'

The light was almost gone, and the young men were tiring of their game. They left the water laughing and dripping; Lillis knocked the ball out of Skafidis's hands and back into the water, and Skafidis, complaining, waded in to fetch it. Their feet were hardened against the beach stones, and they walked easily up the beach towards the captain and the fat man.

'There was another thing,' said the fat man, as they

approached. 'When you went up into the hills looking for the stranger Vassilis Eliadis saw, did you find anything?'

The captain shook his head.

'Nothing. We searched for a good half-hour, but it was a hopeless task from the first. There're a thousand places a man might easily hide himself up there, amongst the scrub. We might pass within feet of someone, and if he kept still, we'd never spot him.'

'Forgive me for saying this, but half an hour to search a hillside doesn't seem very long.'

'There were five of us. We covered plenty of ground. But it was hot, and there was a party going on down here. The boys don't get much in the way of entertainment. It seemed unnecessary to keep them occupied up there for longer.'

The fat man looked at him closely.

'Is it possible,' he said, 'that you never expected to find anything?'

'I have every respect for old Vasso,' said the captain, carefully. 'But he jumps at every shadow. Out of respect for him, we went to see what we could see. But in truth, I didn't expect to find anything, no.'

The soldiers were drawing close, exuberant and heckling, heads high with unselfconscious arrogance.

'Which one is Private Gounaris?' asked the fat man. 'I wonder if I might speak to him for just a moment, before I leave you in peace?'

'That's up to him,' said the captain, and called out to the soldiers, 'You played like a bunch of women! Lillis, fire up the generator. Skafidis, take our guest's flask and put fresh water in it. Gounaris, have a seat. This gentleman wants to talk to you.'

Gounaris pulled a chair up to the table. Kastellanos headed to the bunkhouse.

'We've been talking about Manolis,' said the captain.

'A world-class prick,' said Gounaris. 'A first-class *malaka*.' With his fist, he made a crude gesture to match the insult.

'I understand you two had a falling out,' said the fat man. 'Can you tell me about that?'

Seawater dripped on to the terrace from Gounaris's shorts. Kastellanos came from the bunkhouse with shampoo and a towel, and stopped to listen to what was being said.

'We played cards,' said Gounaris. 'He cheated.'

'Do you mean he won?'

Gounaris sneered.

'No one has that kind of luck without cheating. He cheated when he was on that boat and he cheated when he played here with us. We were stupid to let him sit down to our game in the first place. We should have dumped him on the coast-guard and left him there.'

'I hope you're not questioning my judgement, Gounaris,' said the captain. 'What I agreed with the coastguard has nothing to do with you.'

'I am certainly not questioning your judgement,' said the fat man, 'but as it turns out, that would have been in his own best interests. Alas for him, events have played out as they have. The man is dead, and whoever – or whatever – he was, he deserves the truth around the circumstances of his death to be known. Do any of you remember anything unusual about his time here?'

Skafidis returned with the fat man's flask, and placed it on the table. In its shed, the generator was fired, and Skafidis threw the power switch, lighting the string of dim bulbs along the terrace.

'There was someone in the hills with a rifle,' said Kastellanos. 'The old man spotted him.'

'We talked about that,' said the captain. 'It was a wild goose chase.'

'But there was someone here too,' said Kastellanos. 'I heard someone moving about whilst I was on watch.'

'That's right,' said the captain. 'The incident you failed to record in the book.'

'What did you hear, exactly?' asked the fat man.

'There was music. Sometimes there is. Weird music, really sad. But it was after that.'

'When was this?'

'Two nights ago, three. At what time, I don't know. It's so dark, once the generator's off.'

'And what did you do about this noise?'

'Nothing.'

'Why not?'

'It might have been goats, or rats, or anything. I would've looked a real fool, waking everybody up for a goat.'

'I heard something too,' said Skafidis. He looked doubtfully at the captain. 'I didn't say anything. I thought it was . . .'

'More goats?' asked the captain. '*Theé mou!* What is the point of putting any of you on watch? They'll slaughter us in our beds! You're supposed to be soldiers, alert and responsive!'

'Sorry, Captain,' said Skafidis.

'And when were you on watch?' asked the fat man.

'Two nights ago.'

'So the night before Manolis died?'

'It would have been, yes.'

Gounaris was watching his feet.

'There seems to be a bit of a mystery regarding the object that Manolis took off you in that card game,' the fat man said to him. 'What was it, a chain?'

'A gold chain,' said Gounaris. 'My mother bought it for me.'

'You were careless, then, to gamble with it,' said the fat man. He held up the little finger of his right hand to show a ring with the glint of old gold – a plain band set with an unusual coin, whose visible face was stamped with a rising sun. 'This ring was a gift from my own mother, and whilst I confess to having gambled with it in the past, I have only done so when I have had complete faith it would ultimately come back to me. You, on the other hand, accepted an element of risk, and you lost. That is unfortunate, of course. But what concerns me now, Private, is that your chain appears to be missing. It isn't with the body, or in the room your visitor occupied, whilst he was here. In short, it is nowhere to be found.'

'Maybe it fell down the well,' said Gounaris.

'Maybe it did,' said the fat man. 'And under different circumstances, we might let it go at that. Except that, as I have explained to your captain, I believe we are dealing here with the cruel killing of a man, and as such, we must leave no stone unturned.'

'Killing?' asked Kastellanos. 'He was a *malaka*, we all know that, but who the hell would kill him?'

'Killers always have a motive, and in a small place like Mithros, motives are easy to run to ground. Aren't they, Private?' He looked directly at Gounaris. 'It might happen in a moment, I realise; a flash of temper, an ego bruised, and pouf! – a life is over. Is that how it was, soldier?'

But Gounaris smiled.

'It wasn't me,' he said. 'I had no motive.'

'Can you prove that?'

'As a matter of fact, I can.' He left them for the bunkhouse, and returned a minute later, holding out his gold chain on his open palm.

'Where the hell did you get that?' asked the captain.

Gounaris punched Skafidis in the upper arm.

'Frightened you half to death, didn't I?' he asked. 'I fell over somebody's boots in the dark. I knew you'd have heard me. If you'd challenged me, I'd have come clean. *Poustis*.' He turned to the captain. 'He stole it from me, I pinched it back. Took it while he was sleeping.'

The fat man frowned.

'And did he know you'd taken it back?'

'He was mad,' said Gounaris. 'I passed him going into the showers yesterday morning. He knew I'd got it. He called me a thieving little bastard. That's all.'

'That would explain his filthy mood,' said the captain. 'You'd taken back his ticket out of here.'

'I suppose I had.'

'But if you hadn't, he might have got out of here, and be alive now,' said the fat man.

As the conscripts left them, the fat man rose to go.

'Thank you for your hospitality,' he said. 'Might I return the favour, and invite you to dine with me tomorrow evening? My yacht – the *Aphrodite* – is moored in the harbour. You might enjoy a night away from your charges, and my man is a passable cook. And fingers crossed the Turks won't invade in your absence.'

'It's kind of you,' said the captain. 'Unfortunately, we have no spare fuel to make non-essential trips to the harbour.'

'I'll be happy to have someone pick you up from here. Shall we say about seven, seven thirty?'

'Before you go,' said the captain, 'we seem to have solved the mystery of Skafidis's night visitor. But we still have Kastellanos's report, and the rifleman old Vasso saw. What do you make of both those?'

'I don't know yet,' said the fat man, thoughtfully. 'There are still plenty of loose ends, I have to agree. Your soldiers seem to lack confidence, individually, and perhaps it would be wise to exercise caution, for a while. So might I suggest you put two of them on overnight watch together, until we've answers to all our questions?'

On the road out of the camp, at the brow of the hill the fat man paused, and listened. The gloom of dusk had changed almost to night. Down on the camp, a card game had begun, and the voices of the soldiers carried loud through the still air.

But there was nothing else to hear: certainly no music, and no evidence of anyone who might disturb the soldiers' peaceful night.

Back in the harbour, the bars were busy. Finding no empty tables outside, the fat man took a stool at the counter of a place where the bartender kept the music low, and a television on the wall was tuned in to the news. In a corner, an Italian couple exchanged long kisses.

'What'll you have?' asked the bartender. He was polishing glasses with a damp cloth; he kept one eye on the television.

The fat man asked for a beer. The bartender took a mug from the freezer, and filled it from the pump.

'We're going to be on, in a minute,' he said, nodding towards the television. 'There was a news team in Mithros today.'

'I saw them,' said the fat man. He sipped at his chilled beer. 'What's the story?'

But before the bartender could answer, a shot of Mithros's harbour filled the screen.

The bartender ran to the television, and turned up the volume. A voiceover talked about the island, and gave the background of its famous missing bull. The shot cut to the blonde reporter, standing outside the town hall with the man in the black suit.

'And now the mystery deepens further,' she said, smiling broadly, 'with *another* theft – that of the only true replica of the famous bull, stolen two nights ago from Mithros's museum. Whilst the copy has nothing like the value of the original, officials here are troubled by suggestions unscrupulous thieves intend to pass the copy off as the genuine article, and that it will find its way to the lucrative black market in antiquities. Mr Mayor . . .'

She turned to the man in the suit. He gave an uneasy smile, and curt answers to her questions about the thief's motives, and insisted on the rarity of crime on the island. There were clips of local people, most ignorant of any replica, and all amused at the idea of its theft. Finally, the reporter stood face to face with Uncle Vasso, who seemed relaxed before the camera, and dapper in his seersucker and brogues.

'*Kyrie* Eliadis,' said the reporter, 'it was you who paid for the reproduction of the bull. People are saying history is repeating itself, but what do you make of its disappearance?'

'It's not surprising to me someone would steal it,' said Uncle Vasso. 'The bull is a wonderful object, and whilst the copy can never have the original's magic, it does capture much of its beauty. It's a work of art in itself.'

'And are the people anxious to see the bull returned?'

'Of course,' said Uncle Vasso, spreading his hands to emphasise his words; his kid gloves seemed an oddity in the summer's heat. 'But in our hearts, it isn't the replica we want to see back in Mithros. Every day, we hope for news of the original. And who knows, but that the publicity of this second theft might be the jolt we need to bring our original home.'

'Let's hope so,' smiled the reporter, turning away from Uncle Vasso to face the camera. 'But in the meantime, Mithros's puzzle grows ever more baffling. Now this little island is missing not one bull, but two.'

Fifteen

The stable was no more than a tin-roofed shack, with boards nailed over its glassless window, and a stone floor scattered with droppings and pine-wood shavings. Tethered by a head-collar, the mule twitched its ears to deter the horseflies, and dipped into a bucket holding a few handfuls of oats whose pale dust clung to its muzzle as it chewed.

Milto picked up a broom whose remaining bristles were worn and bent, and swept the night's droppings on to a shovel. Leaning the broom back in the corner with the rake and the pitchfork, he carried the loaded shovel outside.

At the foot of the wall, there were dark rounds of rat holes amongst the thistle roots. Under the lean-to, fragrant new hay was piled high; an oil-barrel of tepid, soupy water was alive with the larvae of mosquitoes. Around the back, over the ammonia-stinking mass of the manure heap, crawled hundreds of flies, which surged up, droning, when he threw the fresh droppings amongst them and thrust the shovel-blade in deep to stand it upright.

Rubbing a few specks of shavings from his hands, he looked across his neighbours' properties – across the chicken runs and green-leaved vines, the goat-pens and the citrus orchards and the house-roofs – down to the sea. A housewife was pegging the day's first washing on a line; her son hoed a row of aubergines. Inside the stable, the mule stamped, and whinnied. Milto took another moment to admire the sea and the early sun laying gold on the placid blues, but the mule had become restless, and hearing its bucket kicked and clattering over, he went back inside the stable.

The fat man was standing by the mule, stroking the polished hair on its neck, speaking soothing words to ease the animal's nervousness. The muscles in its legs and back quivered with tension; its ears were back and its head was high, as if it would break free of the rope which tied it if it could, and gallop away. The fat man's back was to the door, but Milto knew him, by his stature and by his white shoes.

'What are you doing here?'

The fat man turned, and smiled. He was clear-eyed, as if he had enjoyed long and rejuvenating sleep, and had recently shaved; even over the stable's equine smell, the scent of his cologne – the vetivier, and immortelle – was pleasing, and somehow made Milto regret the stubble on his face, and his decision to put on yesterday's unwashed clothes.

As best it could, the mule also turned its head; Milto caught the edge of fear in its eyes. He crossed to its other side, placing his hands protectively on the animal's nose, and under its neck.

'Milto, *kali mera*,' said the fat man, still stroking the mule's neck. 'Your neighbour told me where I'd find you. I am an early riser myself, so I thought that we could talk before I lost you to the fields. You do remember me, I hope?'

'I remember you,' said Milto. He dug in his trouser pocket, and found a slice of carrot which he held out on his palm, but the mule was too anxious to take it.

'Is that your rifle, by the way?' said the fat man, looking up at the case hanging on the wall.

'It was my father's.'

'Are you a good shot?'

'I've never fired it.'

'I shall assume, then, that you are not. You'll be wondering, no doubt, why I want to speak to you, and I shall be only too pleased to satisfy your curiosity. Do you think we might step outside? I should like a cigarette, and these shavings present a fire risk. Besides, your beast has taken a dislike to me. I think my arrival startled it. The animal would be far happier with me on the other side of the door.'

'He doesn't much care for strangers.'

'So it would seem. I ask a few minutes of your time, that is all.'

'As long as it's quick,' said Milto. He stroked one of the mule's ears, and led the way outside. 'Like you, I prefer to travel before the day gets hot, and the fields I'm working today are a good distance.'

'It's fortunate I came early, then, or I should have spent half my day tramping the paths and byways of this island trying to find you.'

The fat man brought out his cigarettes and offered them to Milto, who took one. The fat man took one for himself, and lit them both with his gold lighter.

'I don't understand,' said Milto. 'Why would you go to so much trouble looking for me?' A thought seemed to strike him. 'You're not from the military, are you?'

The fat man laughed.

'No, I'm not from the military. Why? Did you dodge the draft?'

'I was exempt,' said Milto. 'There was only me to care for Mama. But Captain Fanis has designs on me. He seems to think a spell in uniform would do me good.'

'Well, that's nothing to do with me. I'm here on the

business of a higher authority than the military. I'm investigating a case of murder.'

'Murder? Who's been murdered?' asked Milto.

'That, I have yet to find out. He gave his name, I'm told, as Manolis Chiotis. Whether that was his real name, is uncertain. Possibly – even probably – he chose that name as a pseudonym to protect himself when he discovered that Fate had returned him to Mithros.'

'Not a local man, then,' said Milto. 'I thought for a moment it might be someone I knew. I thought you meant old Katzikis. They buried him a few days ago. I don't know anyone else recently dead.'

The fat man studied him.

'No, I don't think you did know him,' he said. 'But I think your father did.'

'Is that right?' Milto drew again on his cigarette. 'These aren't bad,' he said. 'I might get a packet.'

'You won't find them easy to track down,' said the fat man. 'As for your father, little birds have told me something about him. I'm a talkative man by nature, and people often become talkative around me. People chatter away, and within their chatter are kernels of information which interest me. More than one person has suggested to me that this so-called Manolis was acquainted with your father. Or let me speak plainly – they say that this Manolis played a part in your father's death.'

Milto took a last draw on his smoked-down cigarette, and dropped the stub to the ground.

'You know nothing about my father,' he said, coldly. 'You're talking out your backside. And I have work to do.'

He took a step away; but the fat man caught his arm, and even though his touch felt light, Milto found himself unable to shake the grip which held him in place.

'I think you should hear me out,' said the fat man. 'I have plenty to say which is relevant to you, and to your father. Or I should say, more accurately, that I have plenty of questions, and you will do yourself a great service if you answer them honestly. I value the truth very highly. Conversely, where I am concerned, matters tend to go badly with those who offer me half-truths and lies. I hope you understand me, Milto.'

The fat man released Milto's arm. Milto remained where he was.

'Who are you?' he asked.

'You have my name already, as I have yours. Your father's name was, I'm told, Socrates. Do you remember him, Milto? I think you were probably still quite young when he was taken.'

'I've no wish to talk to you about him. No wish, and no time. I have to attend to the mule.'

'You're a lover of animals, I can see that. The mule's well-being is important to you, isn't it?'

'It is,' said Milto. 'You can rely on animals. They ask nothing of you, and give plenty back.'

'I agree with you wholeheartedly,' said the fat man. 'And I have come across some truly remarkable animals in my time. None more so than a mule which belonged to a woman in the Peloponnese, many years ago now, more years than I care to remember. She had bought it as a foal from a travelling circus. Have you had yours from a young age? Forgive me, I don't know his name.'

'I call him Allegro,' said Milto. 'And yes, I had him as a youngster. As soon as he was weaned off his mother's milk, he came to me.'

'And he's a credit to you. This woman also lavished a great deal of care on her mule. I saw him for myself, on one occasion. In fact I made a detour especially to see him. He had become quite famous. He was a beautiful animal, a grey similar to yours, but grey which verged towards silver, and as this silver mule grew, he began to display an intriguing gift, in that he seemed to be able to tell the fortunes of people around him. It began with a single incident, when the mule touched his nose to the belly of a woman who had been trying for some time to become pregnant. Only the following day, a pregnancy was confirmed. A few days later, the beast refused to pass the house of a man with a boil on his back; he refused for so long, his mistress had to take him home by another road. Lo and behold, within a few days, the boil burst and became infected and the man died of blood poisoning. After that, the mule seemed to be able to predict all kinds of things. I took an interest when it was reported in a newspaper that he had predicted the death of a young girl only recently married, who when she heard the prediction, took straight to her bed, and was dead within a month. People travelled great distances to consult the mule. He made his owner a wealthy woman.'

'But how can a mule make predictions?'

The fat man smiled.

'Very simply. Like the ancient oracles, the questioner approached the shrine – in that case, a stable not unlike this one – paid his owner her fee, and she would go inside the stable, consult with the mule, and emerge with the questioner's answer. The answers were, of course, as double-edged as any which came out of Delphi. But what was surprising was, how many of the mule's predictions came true. Those who believed they'd been told they'd recover from illness, recovered; those who thought they'd heard a bad prognosis, grew worse. So there, you see, was an intriguing case of people's fate apparently being announced by a dumb animal. Of course, the woman was behind it all; she was as clever and manipulative as anyone I've ever met. The young bride who died had married a youth whom she had earmarked for her own daughter; indeed, her daughter married the youth only a year afterwards. I admired her ingenuity, and how she had mastered control of a whole community through an allegedly magical beast. The magic was in her own talent in turning him into a source of income. She understood human nature; she read people's strengths and weaknesses, and exploited their gullibility and superstition. But there was no magic in the mule. He was a perfectly normal animal, just like your Allegro. You're devoted to him, I know, and no doubt he is to you, in his own way, as far as a beast may show devotion. I don't doubt it would grieve him if he had the power to understand how he has betrayed you.'

'Betrayed me? What do you mean?'

'I was there, the day Manolis – as we must call him – was murdered. I was there the day he was forced down that well. You were there, too.'

'What of it? Many people were there.'

'Your friends seemed uncertain whether you were there or not. One said you were, another that you weren't. And I saw those many people, but I didn't see you. I only saw Allegro, poor Allegro standing in the sun. He wasn't standing in full sun when you left him, though, was he? You would never leave your animal baking in the sun. When you left him, he was in the shade of the tree he was tied to. But you were gone so long, on whatever errand you were on, that the shade deserted him. Now, what might you have been engaged in to keep you away from him for so long? And how long for the sun to move and leave him without shade? An hour, two hours? So what were you doing, Milto, that stopped you going back to him? You weren't in the church, nor in its environs. I venture to suggest you wouldn't have been more

238

than half a mile away, because no man walks a greater distance than that in the heat when he's got the services of a beast he can call on. No, you were somewhere close by, all that time. The question is, though, where were you?'

'What's that to you?'

'What it is to me, is this. On that day, the alarm was raised about a man on the hillside behind the old village. Someone, as I've heard, with a gun, probably a rifle. It seems to me you're the only one of the assembled party who was absent from the group for long enough to climb up into the hills. I think you were tracking Manolis down. I think whilst the rest of us were distracted, you made your way through the hills round the back of the army camp, marched him to the well at gunpoint and forced him down it. You have a rifle in the stable there. Was that the weapon you used?'

'Many men here own guns! You're mad! If I were going to kill him, why wouldn't I just shoot him?'

'Because the bullet might be traced to your gun. Because if you'd shot him where he stood, people would have come running and he'd have been found much sooner, before you'd had time to drift away and blend back in with the crowd. Because a clean and quick death was not what you wanted for him. And I do wonder whether his death was your intention at all. Still, whether it was or not, that is how it ended up. So, that's what I'm going to tell the police: that you are responsible for Manolis's shocking death, and that it was you who was seen up in the hills, leaving or rejoining the party and thinking your absence had never been noticed. You are quite right, of course – there are many men on this island who own guns. But they lack something that you have. You have a motive for murder.'

'What motive?'

'Clearly, revenge for your father's death.'

239

Milto hung his head; then he looked up, and met the fat man's eyes.

'I believe you mean well,' he said, 'but you have me very wrong, if you think I'm capable of any of it. I told you the truth. I've never fired that rifle in there. I've never even taken it down off the wall.' He sighed a sigh from his very depths, and closed his eyes. 'I'll tell you what I know, for my conscience's sake. God knows I haven't slept these last two nights. I was involved in that man's death, but not knowingly. I was stupid, and was duped into it. I will tell you, even though I'll be made to suffer for it. That much I know.'

'If you are honest with me, I shall ensure you won't suffer for it,' said the fat man. 'Here, sit down a while.' He took a seat on a chopping block indented with the marks of an axe.

Milto removed several empty feed-sacks from an orange-crate, and sat down too.

'Where shall we start?' he asked.

'My preference is always for the beginning,' said the fat man. 'Which I think, in this case, may be some years ago. I think all this began with your father. What do you remember of him?'

'Enough,' said Milto. 'I was nine when he died. Like all boys at that age, I worshipped the ground he walked on. I saw him die, and that was hard. It haunts me still. And they told me what a hero he'd been, how he'd died trying to stop those bad men from getting away. So at first I put him on a hero's pedestal. But I didn't suffer under that illusion very long. The truth of what he'd been doing that night was spelled out to me by the kids I hung around with. They heard what they heard at home; no one bothered to go quiet when they walked in the room, which is how it was at our house. They told me what he'd done, and I put that together with our situation, which wasn't good. My mother was a widow with me to care for, and we had it hard. My father was no hero. I've looked and looked, and I can't find much good in him at all. But he was my father, and so I love and respect his memory.

'I'm not a man who believes in God. No just God would have let a young boy see what I saw that day, my own father taken down to the depths. But I believe we have a soul. My mother used to pay for Masses for him, and have his soul prayed for by the priests. I don't believe that did him any good, but it comforted her. My belief has always been, that his wickedness has trapped him here below, that he's a poor and lonely soul, trapped in that water where he drowned. I've told no one else this. You may think it foolish, but when I can, I go there to Kolona where he died, and I play for him. I play my violin, in the hopes that somehow he can hear me, and take some comfort himself in knowing he's loved and missed, in spite of what he was. And I've taken his ending as a warning in my own life. He died a violent death because of his bad intentions. So I try to make sure everything I do harms no one and nothing, neither man nor beast. That's my penance for him; and some part of me – there's no logic in it, so don't look for any – believes that if I try to be a good man, in every way, maybe I can redeem him. Free him. That's what I'm trying to do. I'm trying to make up for the bad he did, by being a better man myself.'

'There's a word for your beliefs,' said the fat man. 'It's a mindset at the heart of the Hindu's religion. They call it "karma".'

'Karma? I call it living the best life I can. Giving offence to no one, working hard, bringing pleasure if I can, through my music. Taking care of creatures less able to look after themselves. We've a responsibility to them. If we're superior beings, we should act so, but it's my view animals are superior to us in every way. I've been a vegetarian for many years. The people here don't understand that. They think animals are here to serve our purposes, and nothing else – that we can use them and throw away their bones, and they mean nothing. I don't see it that way.'

'I understand your view,' said the fat man, 'and now I see you had no illusions about your father. But I think the rest of Mithros thinks you're still under the spell of a myth they created especially for you.'

'Some of them worked hard to create that myth. They did it to protect me; I know that. They thought it was for my good. Their motives were good, and so I let them think that I believe.'

'So what happened on the name day at Kolona?'

'I was approached by someone, before that day, to do a task.'

'What task?'

'My job was to lure the man calling himself Manolis to the well.'

'And you agreed to do it?'

'Yes, I did. I was given a good reason. What I took to be a valid reason.'

'And did that reason have anything to do with avenging your father's death?'

'It had nothing to do with it at all. I never wanted to avenge my father's death. I wanted to make reparation for him, and for the wrong he did. All my life has been about that.'

'But even so, you lured him there to meet the man who killed him. There's blood on your hands then anyway, isn't there?'

Vehemently, Milto shook his head.

'There was nothing I could do! He had his gun! If I tell you who it was, you'd understand.'

'Then tell me.'

And Milto told.

In its first hour of opening, the museum had no visitors. Professor Philipas sat at his desk, working with a wet toothbrush at the clay-clogged surface of a misshapen coin. From time to time, he stopped scrubbing, and peered at the coin's face, where a figure brandishing a hammer and a horn was beginning to appear.

'Philipas.'

She was smiling in the doorway; the hem of her dress was wet, her hair was untidy and uncombed.

The professor looked up from his cleaning.

'Olympia.'

He left his chair, and went to her. The kiss he gave her was uncertain; when he tried to prolong it, she pushed him away.

'Don't,' she said. 'I only have a minute. I can't leave her too long.'

He grasped her hand.

'Don't go,' he said. 'Stay a while.'

She pulled her hand free.

'I can't,' she said. 'I only came to ask your opinion. She gave me something, and I think I should give it back.' She opened a jewellery box of burgundy leather. The brooch inside was crafted in gold, an oval of small pearls surrounding one much larger. 'It looks old to me. What do you think?'

He took the brooch from her, and held it up to the light.

'It's beautiful,' he said. 'I think they're natural pearls. If so, it'd be worth something. I could get it valued for you, if you like.'

'If it's valuable, it should stay with the family.'

'And where is the family now? It was a gift to you. Take it.'

'I'll keep it for now,' she said. 'But if they ask for it, I'll give it back.'

He touched her hair.

'Can I phone you later?'

'You shouldn't. And it's difficult. She gets so restless, and she needs to know I'm there. She doesn't have much time left.'

'Please. I won't keep you long, I promise.'

'All right,' she said. 'But just for a few minutes, no longer.'

Sixteen

A solitary boy kicked a part-deflated football against the wall of the telephone company offices. When he saw the fat man watching, he bent to pick up his ball and walk away.

'Just a minute, son,' called out the fat man. The boy looked at him. 'How would you like to earn yourself some money?'

The boy shrugged, and approached, and the fat man gave him his instructions.

Whilst the boy was gone, the fat man lit a cigarette, and smoked it with enjoyment in the shade of an overhanging balcony. In the harbour centre, a boat had broken down and was slowly drifting to the south side, whilst on land, interested but ill-informed parties gathered to offer comment and advice. A fisherman jumped into a dinghy and rowed out to offer a tow-rope, whilst others jeered at him, decrying his ability to haul the boat with only the strength of his arms.

The fat man was still enjoying the show when the boy tugged at his sleeve.

'I found them,' he said. 'They're on their way.'

'Thank you,' said the fat man. 'You've done a good job.'

He gave the boy a thousand-drachma note.

* * *

In the coastguard's office, Spiros Tavoularis was inspecting the trap he'd set up the previous day: a plastic bottle sliced in two below its sloping shoulders, and the cut-off top inverted in the bottle's body. The bait was a piece of tinned mackerel, and in the heat the fish was singing its siren call. Having crawled in, and now unable to find the small opening to escape, five wasps and two vicious red and yellow hornets buzzed furiously in the bottle, attacking both each other and the stinking mackerel, which between them they had almost consumed as their final meal.

'I suppose what you do now is to fill the bottle with water, and drown your prisoners.'

Startled, Spiros turned to the doorway, where the fat man stood with his hold-all between his feet.

'For God's sake,' said Spiros, annoyed. 'You frightened me half to death.'

'Forgive me,' said the fat man. 'I move very quietly in these shoes. Did you not hear me on the stairs?'

'No, I didn't,' said Spiros. Smoothing his hair, he crossed to his desk, and sat down behind it. 'What can I do for you?'

The fat man picked up his hold-all, and walked over to the chair in front of the coastguard officer.

'May I sit down?' Without waiting for a response, he did so. 'I saw you – was it yesterday, or the day before? – taking your family out in your speedboat. She's a beautiful craft, isn't she?'

'Yes, she is. What is it that you want?'

'What speed do you get out of her? Forty-five, fifty knots?'

'I suppose she'd do that,' said Spiros, 'if I pushed her.'

'She's an expensive toy, for a coastguard officer,' said the fat man. He glanced down at his shoes, and, frowning at the dustiness of their condition, unzipped his hold-all. 'I suppose there might be those here in Mithros,' he went on, taking out a bottle of shoe-whitener, 'who would question where you'd get the money to pay for her.' As Spiros watched, bemused, the fat man shook the bottle, removed the cap, and dabbed whitener first on one shoe, then the other, until, satisfied his footwear was at its best, he recapped the bottle, tucked it into his bag, zipped it up and leaned back in his chair. 'As you'll have noticed, I'm very particular about my shoes. My winged sandals, as I call them, in honour of my namesake. I know you'll be sympathetic. You of all people understand the problems of wearing white. Has anyone ever made insinuations?'

'What insinuations?'

'About where the money came from. For your boat. In your position, I suppose you have to be careful.'

'I hope you aren't suggesting bribery?' asked Spiros. 'What is it that you want here, exactly?'

'Just take me, for the moment, as a member of the public asking the kind of questions others might easily ask. And I've made no suggestion about bribery. Though others might say that, with regular boat-traffic coming in from Turkey, it would be easy for someone in your position to turn a blind eye to irregular imports. Smuggled imports. Tobacco, as an example.'

'That's an outrageous suggestion!' objected Spiros. 'It's common knowledge, I'm sure, that Vasso – *Kyrie* Eliadis – lent me the money for the boat. He and I are friends. And the boat is second-hand. It didn't cost as much as you might think.'

'He's a generous man, isn't he?' said the fat man. 'Even so, on your salary, with a growing family, it can't be easy. We're all tempted by life's luxuries, and sometimes we will use any means to get them when we should really just do without. Was I right about drowning those insects, by the way? I have seen such traps before. They are ingenious, but cruel. Not unlike the trap Manolis walked into, two days ago. The trap was baited, and the victim walked into it. Once in it, he could find no way out. Is that how it was, Spiros?'

Spiros frowned.

'You've got me at a disadvantage,' he said. 'I've no idea what you're talking about.'

'Really?' The fat man gave him a smile, but without warmth. 'Then let me tell you I have just come from a conversation with Milto. Ah, I see I have set you wondering now. So as a kindness, let me put you out of your misery quickly – though a quick route out of misery was not a kindness granted to poor Manolis.'

Overhead, a ceiling-fan squeaked once in every revolution, but turned too slowly to generate any coolness in the air.

'Which Manolis do you mean?' asked Spiros. 'As you can imagine, I know any number of men who carry the name.'

'I mean the dead Manolis, lying in your friend the butcher's fridge,' said the fat man. 'Don't play games with me, Spiros. The matter is too serious for games. The moment I said I had spoken to Milto, you must have known the truth was out. Or did you think he would be too afraid to speak? No. Milto is a man of conscience, and he has told me all he knows. In return, I have promised him my protection. You may not think that counts for much; but by the time you and I are done, you'll realise that even to consider approaching someone under my protection with intent to harm or intimidate them would be very foolish indeed.'

Spiros leaned forward, elbows on the desk. Despite the heat, the creases in his white uniform shirt were still immaculate.

'*Kyrie* – forgive me, I don't remember your name.'

'Diaktoros. Hermes Diaktoros, of Athens.'

'*Kyrie* Diaktoros, I'm not clear why you're here.'

'The nature of my business,' said the fat man, 'is justice for the man calling himself Manolis Chiotis.'

'That's a police matter, surely – a matter for myself, and for my colleagues in the regular police force.'

Once again, the fat man smiled without warmth.

'In an ideal world, one would expect so,' he said. 'But history seems to be repeating itself. In the way little interest was taken in Socrates Rokos's death and the robbery at Vassilis Eliadis's house some years ago, I see the same lack of activity here. Do I see you making calls to other islands, or out in your launch searching for the boat Manolis came in on? Do I see you moving heaven and earth to find his relatives so he can be taken home? No. I see you sitting here, behind a desk with a silent phone. And if I walk around the harbour to the police station, I know before I see it that the situation will be the same there. I can't say the dogs have been called off, because the dogs were never roused in the first place. Now, why should that be?'

'I assure you, all available resources are being put into his case.'

'You are right,' said the fat man. '*I* am the available resources, as far as the Authorities are concerned, and here I am. Be assured, I am giving this matter all of my attention, and shall continue to do so until I am satisfied that justice will, inevitably, be done. Let us start that process by talking about what Milto had to say. Milto was intended to be a player in this game, but – fortunately for him – Milto lives by a very strong moral code. When the moment came for him to be tested, he didn't abandon that code. Unlike you, Spiros.'

'What do you mean?'

'Two days ago, when we were talking at the festival of St Nikodemos, Milto went missing. He was missing for a while

– long enough to neglect the care of Allegro, which was, for him, most out of character. In fact, I saw Milto with my own eyes, without realising it was him. I saw him from a distance as he was talking to poor Manolis, in front of the guard-house at Kolona. Milto ducked to hide his face from me, but it was he; he has told me so. What was he doing there? He was persuading Manolis to go with him to the well. Why was he doing that? Because someone had asked him to lure Manolis there. And why on earth would he agree to such an apparently bizarre request? Because it came from an official source. It came from you.'

'Me?'

'You told Milto that Manolis was a wanted drug-runner. You told him there would be an ambush set up at the well, a sting operation where you and your colleagues would swoop, and arrest him.'

'But that's absurd! We would never use civilians in that way!'

'Of course you wouldn't. But for Milto and his well-developed sense of right and wrong, it seemed an ideal opportunity to help out with law and order. He went along with it, and talked a good story. He told Manolis he knew where to find your mythical bull, and persuaded him it was hidden at the well. He promised Manolis money upfront, if he'd help him retrieve it. And Manolis, being desperate for money, and no doubt intrigued by the story as well as having his judgement impaired by drink, set off with him without much demur. And when they got there, what did they find? Not a coastguard sting, but you. You, with your gun.'

Spiros shifted in his seat.

'Where is the gun now?' asked the fat man.

'I don't carry it as a matter of course,' said Spiros. 'It's ridiculous to think I would take it to a social event such as that festival.'

'It would be ridiculous if it weren't premeditated,' said the fat man. 'When Manolis appeared, you took control. With a gun to his head, he was yours to command. You announced to Milto that Manolis was his father's killer, expecting, I'm sure, that Milto at that point would immediately convert to your cause, and that years of pent-up rage at the death of his heroic father would come to your service. You expected Milto to join you as a willing accomplice to Manolis's punishment for the death of your friend Socrates, all those years ago. But Milto surprised you, didn't he? Milto didn't want to play along. Milto had no illusions about what his father was, and Milto certainly didn't want any violence in his or his father's name. Milto walked away, and left you to it. I know you threatened him as he went, to make him keep silence. Happily Milto understands something you, I think, do not – that sometimes, a man must act on his conscience. But as it happened, the loss of Milto from your plan didn't much matter.'

There were footsteps on the staircase outside – the slip and click of sandals on bare feet, the heavier tread of loafers. Loskas, the bank clerk, and Makis, the butcher, came into the office.

Spiros smiled broadly.

'*Pedia, yasass*,' he said. 'What can I do for you?'

But before they could answer, the fat man turned in his chair, and spoke.

'*Yassas*. Thank you for coming. You may be surprised to see me when you were expecting to meet Vassilis Eliadis. I must be honest, and say I used a little subterfuge. I had the boy give his name instead of my own. I thought you would be more likely to respond to a request for a meeting from him than to one from me.'

'Meeting?' asked Spiros. 'What meeting?'

The fat man spread his arms.

'This meeting, between the four of us,' he said. 'I thought you would think that we have no common business. But be assured that we do. Spiros, can you find chairs for your friends?'

'We'll stand,' said Loskas. 'Spiros, what's this about? I've shut the branch to be here. I can't stay more than a minute.'

'You're all busy men, I know,' said the fat man. 'Spiros and I have already covered some ground which needn't be gone over again. We've been talking about the death of the man who came here calling himself Manolis Chiotis.'

Loskas and Makis frowned, and the fat man caught a glance between the butcher and the coastguard officer.

The fat man looked at each of them in turn, giving them opportunity to speak, but the men were silent.

'We are off to an excellent start,' said the fat man. 'I expected at least one of you, and possibly all three, to deny any knowledge of a man by that name. But of course that would have been absurd, when the man is lying in Makis's fridge, playing scarecrow with his customers. And you, banker, have spoken to him as a customer, and remembered him well enough the last time I mentioned him to you, whilst Spiros here is probably sick of the name, given the number of official forms he should have written it on in the past couple of days.'

'Why should any of us play ignorant?' asked Loskas. 'The whole island has talked of nothing else since he was pulled out of that well.'

'Even so,' said the fat man, 'you would be surprised how many men in your position begin by denying even the most obvious of facts.'

'What position is that?' asked Makis. 'I'm not aware of being in any position, as you put it.'

'I wonder,' said the fat man, looking at Makis and Loskas, 'if one of you two latecomers would care to offer an opinion as to how Manolis came to be down that well?'

'He fell, plain and simple,' said the banker.

The fat man looked at the butcher.

'Do you agree, Makis?' he asked.

Makis hesitated.

'How can I agree?' he said, at last. 'You yourself showed me what you found on him.'

'And what did you find?' asked Loskas. 'I spoke to the doctor myself. He told me there was no question but that the death was accidental.'

The fat man shook his head.

'Time and again we see this problem in the islands. Doctors fall into apathy, and become lazy. Given the suggestion of a simple, alcohol-induced accident – perhaps by you, Spiros? – I'm sure he was ready to concur, and get back to his chair at the *kafenion*. Maybe he wasn't keen to look too closely anyway. The unfortunate Manolis makes a highly unpleasant corpse, black-faced and blinded as he is. But there are the injuries to the arms, which clearly do not fit with any theory of him having simply fallen down the well. I have already shared the logic for that conclusion with Makis, so if you want to hear the reasoning, I suggest you ask him. The reasoning is in any case academic, and there is no need, either, for me to go into any detail about how he was gagged.'

There was a short silence. The fat man stood up.

'I've taken up enough of your time,' he said.

'Is that it?' asked Loskas.

The fat man looked at him.

'Is that what?'

'Is that what we've come here to hear?'

'And what have you heard?'

253

'That you have some theory about this death not being accidental.'

'Is that really all you've heard, Loskas?'

The banker shrugged.

'What about you, Makis? And you, Spiros? You're a man of the law. Maritime law, admittedly, but surely you can read between the lines of what I'm saying.'

All three remained silent. The fat man picked up his hold-all, and smiled round at them.

'It appears I am going to have to spell it out. There was nothing accidental about Manolis's death, nothing accidental at all. Everything was planned. He was the victim of a conspiracy, and the conspirators were you. All of you know exactly what happened, because you were all there.'

Red-faced, Spiros jumped up from his chair.

'What the hell are you saying?' he shouted. 'What bullshit is this? I'm a respected officer in the national coastguard! What you're saying is actionable, and I'll see you in court!'

'Your threats are empty, Spiros,' said the fat man, reasonably. 'The truth is no libel, as you no doubt know. A gun was used to force Manolis's compliance in his fate: your gun, in your hand. You made him kneel at the well-head, and he was told who you are, and why you were going to do what you did. I expect you named Socrates, and told of his unmarked grave on the seabed. Did you make your case poetic, with talk of crabs eating his flesh, and his white bones? You had the gun to his head, and you made him put his hands behind his back. One of you forced that stone into his mouth to stop him shouting, and two of you tipped him in. That is how it happened. *Kyrie*, I must leave you. *Kali mera sas.*'

The butcher's face was haggard, as if he had aged ten years in a moment.

'Spiros,' he said, 'I think we should . . .'

'Shut it,' said Spiros, and the butcher was silent.

The fat man took a step towards the door, but Loskas blocked his way. The blood had left his face.

'Listen, friend,' he said. 'This is crazy talk, this is madness! You have no proof of these ridiculous allegations! The man's death was an accident, pure and simple. The doctor has already signed the paperwork.'

'I am not your friend,' said the fat man. 'And you are quite right about the proof. I can prove very little of what happened, and I know I'll find no cooperation from the police, or the doctor, if I go to them. Who are they – your cousins, your brothers? What evidence I have would never persuade a court of law, but as it happens, that doesn't matter to me. I act on behalf of higher Authorities, and when they know you have played judge and jury to Manolis, they will allow me to do the same for you.'

'Who the hell are you to talk to us like that?' shouted Spiros. 'You're not above the law!'

'Certainly you are not,' said the fat man, 'though you have acted as though you are. There will be consequences, of course, consequences which will be the same for all of you. Unless, of course, any of you would like to help complete the picture. If any of you would do that, well – we might call this your opportunity for mitigation.'

'Mitigation?' asked Makis of Loskas. 'What does he mean, mitigation?'

'Mitigation is the lessening of intensity of something unpleasant,' said the fat man. 'In short, a way to make your future a little easier, though I make no promises. And I do not mean by trying to push blame on to your partners in crime. It does not matter to me who did or said exactly what. You were all complicit in this. What I am looking for is regret, and remorse.'

255

'I regret it,' blurted the butcher. 'We shouldn't have . . .'

'Shut up, idiot!' shouted Spiros. 'Why can't you ever just shut up?'

'If you have regrets, Makis,' said the fat man, 'then so much the better for you. Maybe you will help me understand why Socrates took the path he took in the first place. That's one question Milto was unable to answer. He was too young at the time to understand his father's state of mind and motivation. What was it that made Socrates an easy target for the men who robbed Vassilis? What made him betray a man who had done so much good for so many, a man so loved and admired?'

'You keep your mouth shut,' said Spiros to Makis. 'There isn't just you to think about here.'

'I'm going to tell him,' said Makis, defiantly. 'What does it matter, anyway? He says he's got no proof. He might as well be told.'

Spiros shook his head, and sat back down in his chair, head in hands.

'Socrates had big ideas,' said Makis. 'He had a plan. He wanted to go to America, and make his fortune. He didn't see himself struggling all his life, scratching out a living at Kolona. But he didn't have the money to get to America. He had not much more than the clothes he stood up in, same as we all did. How could he – how could any of us? – make that kind of money, living as we did? Those tickets were expensive, and he had nothing he could sell. So he thought Vasso was his route out of here. Vasso was going to lend me money to set up my butcher's shop, and Socrates saw no reason he shouldn't lend him money for his ticket to America. But old Vasso turned him down.'

'Really?' said the fat man. 'Why?'

'He made noises about family responsibilities, and the

importance of origins. He told him he'd learned the hard way that there was no place like home, and how he'd save Socrates the trouble of finding it out for himself. Plus, Socrates was a married man with a family – young Milto. Vasso didn't approve of Socrates's plan to go off by himself, and establish himself before he sent for the family. I don't know why he didn't. Maybe he thought it'd be the last anyone ever saw of Socrates. Once they go from here, not many come back, in truth. But it's common enough for men to go away, and it was even more common then. Many men from Mithros used to spend months and months away every year, on the merchant ships. But Vasso had his own ideas about that, and it was his money. So he said no, and thwarted Socrates's plans.'

'Aha,' said the fat man. 'I am beginning to understand the source of his resentment. And Vassilis's reasoning seems strange, given the time he himself spent abroad. It was the route he took to making his own fortune, after all.'

'Socrates was resentful,' said Makis. 'He was jealous, and he was angry. Vasso was a generous man, to everyone else. He seemed in Socrates's eyes to make an exception in his case.'

'I think he had good reason to be resentful,' put in Loskas. Spiros glared at him. 'I could see his point of view.'

'Vassilis's actions sound less to me like the actions of a philanthropist and more like those of a careful banker, analysing his risk,' said the fat man. 'Loskas, would your bank lend money to someone leaving the country indefinitely?'

'Never.'

'Of course not. But I suppose Socrates didn't see it that way?'

'No, he didn't,' said the butcher. 'In his eyes, Vasso was

picking on him, singling him out for disfavour. He thought he was the only man on this island Vasso wouldn't lend to.'

'So when Manolis and his friends came along looking for Vassilis, they found in Socrates a man only too ready to play Judas?'

'They asked us all. They hung around Kolona for a while and sounded us all out. We had no way of knowing what they were about. They mentioned his name, claimed him as some relative. I don't think they knew for certain, at first, they'd hit on the right place. But they described him, and we all knew who they meant. We had no reason not to say the man they were looking for was probably Vasso. That wasn't the name they gave at first, though. He'd been calling himself something else, I think, whilst he was away. No doubt Socrates made some negative comment about Vasso, and then they knew they'd found the right place, and the right man. He told us they'd offered him money to show them the house, and get Vasso to open the door. They knew enough about him to know he wasn't likely to open up for them. We tried to dissuade him; how could they be up to any good? But he had no loyalty to Vasso, only malice; he saw it as a way to take revenge for Vasso's refusal to help him.'

'So why was the outcome so tragic?'

'How can we know, for sure? He took them there; we know that much. So we assume they didn't pay him, or at least not all of what they'd agreed. They came back without him, at great speed, in a big hurry to be gone. Socrates wasn't with them. They'd got themselves back aboard their boat and were ready to take off by the time Socrates appeared, in that old tub of the postman's. And he was shouting, *Kleftes, kleftes* – thieves, thieves. So those that heard him shout – both at Kolona and in Mithros harbour – assumed he was using that term because he was a hero, because he'd witnessed the robbery at Vasso's and was doing the right thing in chasing them. But we knew different. He was after them because they hadn't paid him his dues; they were leaving him still without his boat fare to America, and he was mad. From the way he was shouting and waving his arms, you could tell he was mad as hell. Mad enough to drive in front of them to stop them getting away, and stealing his dream. I suppose he thought they'd stop. But they didn't.'

The fat man was thoughtful.

'They mowed him down in cold blood, and that was despicable,' he said. 'And yet he was on an unpleasant mission, the betrayal of a man because he'd chosen to be careful where he lent his money. Did it never occur to you Socrates put himself in the way of danger, that he reaped a crop of his own sowing? He played with fire, surely, and got burned for it.'

'But it was in cold blood,' said the butcher, bitterly. 'They cut him down in cold blood.'

'Not so cold as the blood I've seen in you three,' said the fat man, sternly. 'Mowing Socrates down was Manolis's reaction in stress; you, on the other hand, plotted and schemed Manolis's horrible punishment. What you did chills the blood, the horror and the cruelty of it. If you wanted the man gone, it would have been enough to shoot him in the head; but to make him suffer that way shows coldness almost beyond belief. Have you so little imagination, you cannot put yourselves in that poor man's shoes, and imagine his agony, and his fear?'

'That's all we intended,' blurted the butcher. 'We just wanted to frighten him, shake him up. We never thought he'd end up dead.'

'Didn't you?' asked the fat man, slyly. 'So how did you expect him to get out of the vicious trap you'd put him in?'

There was silence. In Spiros's bottle, the wasps and hornets buzzed with rage.

'So you thought you'd leave him suffering, until someone happened along and hauled him out? Who did you think would do that?'

'We thought Captain Andreadis would find him pretty quickly,' said Loskas. 'We miscalculated the time they'd spend at the name day.'

'So what Captain Andreadis found was a corpse,' said the fat man. 'And it was all of you who took that man's life. But whatever he had done to you, or anyone else, in the past, it was not for you to exact revenge. Why did you not go to the police, and tell them your suspicions? You had your reasons, I'm sure. But by taking matters into your own hands, you have stepped across a line, into my country.' He looked at each man in turn. 'You're asking yourselves what happens now, so let me tell you. At some point in the future – it may be only days, or it may be weeks, or months, or years – I shall find someone to whom Manolis mattered. He mattered to someone; it is always so. And I shall tell them of your cruelty in his death, and I shall tell them where to find you. So, from now on, be looking over your shoulders! The quiet life you have always enjoyed is at an end. You are hunted, without knowing the faces of your hunters, and every stranger coming to this place could be your nemesis. You may attempt to run, or you may remain here; believe me, it will end the same. You looked for retribution with Manolis; now his confederates will look for retribution from you.'

'But we didn't know it would kill him!' objected Loskas. 'That was never our intention!'

'Cruelty was your intention,' said the fat man, 'and your cruelty went too far.'

He put his hand on the door, and was about to leave them when he stopped.

'There's one last question remaining,' he said, 'though I doubt you know the answer. What is it that they stole from Vassilis?'

'Who knows?' asked Loskas. 'He's never said.'

'Money,' said Makis, bitterly. 'What else does he have anyone would want to steal, but money?'

Seventeen

When the fat man returned from the coastguard's office, Enrico had laid lunch on the rear deck: a frittata made with artichoke hearts and dill, a loaf of bread still warm from the baker's oven, a Mythos beer cold enough to form condensation on the bottle's shoulders.

A breeze flapped the edges of the awning, and drew ripples on the waters of the bay.

'*Meltemi*,' said the fat man, as Enrico poured beer into a chilled glass. 'Maybe we shall have some relief from the heat at last. Are we ready for our guests this evening?'

'All will be ready,' said Enrico. 'Do you want me to serve the mutton?'

The fat man looked across to the harbour, near-deserted at the beginning of siesta. The jeweller was locking the shutters across his shop windows; at the *kafenion*, the *patron* was clearing cups from the empty tables. On the water below the *periptero*, Nondas was climbing into his boat.

'Let's wait and see,' said the fat man.

As he ate the frittata, Enrico sat down with him, drinking beer.

'Has anyone come to claim the man from the butcher's, *kyrie*?' he asked.

'Not as far as I'm aware,' said the fat man. 'And though I know he was not the human race's noblest, and that the world might be the better for his absence, I have to say it makes me sad to think of him still there. Whatever he was guilty of in life, like everyone he deserves honour in death.'

Nondas was motoring slowly towards *Aphrodite*. As the fat man wiped the last olive oil from his plate with a piece of bread, Nondas reached the steps at *Aphrodite*'s stern, where Enrico caught his mooring rope.

The fat man leaned over the rear deck-rail.

'*Yassou*, friend,' Nondas shouted over the noise of his engine. 'I've come to do a trade with you. I'm hoping you still have that mutton, so I can make my wife a happy woman, so she might make me a happy man tonight!'

He stooped down into the boat, and lifted up a wooden box, where – amongst the last shards of melting ice and stinking melt-water – was a splendid snapper, pink-scaled and wide-eyed.

'I had some real luck,' he said. 'I was only on my third or fourth cast when I landed this beauty. He was so heavy, I thought at first I'd caught my hook on the rocks! I was about to get my knife and cut the line, but then I felt him tug. He fought me all the way, and I was sure I'd lose him. But I got him in the boat, and now here he is. Just have a look, friend, and tell me if we have a trade!'

'We certainly do,' said the fat man. 'Enrico, fetch Nondas our leg of mutton.'

'Wait a minute, friend, wait a minute,' said Nondas, and from under one of the boat's benches, he brought out a jar of sea-snails preserved in brine. 'I brought this for the gentleman too. A gift from me to him.'

The fat man smiled.

'Excellent!' he said. 'Nondas, thank you. You have done me a favour, and now I owe one to you.'

The fat man slept away the afternoon, and spent the earliest hours of the evening with a volume of poetry. The hillsides were still warm from the day's heat, and the perfume of the herbs that grew there filled the coming night; as darkness fell, stars glittered on the black sky, and the reflection of an orange moon glimmered on the sea.

Just after seven, Ilias brought over Professor Philipas in the prow of the dinghy, and when the professor had stepped aboard, Ilias slowly backed into the bay, and set off in the direction of Kolona.

'Welcome,' said the fat man, offering his hand.

He led the professor to *Aphrodite*'s prow, where canvas chairs stood round a pretty table inlaid with pear wood. The fat man indicated one of the chairs to the professor, and took one himself.

'This is a beautiful yacht,' said Professor Philipas.

'She's not young any more, but she has lost none of her charm for me,' said the fat man. 'Like a beautiful woman, age has softened and mellowed her. She is supremely comfortable, and if properly cared for, gives reliable service.'

Enrico approached with a tray in the Turkish style – engraved brass swinging from three chains, so it could be carried without spillage. He gave a small bow to the fat man, and placed a drink from the tray before him, then did the same for the professor. He put a bowl of roasted sunflower seeds between them, and gave another small bow as he left.

'I hope Campari is to your taste?' asked the fat man. 'I find it a very agreeable aperitif for the heat of summer.' He picked up his glass, where a lemon slice floated amongst ice cubes, and held it up to the professor, who did likewise. '*Yammas*.

Your wife decided not to join us, I assume?'

'I never thought she would,' said the professor. 'I did ask her. As I said, she's not a sociable woman.'

'Perhaps she's the exception that proves the rule. I drew a parallel a moment ago between this craft, and the mellowing of a beautiful woman. I have the impression from you that your wife is not the mellowing kind.'

The professor looked out across the water, where the moon cast its strange light.

'If I had a boat like this,' he said, 'I'd sail away. You could go anywhere, in a boat like this.'

'You could,' said the fat man, 'and she has taken me many, many places. But it is a fallacy that in leaving a place, a man can leave his problems behind. Rather, solve the problems that trouble you, and find peace in the place that's home. What about your son? You wouldn't want to leave him, I'm sure. Though no doubt he'll be leaving you, shortly. He'll be of an age to join the army, before too long.'

'We'll apply for a deferment. He's a bright boy, and there might be university or college. I never had those chances, and I'd like to do my best for him.'

'He seems a solitary young man, if you don't mind my saying so. Maybe the army's camaraderie would do him good.'

'He would hate it, I'm sure. I hated it, when I did my time.'

'But not everyone hates it. The discipline and the team-work appeal to some. And for many it's an excellent rite of passage, an introduction to the world of men. In the past, Greece bred some of the finest armies in the world, and though our forces now may lack the glamour of the Spartans, in their own way, our modern generals do the same work, with the same aims at heart – the protection of Greece's boundaries against her enemies.'

'We have no enemies, surely?' said the professor. 'Not declared enemies, anyway.'

'We all have enemies,' said the fat man. 'Sometimes we fail to recognise them as such. And sometimes those we think of as our enemies turn out to be our truest friends.'

The buzz of the dinghy's engine was drawing close.

'I saw the museum on the television, by the way,' said the fat man. 'Mithros as the island with two missing bulls made a good story. Is there any news of the replica?'

The professor shook his head.

'None,' he said. 'I'm absolutely at a loss as to who would take it. It seems to make no sense.'

They felt the touch of the dinghy's nose as it reached *Aphrodite*'s steps.

'That will be my other guest,' said the fat man. 'Come, bring your drink, and we'll go and meet him.'

Enrico had covered the table with a white cloth and laid three places. The candle lamps had been lit; the candles were of caramel-coloured beeswax, and gave off pollen's essence of spring meadows. The silver-bladed knives had handles of ivory, carved with vine leaves set with grapes formed from tiny amethysts, with two-tined forks to match. The spoons were shaped like scallop shells, and the wine-goblets were in the Venetian style, their stems wrapped in engraved silver.

The professor's attention was on the cutlery; the forks were similar to one displayed in the Herakleion museum. He heard footfall on the steps, and the fat man offering a welcome.

'I believe you two know each other,' he said.

Even in civilian clothes, Capain Fanis could only be a soldier, with his military haircut and his straight-backed, at-ease stance. He was smiling to greet his fellow guest; but when he saw the professor, his smile fled, and a flash of anger spread over his face. The anger, though, was quickly repressed, and replaced by an expression of indifference.

On seeing the captain, the professor offered an uncertain smile, and, equally uncertainly, his hand; but reading the captain's face, he dropped his hand, and himself took on an attitude of detachment.

When both wore similar expressions, the resemblance between them was marked.

'Captain,' said the fat man, coaxingly, 'please become reacquainted with your brother.'

The captain remained cold, and spoke to the fat man as if the professor were not there.

'Forgive me,' he said. 'I don't want to offend you, but I can't sit down at a table with this man. So as not to spoil your evening, I thank you for your invitation, but ask that you get your man to take me back to Kolona.'

The fat man gestured at the table.

'Please,' he said. 'My crew has gone to some trouble. And there's too much food for only two of us.'

'It's impossible,' said the captain, and turning his back on both the fat man and the professor, he made for the stern steps. The dinghy wasn't there.

'Ilias has another errand to run,' said the fat man, 'but if you still feel the same when he returns, of course I will have him take you. I will not force you to stay.'

'Fanis,' said Professor Philipas, quietly. 'My brother. Forgive me.'

With his back still to his brother, the captain's head lifted as though he had been struck.

'Please, listen to him, Fanis,' said the fat man. 'I have gleaned a little of his story, and I don't believe it has been happy.'

267

Fanis turned towards his brother with tears in his eyes, struggling to control rage, or grief, or both. He waved a threatening finger at Philipas, but the words he spoke through clenched teeth were to the fat man.

'You see this man?' he asked. 'This snake, this vermin? I loved that woman, and he knew it. She was going to marry me. She'd given her word, her family had given its agreement. We would have been happy, she and I, if my own brother hadn't cut in, and stolen the woman who was to be my wife! *My* wife!' He looked now at Philipas. 'Why?' he asked, shaking his head. 'Why did you make such a fool of me? Why couldn't you have left her alone?'

Tears came to Philipas's eyes.

'Oh Christ, I wish to God I had! It was a black day when either of us laid eyes on her! I did you wrong, and I admit that, freely, now. But believe me, I've long ago come to my senses. You didn't deserve her, Fanis. I deserved her.'

Fanis sneered.

'How dare you!'

'I mean it,' said Philipas. He spread his arms wide. 'Hit me if you want to, give me the beating I've earned. But you are too good a man for her! You're right, I was the lowest and the dirtiest kind of snake, and I've been reaping the rewards of that for years. She's the sourest, most disagreeable woman you could ever meet! It was madness to steal her, and make you wear a cuckold's horns. Don't ask me what I was thinking, because I don't know. You are my brother, by blood and birth, and I disregarded that to get to her. But God sees all, Fanis, and by Christ, I got my just reward! Outside a doll, inside the plague! She's a bitch of a woman, who makes it her duty to make me miserable. If there can be anything noble in what I did, it's that I spared you the misery of her company. Believe me, I've been punished for my sin against

268

you. Every day is a punishment. Not least of all because now I've met the woman I should have married, and I'm not free!'

'I can vouch for the truth of what your brother says,' said the fat man. 'The lady you fell out over is difficult, to say the least. You had a narrow escape, Captain.'

But the captain shook his head.

'I had no escape,' he said to his brother. 'You and she together broke my heart. I've never since then looked at a woman, in any serious way. How could I ever trust one of them again? And for my own brother to betray me!'

'I'm so sorry!' Philipas moved towards Fanis, but Fanis flinched, and held up his hand to stop his brother coming closer. 'Fanis, forgive me, and let bygones be bygones. You have a nephew, did you know?'

'I've seen him,' said the captain. 'I've seen him with her, and I've seen him with you. It makes me sick to see him, because he should have been my son. And if you're so sorry, why didn't you come and say so, years ago?'

'I've tried,' said Philipas. 'But every time I see you, you disappear down some back alley. How could I apologise to you, when all you do is run away?'

'I wish to leave now,' said the captain to the fat man. 'If your man isn't ready to take me, maybe there's somewhere I can wait until he can.'

'Fanis.' The fat man placed his hand on the captain's shoulder; the soldier stiffened, but then seemed to lose his will to fight, and slumped a little. 'Your brother did you a great wrong, but he has paid double for it, with the misery of the bad marriage that might have been yours, and the heart-ache of loving a woman he is not free to be with. You might still – if you wish, if you choose – make your nephew the son you didn't have. Between us, from what I have observed, he would benefit greatly from your company. The boy's on

269

course to be his mother's son; time spent away from her influence would change him for the better. You have a gift with boys and youths; you gain their trust easily, and bring out the best in them. Don't ever think of your life as wasted, because you lost that woman. If you had married, it's unlikely you'd have pursued the career you did, and hundreds of young men would have lost the benefit of your care. Losing her put you on the right track for your life, and made you the exceptional man you are. Your brother hasn't had it easy, by any means. Now, I know human nature, and I know that knowledge will bring you bitter pleasure. That I can understand; but bitterness is corrosive, and will burn away a heart's finer emotions.

'You have lost many years of family life, and the love you had for each other as brothers must seem the husk of what it was. But think of that husk as charcoal, which seems the black and soulless form of the growing tree. Charcoal keeps the form it had in life, and given the right conditions – oxygen, and a spark – will burn twice as long and twice as hot as green wood. It is not too late.' He grasped Fanis's wrist, and so made him hold out his hand, then beckoned Philipas forward. Cautiously, Philipas touched his brother's hand; and the captain reluctantly took it in his own, and let Philipas hug him to his chest.

They ate Nondas's snapper, and drank a bottle of good wine.

'A friend of mine has a vineyard in Santorini, where they have perfected the art of growing Assyrtiko grapes,' said the fat man, in response to the professor's question on its origins. 'I have vineyards of my own, in the north. If the Assyrtiko is finished, maybe you'd like to try a bottle from there?'

But when Enrico filled Fanis's and Philipas's glasses from a second bottle, the fat man gave a subtle shake of the head, and Enrico replaced the wine in the ice-bucket without pouring for him.

Enrico brought out dessert: pink sugared almonds, rose-flavoured Turkish delight, sliced cantaloupe.

'I have to ask you,' said the professor, 'how did you know we were brothers?'

'I rely heavily on what you might call intuition,' said the fat man. 'It's a skill I have worked hard to develop, over the years. But you'll remember you drew a map for me, on the back of an envelope. The envelope was addressed to you, and your family name was the same as Fanis's.'

The brothers drank more, until the second bottle was gone. As they stood up from the table, they embraced, and the fat man shook both their hands.

'I cannot tell you what pleasure it gives me to see you reconciled,' he said. 'Blood is always thicker than water, and family ties are the heart of a happy life. Put what's passed behind you, and move on. Make up for the time you have lost, and befriend each other again. Fanis, spend time with your nephew. He needs your influence to make him the young man he might be. And Professor, now the boy is older, you might perhaps consider that your church permits divorce. Since you have acknowledged the grossness of your offence to your brother, maybe the time is right to move on.'

He called Enrico to his side.

'Our guests are ready to leave,' he said. 'Tell Ilias to bring round the launch. I shall go ashore with him; I have business I must conclude tonight. We shall leave Mithros at dawn, so be sure we're ready. And make sure nothing delays our departure. There are matters elsewhere demanding my urgent attention.'

The butcher's wasn't open for business. Makis had opened in the morning, but trade had been too slow to be worth his time. The first hours after siesta had been no better. Then visitors had arrived, and ordered him to close the doors.

The contents of the freezer – trussed chickens and trays of their livers, skinned rabbits, pork hocks and filo pastry, green beans, prawns and minced beef – were on the floor, and the butcher's stock was defrosting by his feet; the rime of frost on the wrappings, the artificial snow that came out with the boxes and bags, were already puddles of water on the stones.

With some sympathy, Spiros in his white uniform patted Makis's shoulder. The police sergeant and the constable with him were keen to be gone.

'Open it up, then, Makis,' said one, gesturing towards the fridge. 'Let's get this done, if we have to do it.'

With reluctance, Makis lifted the refrigerator handle, and opened the door a crack. The cold air took a moment to reach them. When it did, it carried the corpse's stink.

'*Panayeia mou*,' said the sergeant, wafting his hand in front of his face to disperse the smell. 'He's a bit overripe, wouldn't you say? For God's sake, let's get him out of there. If we leave him much longer, he'll be slipping off the bone.'

'Have some respect,' said Spiros. Under his tan, he didn't look well; sleepless nights had left him drawn. 'Makis, open it wide and let's get him out of there.'

'I still don't see why he has to stay in my shop,' complained the butcher. 'My business will never recover! All my frozen stock will be lost! And there'll have to be a new freezer when he's gone, but how long will I wait for compensation? Why can't they just come and take him away?'

'They've no one to send,' said the constable.

'They're still trying to trace his relatives,' said the sergeant.

'We should just bury him,' said Spiros. 'Have a collection to pay for a grave, and give him a decent funeral. He deserves

272

that, surely? Why can't we do that, and have the business over with?'

'No confirmation of identity,' said the sergeant. 'He might be anyone. If you're thinking of compensation, Makis, you'll have to fill in the forms.'

'There are a lot of forms,' said the constable.

'I'm sure there are,' said the butcher. 'Don't think they'll put me off.'

'There's no point in delaying,' said Spiros. 'Shall we get on with it?'

The butcher pulled back the bedsheet. Seeing the blackness of the dead man's face, the constable grew pale, and crossed himself.

'Lift at the shoulders and the thighs,' said the butcher. 'One at each corner.'

The corpse seemed very heavy; to Makis, Manolis seemed more weighty than any animal. Grimacing at the smell, they heaved him up. Manolis's head dropped back, and his mouth fell open. The pebble that had silenced him was gone. They carried him to the centre of the shop, and tried to lay him down as carefully as they could; but his weight made them awkward, and his head cracked on the floor. Panting, they rested. Makis studied the palms of his hands, as if they might be stained from what he was doing.

'One more lift,' said Spiros, wiping sweat from his forehead. 'On three.'

Again they raised Manolis up, high enough to get him into the freezer, and lowered him on to his back.

He was too tall to fit, stretched out.

'We'll have to bend his knees,' said the sergeant. 'Makis, bend his knees.'

One at a time, Makis pulled under Manolis's thighs, and bent his legs so his feet were flat on the freezer's base.

Manolis's left leg dropped to the left, his right fell to the right.

'He doesn't look decent, with his legs spread like that,' said Spiros. 'What'll the relatives say, when they come? Can't you do any better?'

Makis hauled Manolis's right leg over to rest on the left. He crossed the arms over the chest, and draped him with the sheet. Spiros slammed the glass cover on the freezer.

'Done,' he said.

'What if the relatives don't come?' asked the sergeant. 'If they can't find them, he might be with you for a long time, Makis.'

'You could make him an attraction,' said the constable. 'Charge the tourists a hundred drachma to see him.'

The sergeant and the constable laughed. Makis looked despairing. Spiros glanced around for somewhere to wash his hands, but there was nowhere.

The defrosting food sat in a pool of its own melting.

'Well, if we're done here, we'll get out of your way,' said the sergeant. 'What're you going to do with all your stock?'

'I'll give it away,' said the butcher. 'Take anything you'd like.'

'Are there any *ambelopoulia*?' asked the sergeant. 'Not that I'd say where I got them.'

'Larks, blackcaps, help yourselves,' said the butcher. 'Take whatever you want. I don't care.'

'Thanks very much,' said the policemen.

And they did.

Eighteen

The courtyard door was open, and the music from a record-player – Dragatakis's sinister Concert for Oboe and Strings, with its troubling melodies and cadences of heartache – reached from the Governor's Villa into the empty lanes outside. Lemonia poured water on the roots of the jasmine and honeysuckle, splashing the delicate white and lemon flowers to intensify their scent and mask the stink of tomcats. A warm wind blew up from the sea, carrying notes of pinewoods and mountainside thyme. The open door emitted enough of the courtyard's light to cast shadows, and her own fell on the jasmine, moving as she moved.

An owl screeched.

In the tree where the bird must be, she caught no sign of movement in the branches; but as she lowered her eyes, the tree's trunk was distorted from its usual form.

Someone was there.

She felt the unpleasant flutter of fear. The courtyard door was near to hand, and she might within seconds have been through it, and slammed it shut; but disbelief in her own senses made her stay and look again.

The fat man stepped out of the dark beneath the tree, and into the outer limits of the courtyard's light-spill.

'*Yassou*, Lemonia,' he said. 'I'm sorry if I frightened you.'

She recognised him, but recognition did not dispel her fear.

'You did frighten me!' She glanced at the open door, balancing an instinct to run with the training of politeness and good manners. 'Of course you frightened me, hiding there like that! What are you doing here?'

'I brought you a gift, a parting gift. I leave Mithros tomorrow, and I wanted to give you the volume of poetry I promised you. In fact I have gifts for both you, and Vassilis.'

'He won't see you,' she said. 'I told you that when you were here before. He never sees anyone at home, and certainly not at this hour.'

Though it remained in shadow, Lemonia thought a smile might have crossed the fat man's face.

'If I want to see him, I will see him,' he said. 'The choice is mine, not his. But he's an old man, and there may be no reason to disturb him, if you will be my messenger. I thought he was deserving of a gift – a token suitable to reflect the gifts he has so often made to others. Shall we go inside a moment?'

'No!'

She shook her head in emphatic refusal. Again, she sensed him smile.

'You have nothing to fear from me, Lemonia,' he said. 'But if you prefer, we can talk out here.'

He walked two paces forward to where the light was better; she matched him, moving two paces back. He placed his hold-all at his feet, and unzipping it, searched out a paperback book and held it out to her. She took it, and twisted the cover to the light to read the title: *The Odes to Nemesis*, by Volonakis.

'It is my personal copy, and you'll find it well read,' he said, 'but the words are not diminished by having been viewed by other eyes. I knew Volonakis, once. His was a remarkable talent, and his loss from the world was unfortunate. He came to a humbling end for a great man. The story of course was that he choked on an olive. But whatever his ending, his poetry stays with us. I hope you enjoy it.'

He fell silent, watching her. The pins in her hair were coming loose, and she brushed a long strand from her forehead. At the neck of her dress, her skin was damp with sweat. She looked briefly into his face, then lowered her eyes.

'It's hot,' he said. 'There seems to be no relief from the heat this evening, does there? I don't want to compromise you, but might I trouble you for a glass of water, before I go? I assure you, Lemonia, I am the same man I was when I was here before, weaponless and not intending any violence. If you would let me have a glass of water, I can give you my gift for Vassilis, and I'll be gone.'

'I told you,' she said, 'he always tells me to let no one in.'

'And you are an excellent gatekeeper. But you're capable too of making your own judgements. Aren't you? I could come no further than the courtyard. He need never know I've been there, unless you choose to tell him.'

'He'll know,' she said. 'He has hearing sharp as any dog. But as far as the courtyard, all right. I'll get your water.'

She led him through the courtyard door, and laying the book of poetry on the outdoor table, indicated he should take a seat there; but as she took down a glass from the kitchen shelf, she turned to find him standing on the threshold.

He caught her apprehensive glance at the *salone* door, through which Dragatakis's music was reaching a crescendo.

She ran water into the sink, holding her finger under the stream until it ran cool.

'You seem afraid of him,' he said, softly, as she filled the glass. 'Is that why you stay? You're an attractive woman, Lemonia, who must have other options. Yet somehow he –

old though he is – keeps you in this mausoleum as his gate-keeper and protector, his cook and his mistress.'

'You have no right to speak to me that way,' she said, and held out the glass. 'Drink this, and then please go.'

He took the glass, but instead of drinking, placed the glass on the kitchen table, alongside the closed ledger and a parcel wrapped in candy-striped paper, decorated with florist's ribbon.

'I have no right to speak, of course, and what I say is no more than my opinion. But I wonder what will be left to you, when he is gone? I see no ring on your finger, and so I assume he has not made you his wife. When he dies, who will take care of you then? What I am asking you is, does he deserve the loyalty you offer him?'

Her expression was defiant. The last notes of the music came through the speakers. In the absence of the music, the house seemed silent.

'Let me tell you about that man through there,' she said, keeping her voice low. 'When I first knew him, he was a lion of a man, a lion who dared to roar, a lion who had seized life and lived it in a way few men do. He was a fire-ball, he took risks, and he made things happen even in this place, where these idlers will do nothing troublesome or hard. Now he's failing; he's weak, and he's afraid, and his lion heart has deserted him. When I first knew him, I worked for him through obligation, because I needed money, but he earned my affection because of what he was. I cared for him when he was that lion; how can I desert him now he can no longer roar?'

'In the same way, perhaps, that he may leave you vulnerable when he goes.'

She shook her head.

'You have us wrong. It's he who's the vulnerable one.

Night after night he sits there, waiting for whatever it is that scares him. I know the thought preys on his mind every minute, that those men who came and tortured him are coming back. I did whatever I could for him, after he was burned. I changed his bandages, and rubbed honey and ointments into his skin to help it heal. That's when he and I grew close. And slowly I began to realise, I could help to heal his physical wounds, but there was nothing I could do in here.' She pointed to her temple. 'He's damaged, as I was damaged goods when he took me on. I might seem matronly and honourable to you, but my past is black and shameful. Small wonder he wouldn't marry me. No one would blame him for that, least of all me. I made choices in life which made marriage to any decent man impossible. But to see him this way breaks my heart, and it is my duty to try and stand between him and whatever or whoever it is he fears. His fears are growing worse, I know. He always keeps his gun by him now, even though it can do him no good. He used the bullet that might have saved his own life to end the suffering of a fellow creature. That's why I love him, and that's why he has my loyalty.'

The fat man reached forward, and opened up the ledger, and ran his hand over a page of the columns, of the figures and the names.

'And this?' he asked. 'What's your explanation for all this?'

She shrugged, indifferent.

'He's always been a businessman. I keep his books for him. He pays me to do it.'

'And this?' He picked up the candy-stripe wrapped parcel. 'If I were to guess, by its size and weight, this is a pair of shoes for a little girl, very pretty and decorated with butterflies. A name-day gift for somebody, no doubt.'

'It is,' she said. 'What of it?'

'I have no criticism at all of the gift,' said the fat man, 'or of any of the gifts he is famous for, or of the generosity on which he builds his reputation. Except that he didn't choose this gift, did he? You did. It's you who has the talent for choosing gifts, for finding the perfect present for his godchildren. No doubt it was you who found the violin for Milto Rokos, and gave him his very successful musical start in life.'

'Is that a crime?' she asked. 'A woman's sensitivity can be a help.'

'A help, yes. But between you, you have cooked up a deception surrounding his reputation. Which begs the question, what other deceptions might have been dreamed up in this house? I think it's time I showed you the gift I brought for Vassilis.'

From his hold-all, he brought out an object wrapped in pale-blue tissue paper. She took the packet from him, the paper rustling at her touch.

'Open it,' he said, and she did so, being careful not to tear the delicate wrapping as she peeled back the tape which held it closed. She opened up the tissue paper, and revealed an ebony bull, with golden horns and a gold crocus at its mouth.

For a long moment, she looked at him.

'I think you need to talk to him yourself,' she said.

She sent him into the *salone*, where the lamp made of shrew-skins was lit, and the long, black tribal masks stared disquietingly from the walls. The room, though, was empty, and so the fat man passed straight through it towards the balcony, where Uncle Vasso sat at the cast-iron table, his binoculars out of their case and ready for use alongside his pistol. He had a glass of brandy in one hand, and between the fingers of the other a burning cigar, and laid across his thigh, his cream kid gloves.

The fat man moved almost silently in his tennis shoes, but as he drew close, Uncle Vasso became still in his chair, his cigar part-way to his mouth.

'Has he gone?' he asked. 'Lemonia?'

The fat man stepped on to the balcony.

'No, Vassilis,' said the fat man. 'No, he hasn't gone.'

Shocked, Uncle Vasso turned his head, and put his hand on the gun. Almost half the hand was covered with scarring, a glossy red welt which spread from the knuckle of the thumb, down to the wrist and across to the central metacarpals. The tightness of the skin made him awkward in gripping the weapon, and with his stick-hand holding the gun, he was slow to get out of his chair. In the time he was ready to aim and pull the trigger, the fat man might have snatched the gun, or walked away. He remained, however, where he was – the easiest of targets, yet unconcerned.

'Get out,' said Uncle Vasso. 'Get out, or I'll shoot.'

'Shoot all you like,' said the fat man. 'You'll do me little damage with an empty gun. Why don't you sit down? I have not come to offer violence, and I shan't burn you or beat you. I am here only to talk. Come, let us behave like civilised men.'

A moment passed. Uncle Vasso sank back down into his chair, and let the gun fall on the table.

'I'll join you, if I may,' said the fat man, taking a chair. He placed his hold-all at his feet, and put the tissue-wrapped bull before Uncle Vasso.

'I brought you something,' he said. 'A work of genius.'

Uncle Vasso studied him.

'Remind me who you are,' he said. 'I'm an old man, and my memory's unreliable. What's not important, I forget.'

The fat man gave a slow smile.

'I will allow you to forget me once,' he said, 'since I made it my business with you to be unobtrusive. My name is Diaktoros, Hermes Diaktoros. I don't think you'll forget me again, Vassilis. You'll be carrying me with you for the time you have left. Why don't you look at what I brought you?'

As Uncle Vasso picked up the package, the fat man saw the scarring on his palm: a hollow burned almost to the bone, following his fate line from the mount of Saturn to the mount of Neptune.

Keeping a close watch on the fat man, Uncle Vasso opened out the tissue paper. When he found the bull, he frowned.

'Where did you get this?' he asked.

'From the place where it was,' said the fat man. 'What will you give me for it?'

Uncle Vasso stood the bull upright on the table between them; he crushed the tissue paper into a ball, and tossed it over the balcony, into the night.

'Nothing,' he said. 'I'll give you nothing for it.'

The fat man seemed surprised.

'How can that be? Here I present you with the original bull of Mithros – he is the original, I assure you – and you will offer me nothing for it? Why not, Vassilis?'

Uncle Vasso drew on his cigar, and blew a cloud of smoke high into the air.

'I know why not,' said the fat man. 'I know Mithros's great secret, and I know the truth behind the legend of your famous bull. You might have fooled all the hopefuls who come here looking for the treasure, but you do not fool me, nor my friends in the archaeological museum, whom you never succeeded in duping. You know without even a second glance this cannot be the fabled bull of Mithros, because the bull of Mithros doesn't exist. He is a fake, an invention. He was never found during building work, and he was never stolen or lost. You know that the bull there before us can only be the replica – the so-called replica – stolen from the museum. Not truly stolen, perhaps. He was removed temporarily by my man Ilias, on my instructions, and it was he who tipped off the television newsroom. It was a little game I played with Mithros, whose people seem to enjoy games and trickery. They have, after all, tricked most of the world into believing in your tale of lost antiquities.'

'Go, friend,' said Uncle Vasso. 'The evening's getting late. I'm an old man, and I'm tired.'

He turned away from the fat man, dismissing him.

'Are you disappointed in my gift to you?' asked the fat man. 'Did you think I might have brought something of value? But disappointment is what I feel about you, Vassilis. I was sold you as a man of high value, of integrity, a philanthropist and the most generous of men. Your packaging persuaded me. See, here you are, masquerading as an old man who needs his sleep. But you are none of those things that you appear. You are a schemer, a user and a deceiver. The bull was your invention, wasn't it? And I don't deny it was a clever one. The bull and the industry round it, all your idea. You sponsored a museum to give credibility to a lie, and made that lie a source from which the whole island might draw its living. Tell me, who did you recruit as the bull's finder? Who was it who came into a legacy, and disappeared from Greece so no questions could be asked?'

'My cousin and her husband,' said Uncle Vasso. 'What of it? They wanted to make a new life in America, and I gave them a way to finance it. They couldn't possibly have stayed here. Too many questions would have been asked of them.'

'And all the rest of your fellow islanders were persuaded to be part of your hoax, which would bring in the tourists, and make them easy money. Your accomplices play their parts very well – they are gifted actors and pretenders, talented purveyors of what you sell as a modern myth. But myths have their roots in truth, and your bull isn't a myth. It's nothing but a racket.'

Uncle Vasso blew out more smoke, and smiled.

'What if it is?' he asked. 'What other way was there to get these idlers out of their poverty? They won't work, if the work's hard. But present them with something they can sit on their backsides and sell, it's easy pickings and they'll do it. My interest in this island is quite genuine, friend. I went away poor and I came back with money in my pocket, and I found Mithros the same hopeless backwater that I left. This is the land of my birth, and for that reason, I love it. You look at it now, prosperous and flourishing, and tell me what I did was bad.'

'You recruited them all in a lie.'

Uncle Vasso waved a dismissive hand.

'They lacked leadership, direction, and I provided it. No more than that. And the public loves a good story. If people insist on being gullible, they must expect to be milked.'

'You use the word gullible where others might say trusting,' said the fat man. 'And that is not the only instance where you've misused the trust of others.'

'I dare say not. I've been blessed with a long life, and I've made no claims to sainthood.'

'A long life, and a full one, apparently,' said the fat man. 'Your collection in the *salone* is impressive. Souvenirs of your travels, I assume?'

Uncle Vasso examined the end of his cigar, and found it had gone out.

'Do you have a light?' he asked. 'Maybe I should offer you a drink. Lemonia!'

As the fat man passed Uncle Vasso his gold lighter, there was a quick step on the floorboards, and Lemonia appeared.

'A drink for the gentleman, *koukla mou*,' said Uncle Vasso. 'And another for me.'

In the *salone*, Lemonia crouched to open a dark-wood cabinet, and removed a bottle of brandy. Uncle Vasso was watching her. He licked his lips.

Lemonia brought the bottle and a glass for the fat man, and poured the brandy. As she left them Uncle Vasso watched the swing of her hips, and smiled.

'In my own mind, I'm still a young man,' he said. 'And sometimes, my old body still plays along.'

'You were going to tell me about your memorabilia.'

'Is that what you're here for, a traveller's tales?'

'I've heard several stories about where you made your money,' said the fat man, 'but I never heard the same story twice.'

'You've been taking an interest in me, then?'

'Almost since the moment I arrived. The first story I heard was that you'd made your money in the Congo. Coffee, I think they said.'

'If you're interested in my travels, I should be flattered.' Uncle Vasso sipped his brandy. 'There's money in coffee, for certain. But I know nothing about the coffee trade.'

'Were you ever in Egypt, selling cotton?'

'Egypt? I've been there. I wanted to see the pyramids. They're fabulous feats of engineering, and I have a great appreciation of man's ingenuity. But I was only there a week. The place was hotter than hell, and the flies bit badly enough to make a man cry. No, I made not a cent in Egypt.'

'It must be copper, then. I heard you made a fortune in precious metals.'

Uncle Vasso laughed.

'Commodities, all,' he said. 'But I did make my money in a commodity.' He gestured to the *salone* with his left hand. Like the right, the back of it was sworled with dense, red scars; the last two fingers had no nails, but were fused together by taut skin, smooth as plastic. 'My little collection there, my memorabilia, as you call them, the jungle drums, the beads and the masks. All of it, I got as a job lot. I had a friend who was in the import business, and I used to go to his warehouse from time to time to play cards. We had a couple of packing cases we used as our table, cases someone had shipped from Africa and never came to claim. One night we'd been drinking, and we got curious as to what had been shut away in those boxes, all those years. So we got a crowbar, and opened them up, and there was my collection. I gave him something for it and took it away. We nailed the lids back on the packing cases, and still used them as our card table. When I came back here, I said nothing at all. Rumour and speculation built my background, using the bric-à-brac in there as props. Happily what they invented for me was all legitimate.'

'Were your business interests not legitimate, then? What commodity did you deal in?'

Uncle Vasso smiled, and ground out his cigar in the ashtray.

'Do you know,' he said, 'in all the time since I returned to Mithros, no one has asked me that question. Why do you suppose that is?'

'People make assumptions. They hear rumour, and take it as truth. Whereas I discount rumour, and make it my business to ask questions directly, as I am asking you now.'

'You're bold, my friend, asking such things of a man you don't know,' said Uncle Vasso. 'But I like boldness, and so I'll answer you. The commodity I dealt in was a live one. I sold women, in the most successful chain of brothels Albania ever saw. The side benefits were, of course, considerable. But you, friend – what line are you in? You strike me as a man of the world. Maybe you've wandered into one of my establishments, on your travels.'

'No,' said the fat man. 'I guarantee you absolutely I have not. The women I have known have come to me freely, and as friends. As to whether I am your friend or not, we shall yet see. I work for the Authorities.'

'Which authorities are you with? Are you going to arrest me? Because if you try, I should warn you I won't go quietly. Under the law of this country, I've done nothing wrong. Disapprove of my trade as you may, I conducted it on foreign soil. I've committed no offences under Greek law.'

'I have no interest, at this moment, in your dirty little businesses in Albania. And you mistake my credentials. I am no officer of the law, no policeman, and I'm not here to arrest you. But I am here to see justice done. I have seen the ledger that Lemonia keeps for you, where you record debts and repayments. The Authorities who employ me are record-keepers too, and they believe that you have debts outstanding.'

Uncle Vasso put down his glass.

'I see. Do you bring trouble, then?' he asked.

'On the contrary. I bring an end to the trouble you have brought to this place.'

'You've got me wrong, friend. I've brought nothing but prosperity to Mithros. I've a businessman's acumen, and I've used it for everyone's benefit.'

'But that isn't true, is it?' asked the fat man. 'The only man who has ever really benefited from your business acumen is you. On the surface, you have been generous with your money, but you have given it out as loans, rather than gifts – loans which all have strings firmly attached, and you have no qualms about calling in disproportionate favours as repayment. Favours of such magnitude as demanding help in an act of murder.'

'Murder?' Uncle Vasso shook his head. 'You're deluded, coming here and talking to me of murder.' He held up both his hands to show the fat man the extent of his disfigurement. 'I am a victim of crime, my friend, not a perpetrator. Now, you've shown me that trinket in the packet there, and I've been honest with you, and admitted the truth in relation to that. Take that back to your authorities, whoever they are. I'm an old man, and I need my bed. If you'll excuse me.'

'Not yet, Vassilis,' said the fat man. 'We are here, you and I, at the end of the line. This is the tail-end of a story which began many years ago, when the robbers who gave you those injuries came to your house. But it was no random break-in, was it? Those men did not just happen to land in Mithros, ask around for the nearest wealthy man and come and rob you. You knew them, and they tracked you down. Why?'

'Why should I tell you?'

'Because it's time. Because you're tired of keeping the secret. Because, why not? Your time grows close; I know you sense that. You are no different from any other man, Vassilis. When you leave this earth, you want to go with your heart unburdened.'

'So you want to act as my confessor? If I ever wish to confess my sins, I'll call a priest. Go.'

'I shall not go,' said the fat man. 'Not until you have told me everything.'

Uncle Vasso sipped his brandy, and looked away. The fat man let the silence between them grow long.

'I have a feeling about you, friend,' said Uncle Vasso, at last. 'I have a feeling of wanting to tell the truth. The truth about the bull is a long-kept secret and an excellent joke, which I've shared with everyone here. But I've never shared the truth about what happened that night, not even with my Lemonia, because it would have shamed me to tell her.'

'Tell me, then,' said the fat man. 'We are, as I have said, at the end of the line. Why did they seek you out?'

Uncle Vasso sighed.

'Fire with fire, that's what they said. My empire grew too big, and I lost control of it. No, that isn't true. I didn't take the time to control it. I developed a taste for poker, and sleeping late. I got careless. I let things slide. I didn't bother with the details of the mundane and day-to-day. My businesses being what they were, I wasn't subject to checks and controls. If I'd been in the hotel business, there'd have been official interference: the fire department, environmental health, all of them. But my business was brothels, and no one cared about the well-being of whores. We kept the lights turned down, and no one saw the problems. I had some wiring done on the cheap. There was a fire, on the ground floor. This place had three floors. The girls upstairs, they couldn't get out. I was asleep when they came for me; I'd had a heavy night at the poker table, and I'd lost, badly, so I'd drowned my sorrows in whisky. They came for me, and I told them to go away. They came back and gave me the news, four women dead. I knew that wasn't good. I didn't pack. I went straight to the bank, and cleared out the accounts. I bought a car, paid cash, and drove away. One of the girls who died, we were close for a while. Tamara, she was called, a Greek girl from Livadia. I wasn't in love with her, but she was easy company, we got along. We had a child, a son. I married her when she got pregnant, to give him a name. I don't know what happened to the boy. I never asked, I never troubled to find out. And then they found me – Tamara's sister's boy, he brought them here. They did what they came to do, which was to hurt me, but they were clever. They didn't finish me off; they made me wait. That's what my nephew said to me, that I'd have to wait. He was a damnable man, a Greek working as a heavy for some Albanian mob. Half now, half later, he said, and they'd be back when they got round to it. And I've been waiting ever since. But he made a bad mistake whilst he was leaving, and killed Socrates, my betrayer. I half-thought his death would make me safe, would keep my nephew from coming back. I was starting to believe he'd gone for good, or come himself to some bad end.'

'What did they steal?'

'Nothing of importance. Money, the deeds to some property. He said it was for my son, but I'm sure my son never saw any of it. I hope my son has spent his life far away from that world.'

'And what do you keep that's so precious in the bank vault?'

'My insurance policy. I suspect it's worthless now. There are photographs of important men in compromising positions. It was easy to get footage whilst they were occupied with the girls. There are tapes, and videos. If there were ever trouble, I had all I needed to keep me out of jail. Except the men I used for my insurance must have moved on. New men have replaced them, I have no doubt.'

'Then your nephew came back.'

Uncle Vasso smiled.

'You're a sharp one, *Kyrie* Diaktoros. If circumstances were different, we might have done business, you and I. Yes, these past few days, here he was again. What were the chances of him being ditched here, in Mithros?'

'The Fates have long memories. It seems they had not forgotten him, or you.'

'Call it Fate if you like, or the worst of bad luck. I was

brought the news that he was back. It doesn't matter by whom. There was talk of the police, but what was the point in them? They're still the lazy, useless fools they were when this was done to me.' Once again he held up his hands. 'Nothing has changed in that regard. But I wanted no arrest then, and I didn't want one now. If he was arrested, the first thing he would have done would have been to talk about me. What would he have had to lose? There might have been extradition for me, and criminal charges for negligence, and I didn't want to end my days in an Albanian jail. A great deal of my money is already spent, and I don't have the necessary funds to buy off Albanian policemen. They have expensive tastes, and my insurance policy, as I've told you, is out of date. It used to be easy with them; I gave them free run of my girls, and they took full advantage. But I don't have the girls any more, only my Lemonia. My lovely Lemonia, who has been such a help with the fiction of my background. She grew up in the Congo, and I adapted her stories as my own. She tells me you tried her cooking, that you enjoyed it. I've developed quite a taste for it, over the years.'

'You never married her, though.'

'No, I never did. I'm much older than she is. When I die, I don't want her to put on widow's weeds for ever. I want her to find another man, someone who'll take care of her.'

'Have you taken care of her? If anything happens to you, what would she do?'

'She'd find herself a woman of property, through my will. I've never told her so. I had one threat hanging over my life. I didn't need to wonder if she was poisoning my food to get at my cash. It'd be easy to disguise poison in a curry.'

'I've heard people say you're paranoid. That sounds like paranoia.'

'My life has been under threat for seventeen years. It can't be any surprise if I see danger in everyone.'

'But you knew the source of the danger.'

'My nephew. A man the world is very well rid of.'

'That may be your view, and it may be the truth. But that doesn't give you the right to judge him, and sentence him, and be his executioner. And you made your offence worse by recruiting others into your plans. Your hold on them was tight, and you abused that. All of them owed you money, and favours, and they were grateful, in the beginning, for your making their lives easier. You gave Makis a start in business, and helped Loskas with the burden of his daughters' dowries. You helped Spiros buy his boat – a luxury he would never have afforded alone. Your cigars, by the way – where do you buy them?'

Uncle Vasso picked the stub of his cigar from the ashtray, and sniffed at it.

'From Nicaragua,' he said. 'I find the quality is finer than anything Cuban. I've developed my own little business, importing via Turkey. I keep a few, and send the rest on to a contact in the north.'

'And your import business involves no taxes and attracts no attention from the coastguard. All of them – Makis, Spiros, Loskas – saw your loans as generosity, but your money chained them to you tight as Prometheus bound to his rock. And once you had them, you would never set them free. You milked them, and fed off them, calling in favour after favour.'

'Your words are very harsh. I don't see that I milked them. We had business arrangements, surely? They are men of the world, as am I.'

'But they are not men of the world, Vassilis, they are men of Mithros, and what you saw as business, they saw as friendship. The template for your commercial dealings might have been appropriate once, but you brought that same model here, and it was in no way appropriate to the gentler men of this island. Surely you must see that?'

Uncle Vasso laid the cigar stub back in the ashtray.

'You may be right,' he said, pensively. 'Maybe I have misused them.'

'Most certainly you have. You made them killers. You misused them and misled them over a border they would never in a hundred lifetimes have crossed without your influence.'

'But what could I do?' asked Uncle Vasso. He spoke with a hint of contrition. 'I had no choice but to recruit them. The job had to be done, and I needed help. I wanted him to suffer in the same way I had suffered. He put me through agonies, waiting for his retribution; he left me a legacy of never a moment's peace. He made Death stand always at my shoulder, and I wanted him to have time to get well acquainted with Death, on his way out. I saw a man once, strung up by his feet. He'd given offence to some mafioso, and he was shown to me as a warning. I didn't understand that hanging there could kill him, but the horror of his death was in his face.'

'How did you get your nephew down the well?'

'Simple enough. Once Milto had brought him to the spot, I held the gun to his head.'

'And none of them betrayed you in that. Your hold on them is strong. They stuck together, and said the gun put to his head was Spiros's. But it wasn't. It was your empty weapon.'

'He didn't know it was empty. I made him kneel, and they tipped him in. I sent them away then, and they made their escape in the coastguard launch. I gave them my promise he'd be down there only a while, that I'd fetch Captain Fanis to get him out. They're slow thinkers, or perhaps they don't think at all. My nephew had seen them, and would point the finger, if he came up alive. They left, and I walked away, back to the celebrations. That's how it was. Except for Milto. He had no guts, no stomach for any of it. It was his duty to be there, to avenge his father, and he shirked that duty. I wasn't surprised. You expect no spine from a man too soft to eat meat. It's not natural for a man not to eat meat. Meat makes the blood red, and gives strength and stamina.'

'I was there when you tried to force a dish of lamb on him. You seem keen to force people into your way of thinking, even down to choosing the foods they eat. Milto had no illusions about his father. He knew his father deserved no retribution. Socrates was involved in bad business, and came to a bad end.'

'Bad ends, good ends, they're endings, all the same.' Uncle Vasso drained his glass. 'Are you done with me?'

'Not quite,' said the fat man. 'There have been many mentions of strangers, since I've been here. Most are accounted for. I was told up near the museum a stranger had been seen, but that was my man Ilias, taking the bull on my behalf. I have made him practise, and he picks a lock as cleanly now as I do myself. Then at Kolona, two soldiers heard strange things in the night. One I think was Milto, comforting the soul of his dead father. The other was Gounaris, who'd lost the chain his mother gave him, going to your nephew's room to steal it back. But the stranger you saw – how do we account for him?'

Uncle Vasso laughed.

'There was no stranger, of course. That was a mere decoy for the captain. He headed in one direction, we went in the other. I'm sure you can see it would have complicated matters, if they'd returned to camp at the wrong time.'

'And now your nephew's gone, do you feel a free man?'

Uncle Vasso's expression was philosophical.

'Do you know,' he said, 'I don't. I rejoice that he's gone; but he has friends, or what pass for friends in those circles. In time, they'll come looking for him, and they'll find me. No. I'm not free.'

'No, you are not,' said the fat man. 'There will be further retribution, worse than before. And now you've put the lives of previously innocent men at risk. Tell me, what happened to your last bullet? Wasn't it foolish to use what might save you?'

'It was needed. A donkey, beyond help. I put it out of its misery.'

'You did the right thing. And you can help those others you have led into danger by doing the right thing now. They did not betray you, but I know they did not think they were help-ing in an act of murder, only of punishment which they believed justified. Now they carry a great weight on their consciences, and I have told them their lives are under threat. For a time, it's appropriate they believe that; they should suffer for the wrong they have done. But because murder was not their intention, if you will do the right thing, you may buy them a lessening of their burden, in due course. If you do the right thing, I will let it be known in the right quarters that you have done so, and your accomplices' lives will not be at risk, despite what they believe. When I feel the time is right, I shall let them know – either by coming here myself, or by getting word to them – that the danger is past. All they will have to wrestle with then is their memories and their consciences – lessons that must be learned by anyone who takes matters that are not theirs to judge into their own hands.'

He reached into his pocket and pulled out a matchbox. He placed it in front of Uncle Vasso.

'Another gift,' he said, 'to help in your decision.' He stood to go. 'I have not asked you one crucial question. What is your nephew's real name? Whatever wrong he has done, he deserves to have his relatives claim him and bury him in his home soil.'

Uncle Vasso shook his head.

'That will be my final revenge on him,' he said, 'and I will never tell. If you want to know his name, you must find out for yourself.'

When the fat man had left, Uncle Vasso smoked another cigar, and gazed out into the night. The matchbox lay beside him on the table.

Lemonia came and stood behind his chair, and kissed the top of his head. He took her hand, and kissed it.

'I'm going to bed,' she said. 'Don't be too late.'

When she had left him, he slid the matchbox open.

It contained a single bullet.

Nineteen

At dawn, the firing of *Aphrodite*'s engines disturbed the peace of the bay. The chains rattled as her anchors were raised, and she executed a slow turn to point her prow to the east, and a rosy horizon.

As she motored towards the first sunlight, a single shot rang out.

As daylight filled the bedroom, Olympia read Philipas's letter again, though there was no need; the words were few, and memorised. Turning out the lamp which had burned all night, she wondered whether a ring would suit her finger.

There had been little pain, and the sick woman's face was peaceful, almost smiling. When finally her breathing stopped, Olympia released her hand.

She tucked the letter inside her dress, and slid open the dresser drawer to find the clothes the woman had chosen as her last. Over the body, a fly buzzed.

Olympia went to find the neighbour, to tell her to have them ring the passing bell.

Along the island's east coast, where the fat man had been swimming, Nondas was hauling up nets he had laid the previous evening. Drawing them in hand over hand, the nets were heavy; he was optimistic of a good catch, hoping to emulate the luck he'd had with the snapper two days before.

Towards the skyline, *Aphrodite* passed; the figure leaning on the deck-rail waved a hand in farewell, but was unseen.

There was no wriggle in the nets, no struggle, only weight; and as he hauled them in, dripping and stinking of the fishy depths, Nondas saw why.

At first, he cursed, thinking he had landed a boulder, some worthless stone. But as he unwrapped the object from the nets, he saw, despite the corally growths and weeds which covered it, the stone had a form created by human hand; and when freed from the mesh, though long submerged, the object's beauty was clear to see: an ancient statue of a leaping dolphin, fighting to break free from the sea.

ACKNOWLEDGEMENTS

For their enthusiastic and diligent help in the choosing of suitable firearms, my thanks to Myles Allfrey, and author Zoë Sharp.

For her kind sharing of Greek family recipes, thank you to Angela Demetriades Schwartz.

And once again, many thanks to John Gilkes for his cartographic skills.

A NOTE ON THE TYPE

The text of this book is set in Linotype Sabon, named after the type founder, Jacques Sabon. It was designed by Jan Tschichold and jointly developed by Linotype, Monotype and Stempel, in response to a need for a typeface to be available in identical form for mechanical hot metal composition and hand composition using foundry type.

Tschichold based his design for Sabon roman on a font engraved by Garamond, and Sabon italic on a font by Granjon. It was first used in 1966 and has proved an enduring modern classic.

ALSO AVAILABLE BY ANNE ZOUROUDI

THE MESSENGER OF ATHENS

Shortlisted for the ITV 3 Crime Thriller Awards

When the battered body of a young woman is discovered on a remote Greek island, the local police are quick to dismiss her death as an accident. Then a stranger arrives, uninvited, from Athens, announcing his intention to investigate further. His name is Hermes Diaktoros, his methods are unorthodox, and he brings his own mystery into the web of dark secrets and lies. Who has sent him, on whose authority is he acting, and how does he know of dramas played out decades ago?

'Powerfully atmospheric . . . Zouroudi proves a natural at the dark arts of writing Euro-crime'
INDEPENDENT

THE TAINT OF MIDAS

For over half a century the beautiful Temple of Apollo has been in the care of the old beekeeper Gabrilis. But when the value of the land soars he is forced to sign away his interests – and hours later he meets a violent, lonely death. When Hermes Diaktoros finds his friend's battered body by a dusty roadside, the police quickly make him the prime suspect. But with rapacious developers threatening Arcadia's most ancient sites, there are many who stand to gain from Gabrilis's death. Hermes resolves to avenge his old friend and find the true culprit, but his investigative methods are, as ever, unorthodox . . .

'More transported Agatha Christie here . . . Hermes is a delight. Half Poirot, half deus ex machina, but far more earth-bound than his first name suggests . . . A cracking plot, colourful local characters and descriptions of the hot, dry countryside so strong that you can almost see the heat haze and hear the cicadas – the perfect read to curl up with'
GUARDIAN

BLOOMSBURY

THE DOCTOR OF THESSALY

A jilted bride weeps on an empty beach, a local doctor is attacked in an isolated churchyard – trouble has come at a bad time to Morfi, just as the backwater village is making headlines with a visit from a government minister. Fortunately, where there's trouble there's Hermes Diaktoros, the mysterious fat man whose tennis shoes are always pristine and whose methods are always unorthodox. Hermes must solve a brutal crime, thwart the petty machinations of the town's ex-mayor and pour oil on the troubled waters of a sisters' relationship – but how can he solve a mystery that not even the victim wants to be solved?

'If you don't find yourself in Greece this summer, then Zouroudi's latest mystery brings the Hellenic vibe tantalisingly close . . . Once again Hermes Diaktoros – a reassuringly earthbound investigator – finds himself dealing with a chorus of colourful locals'
INDEPENDENT

THE LADY OF SORROWS

A painter is found dead at sea off the coast of a remote Greek island. For our enigmatic detective Hermes Diaktoros, the plot can only thicken: the painter's work, an icon of the Virgin long famed for its miraculous powers, has just been uncovered as a fake. But has the painter died of natural causes or by a wrathful hand? What secret is a dishonest gypsy keeping? And what haunts the ancient catacombs beneath the bishop's house?

'Anne Zouroudi writes beautifully – her books have all the sparkle and light of the island landscapes in which she sets them. *The Lady of Sorrows,* her latest, is a gorgeous treat'
ALEXANDER MCCALL SMITH

BLOOMSBURY

THE WHISPERS OF NEMESIS

As snow falls on the tiny village of Vrisi, a coffin is unearthed and broken open and, to the astonishment of the mourners at the graveside, the remains inside the coffin have been transformed. News of the bizarre discovery spreads through the village and sets tongues wagging and heads shaking. Then, by the shrine of St Fanourios, a body is found, buried under the fallen snow. Rumours of witchcraft and the devil's work abound, and when Hermes Diaktoros arrives in Vrisi he soon finds himself embroiled in the mysteries. But the truth may be far, far stranger than even he could possibly have imagined . . .

THE FEAST OF ARTEMIS

The olive harvest is drawing to a close in the town of Dendra, and when Hermes Diaktoros arrives for the celebratory festival he expects an indulgent day of food and wine. But as young men leap a blazing bonfire in feats of daring, one of them is badly burned. Did he fall, or was he pushed? Then, as Hermes learns of a deep-running feud between two families, one of their patriarchs dies. Determined to find out why, Hermes follows a bitter trail through the olive groves to reveal a motive for murder, and uncovers a dark deed brought to light by the sin of gluttony.

ORDER BY PHONE: +44 (0)1256 302 699; BY EMAIL: DIRECT@MACMILLAN.CO.UK
DELIVERY IS USUALLY 3–5 WORKING DAYS. POSTAGE AND PACKAGING WILL BE CHARGED.
ONLINE: WWW.BLOOMSBURY.COM/BOOKSHOP
FREE POSTAGE AND PACKAGING FOR ORDERS OVER £20.
PRICES AND AVAILABILITY SUBJECT TO CHANGE WITHOUT NOTICE.

WWW.BLOOMSBURY.COM/ANNEZOUROUDI

BLOOMSBURY